TEN BELLS
STREET AT WAR

Mary Collins

piatkus

PIATKUS

First published in Great Britain in 2019 by Piatkus

1 3 5 7 9 10 8 6 4 2

A CIP catalogue record for this book
is available from the British Library.

ISBN 978-0-349-41617-5

Typeset in Palatino by M Rules
Printed and bound in Great Britain by
Clays Ltd, Elcograf S.p.A.

Papers used by Piatkus are from well-managed forests
and other responsible sources.

Piatkus
An imprint of
Little, Brown Book Group
Carmelite House
50 Victoria Embankment
London EC4Y 0DZ

An Hachette UK Company
www.hachette.co.uk

www.littlebrown.co.uk

To my grandparents and to all the bona
omis *and* palones *I've known*

Prologue

14 September 1940
Savoy Hotel, London

They'd been drinking Dry Martinis: half French vermouth, half dry gin, with a dash of orange bitters. The bar had been full of noisy hacks hell-bent on a night of Hitler-defying boozing. People just like Bernie Lynch and Heinrich Simpson.

An ancient news editor from the *Daily Mail* raised his glass and shouted, 'If Fritz comes tonight, I'll knock him dead with my breath!' when the sirens began to wail. Heinrich drained his glass. Bernie was just about to follow suit when one of the exquisitely dressed barmen put a hand on her shoulder and said, 'Please, miss, feel free to take your glass down to the shelter.'

'Oh.' She looked up at Heinrich, who shrugged. Although he had, over the years, patronised the Savoy's famous American Bar many times, he'd never been there during a raid. In common with most of the other reporters at the bar,

Heinrich had not long finished attending a press briefing with civil servants from the Ministry of Information.

With quiet but insistent efficiency, Savoy staff led their guests plus the patrons of the hotel's bars and restaurants down what felt to Bernie like hundreds of stairs, and into the hotel's basement. Dimly aware of some sort of commotion going on up above, it wasn't until she had been sheltering for some minutes that she found out what it was about.

Men and women, poorly dressed and smelling of sour soap and coal-dust, burst into the basement. She recognised Phil Piratin's face first. As red as his politics – he worked as an organiser for the Communist Party in Britain – he was shouting about how people in the East End were dying every night due to the lack of adequate bomb shelters for them. Then she saw, at his side, Solly Adler, and Bernie Lynch froze.

Chapter 1

It had been over two years since Bernadette Lynch had been back home to the East End of London. The last time, back in spring 1938, she'd been hailed as a local heroine for taking what had become one of the most well-known and chilling photographs of Hitler's Berlin – the swastika-topped Christmas tree in Wertheim's department store. She and reporter Heinrich Simpson, a Jew of German origin, had broken the story of how Hitler planned to replace Christmas with a Winter Festival, celebrating old Germanic gods and goddesses and, of course, the Führer himself. It had been a massive reporting coup and Bernie's family, especially her mother Kitty, had almost burst with pride.

Then Bernie had been honest and told her mother another piece of news, which Kitty hadn't liked one bit. Neither Bernie nor Heinrich had sought a relationship. But in the charged atmosphere of Nazi Berlin, they had been drawn to each other. That he was a married man of fifty and she a girl approaching eighteen hadn't mattered and still didn't. Except that it did – especially when Bernie came face to face with her past, as she was doing now.

When she'd been a kid, Bernie had been sweet on a young man called Solly Adler. Dark and good-looking, Solly had been one of the Communist Party members who'd gone to fight with the Republicans in Spain back in 1936. Just before he'd left, he'd kissed her. But when he came back, traumatised by what he'd witnessed and having had a leg amputated, he hadn't wanted to see her – or anyone. Now here he was – shouting and protesting – and, to her horror, Bernie's heart skipped a beat at the sight of him. Still handsome, still passionate, to her Solly remained the dashing firebrand she'd fallen for back in 1936. She felt physically sick at the realisation.

'Do you know that people down the East End die every night because they ain't got places to shelter?' he yelled.

'Kiddies included,' Phil Piratin added.

A woman, who remained rather grand despite being dressed in a flannelette nightdress, said, 'Well, then, you should evacuate your children, like decent people.'

Solly bore down on her. 'Firstly, women nursing babies can't send them away, and second, people out in the country don't want us or our kids,' he said. 'You want our women on war work, you get our kids an' all. Unless you wanna work in munitions youself, missus?'

At this point the hotel manager intervened.

'Now there's no need for any unpleasantness ... '

'I'm not being unpleasant, mate,' Solly said. 'If I was being unpleasant you'd know about it.'

Coldly aware that Heinrich was watching her watch Solly, Bernie made herself look away. The floor shook as bombs dropped on the streets of London above them and everyone automatically glanced up. No one spoke for several seconds.

Phil Piratin eventually broke the silence. Though a man of action and a passionate Communist, he was nevertheless a pragmatist and so he said, 'I think what we all need now is a nice cuppa.'

The manager, visibly shaken, said, 'Oh, er, yes, yes . . .'

'We'll pay our way,' Solly put in. 'We may be poor but we ain't spongers.'

The manager gave a weak smile. 'No, indeed. But that won't be necessary, sir, not during an air raid.'

Heinrich whispered to Bernie, 'Do you know these men?'

They squashed in around Rose, as if protecting her from every side: Mr G at her back, Tilly to the left, Rupert to the right, while the Duchess of Greek Street lay in her lap.

'Gawd blimey,' Mr G said during a lull in the bombing up above, 'don't they ever bleedin' give up?'

Tilly lit a cigar and said, 'They're the bloody Luftwaffe, Stan, not a load of old dears making too much noise down the pub!'

The cellars of the Windmill Theatre in Soho attracted an eclectic group of shelterers. There was Mr Talent, the One-Man Band, Tilly, Mary and a group of their fellow drag queens, little Harry the South African kid from the salt-beef bar, various duchesses, baronesses and ladies – all euphemisms for those living life on their backs – plus, of course, the staff and the showgirls from the Windmill Theatre. And prominent amongst these, sitting on the floor surrounded by Soho's finest, was one of the Windmill's most popular artistes, Rosie Red. Though little and slightly plump, she stood naked on stage every night as part of impresario Vivian Van Damm's famous *tableau-vivant* show at the Windmill. Unknown to Mr Van Damm, she wasn't yet twenty.

Born Rose Larkin in the East End of London, Rosie Red

had left her mother Nelly and her home in Spitalfields two years earlier under a big black cloud. Admittedly for a good reason, which had been to stop her alcoholic mother from being evicted from her flat for non-payment of rent, Rosie had stolen fifty pounds from a local Jewish matchmaker for whom she'd worked as a servant. On the run from the law, she'd found herself homeless, sleeping in St James's Park and eating the bread people threw for the ducks, until she'd been taken in by Tilly – or rather Herbert Lewis, office clerk by day, glamorous Gloria Swanson lookalike by night. Once she'd realised that Tilly didn't want to sleep with her, Rose had come to trust and even love her. Tilly had helped her get her job. And before this terrible war began, life with Tilly, her drag-queen friends and the Windmill girls had been nothing but fun. The only people Rosie really missed from back home were her mum and her two best friends, Bernie Lynch and Becky Shapiro.

The earth trembled and a deep thrumming sound told the shelterers that a bomb had dropped somewhere nearby. A trickle of rubble and dust pitter-pattered down from the ceiling.

Vivian Van Damm muttered, 'If they've damaged my theatre ...'

'Oh, do pipe down, Viv darling,' one of the girls said.

A vast rumble like an earthquake silenced everyone.

Rose whispered into Tilly's ear, 'Do you think we're going to die?'

Tilly smiled. 'Not today, love.'

'Where do you know the dark one from?' Heinrich asked her.

Bernie felt her face colour. 'Oh, he's a local Commie,' she said. 'Everyone down Spitalfields knows Solly Adler.'

Although she wasn't looking at him, Bernie knew that Heinrich was frowning. Now they were living together she had come to realise that her lover was not as easy-going as he had first appeared. He may not be married to her, but Heinrich Simpson was her husband in all but name. And sometimes a jealous one at that.

'He's a handsome fellow,' Heinrich observed thoughtfully.

The hotel staff were serving tea and cake to both the East Enders and their own guests. Solly, she noticed, was slurping down his tea as if his life depended on it. She saw him looking at her and so she turned away.

A huge thud somewhere nearby momentarily dimmed the lights in the basement and Bernie moved closer to Heinrich. If the lights went out she was sure the hotel staff would 'fix' that problem. They probably all walked about carrying pocketsful of candles. But she feared being in the pitch blackness; she always had done. Things happened in the dark, things unsought . . . She glanced quickly at Solly, who was now staring openly at her.

Technically they were in the basement, but Nurse Rebecca Shapiro and her patient were stuck in one of the corridors there and the noise from above was deafening.

Old Mrs Palmer, her patient, was dying. She had what was known locally as the 'Barking cough', which meant her lungs were riddled with cancer. It was called the Barking cough because so many people in the area suffered from it. Nobody really knew why although there were rumours about the Cape Asbestos factory, which was where Gladys Palmer had worked for the past ten years. The old girl breathed shallowly. Becky, holding one of the candles that were the only sources of light down deep underneath the London Hospital, looked at the young man who had followed her. A posh boy from Surrey, Dominic Winter was a dedicated junior doctor if, sometimes, a little forgetful.

Becky said, 'You did bring Mrs Palmer's medication, didn't you, doctor?'

He said yes, but he checked his pockets too. Nurse Shapiro, though not much more than a girl, was a little bit frightening to Dr Winter.

Becky turned back to her patient who, to her horror, opened her eyes. Becky stroked her forehead. 'It's all right, Mrs Palmer, just another raid. We've brought you down to the basement, like we did last night.'

How long would it go on for this time? It had gone on all of the previous night. Ernie Jones, a docker from Canning Town, had died in the middle of the raid and, apart from the half-hour Becky had snatched just before coming on shift, she hadn't slept since.

The old woman mouthed something at Becky, who bent down so she could hear. 'We are going to win this war, ain't we?' said her patient.

Becky squeezed her hand. 'Of course we are.'

Two explosions rocked the building then and Becky hung onto Mrs Palmer's trolley as the blast punched its way through the hospital and down into the shelter below. Dr Winter lost his footing and ended up on his back, while Becky just about managed to stay upright. Everyone's candles blew straight out. In the thick, almost tangible darkness, Becky heard people swear as they fiddled to light matches and find cigarette lighters. Eventually, to his credit, it was Dominic Winter who saved the day for them.

'Had my lighter in my pocket,' he said as he stood up and let Becky light her candle from his. 'Good, eh?'

'Yes, Dr Winter.'

She passed her candle to the nurse in front of her and then took it back. Mrs Palmer's face had paled still further since the blast. Becky leaned down to listen to her breathing. But there was none. Becky closed the old woman's eyes. The only consolation was that the last thing she'd said to old Gladys had been hopeful.

Not that Becky felt any hope at all. She was beyond that.

Rose didn't know how she'd managed to sleep. And with the Duchess of Greek Street sprawled on her lap too! Not that the Duchess, or Dolores to use her proper name, was heavy. But she did snore.

Once awake, Rose strained her ears for the sound of explosions. She wasn't alone. After who knew how many hours down in that damp-scented, blast-absorbing, uncomfortably full basement, everyone now seemed to be perfectly silent. She looked over at Tilly, who put her finger to her lips. Glancing around, Rose saw that everyone else was looking up at the ceiling as if expecting something to emerge from it. In reality they were waiting for the All Clear which, when it came, finally loosened tongues and made strained faces relax.

Vivian Van Damm brushed dust from his suit trousers and stood up. 'Well, thank Christ that's over,' he said.

'I always give thanks to the spirit of Madam Rinaldi myself,' Tilly said as she got arthritically to her feet.

'Who's she?' Rose asked.

'My mum's old spirit medium,' Tilly said. 'Mad as a wagon-load of monkeys, now dead as a doornail. Poor old fraud. Came from Colchester, but she had a heart of gold.' He looked up at the ceiling. 'Thanks, Rene.'

'Rene?'

'That was her name,' Tilly said. 'Rene Smith from Colchester.'

'Oh.' Rose got to her feet.

Mr Talent, a bugle in one hand and a drum in the other, said, 'I s'pose we ought to go and see what's left?'

'As long as I can buy a packet of fags, I don't care,' the Duchess said.

Rose hoped her flat had survived. It was only a room in reality and she had to share that with a girl called Sarah, but it was the only home she had. Except, of course, for the one she'd left over in Spitalfields. If indeed her mum still lived in that dark, cold basement on Fournier Street.

Her mum, Nell, had always called their road 'Ten Bells Street' after the pub on the corner with Commercial Street. Unlike Rose, who was only partially illiterate, Nell couldn't even write her own name, much less decipher street signs. But she did know pubs, which had been one of the reasons why she'd never been able to get a proper job.

Rose stepped over the empty cups and bulging ashtrays they'd used the night before and shook her head when she saw a ladder in one of her nylons. The show had only just fin-ished when the sirens had sounded and so she'd got dressed too quickly and put her finger through her stocking. Luckily she had another pair but she'd have to sew these up when she got home.

As she walked out into the grey morning light, Rose won-dered how her mum and her friends were faring out in the East End. Then she dismissed that thought. She could never go back there and see them so what was the point in wondering?

The morning air was thick with brick dust and smoke. As Bernie stepped out of the Savoy and onto the Strand she saw that the pavement was shining with broken glass from all the windows that had blown out during last night's raid. As she walked it crunched under her feet. She lit a cigarette and waited for Heinrich to join her. He'd spent much of the night in conversation with other journalists down in the basement and he was still at it now. Because so many warehouses and refrigeration plants had been bombed, mainly in the East End docklands, food stocks were low. Would that mean even stricter rationing? And, more to the point, what did such devastation say about the condition of the people in the East End now?

Phil, Solly and the rest of the Commies had come to the Savoy to protest about the lack of shelters in their area. It was terrible. While the rich could hunker down underneath posh hotels and nightclubs, the poor died in stupid above-ground shelters or in their own jerry-built homes. Bernie watched the protesters leave: a ragged troupe of thin men and women ground down just by trying to live with the twin evils of poverty and war. What had happened to their dreams of a society where everyone could be safe, free and have enough? It wasn't just Hitler who was to blame. Things had been rotten even without him. While people were homeless and starved on the streets, things always would be rotten for the poor and unfortunate.

Heinrich was still talking to an old man in a Homburg, writing down what he said on the back of his fag packet. Bernie suddenly wanted to go home like never before. Not to the flat she shared with Heinrich in Pimlico but *home* – to Spitalfields, to her mum and dad's old flat in what little Rosie's mum had always called Ten Bells Street, though properly speaking it was Fournier Street. In spite of everything, Bernie smiled. Oh, for a moment, just a moment, with Rosie and

Becky and Mum and Dad and all her brothers and sisters . . .

But that wasn't possible. Rosie had stolen money and gone on the run back in 1937 and God knew where she was now. Becky was a nurse with no time for anything beyond her patients, and Bernie's family . . . well, they had disowned her. Sleeping with a married man wasn't what a nice Catholic girl did.

The only exception to this was her brother Dermot. Never one to judge others, he'd kept in touch by letter and had even been to visit the flat once. He'd shaken Heinrich's hand too. But just because Dermot didn't hate her, didn't mean the others had forgiven her. How could Bernie go home to them while she was seen as not just a bad Catholic girl, but also a home-wrecker? Heinrich had two children, both older than Bernie, and a wife to whom he was, and probably always would be, married. What was she doing with her life?

She stubbed out her cigarette with her foot and smiled as Heinrich approached.

'Sorry, darling,' he said. He kissed her. 'Old Wal Watters has been around Fleet Street since before the Flood. He knows everyone and everything.'

They began to walk towards Aldwych.

'What did he say?'

Heinrich shook his head. 'If the raids keep up at this level for much longer we could have serious food shortages.'

'And fuel?'

'That too.' Heinrich averted his eyes as he always did when he was about to mention his family. 'I'd better make sure that Adrienne and the kids have enough . . . '

'Of course.' Bernie squeezed his hand. Then she said, 'And I'd like to give Mammy . . . '

'Send your mother some money, yes.'

'No, Heine, I should go and see them.'

She watched his face turn pale. The East End was dangerous in all sorts of ways now. Not just because it was being carpet bombed, but also because of the risks it posed: of disease from its ruptured sewers, injury from falling masonry, and, as she knew Heinrich felt, danger from Solly Adler too. Even though she'd never told him about Solly, she knew her lover had seen the look that had passed between them last night.

And if Bernie was honest with herself, she too knew that seeing Solly in his own environment was dangerous to her.

Well, at least the old man was still alive: walking slowly but as upright as ever. Moritz Shapiro didn't have to meet his daughter at the end of her shift, but ever since the Blitz had started he always had. In one way, she wished that he wouldn't, but in another Nurse Becky was so pleased to see him.

'Papa!'

She ran into his arms and hugged him. He smelled of damp and brick-dust. She hoped he wouldn't smell the taint of death that she knew hung about her slim shoulders like a shroud. After Mrs Palmer, other old people had dropped like flies. Five deaths on her ward alone in the space of eight hours. It was as if they'd just given up. Maybe the noise and the dust and all the horror of the raids had finally been too much for them. She could understand it. Even going home provided no comfort for her these days. Although still intact, the Shapiros' house had been damaged. The kitchen window had blown out and the cellar had been flooded for two days.

'Rebekah.'

Her father hugged her to him. Time was when he would never have done such a thing out in the street. That wasn't how Orthodox Jewish men behaved. But when people knew they could die at any minute, a lot of the rigid codes they'd

13

once upheld were abandoned. He pressed her to his chest. 'Are you all right?'

Becky gently freed herself. 'Yes, Papa,' she said.

'Your eyes . . . they're full of tears.'

She knew that. All night she'd held them in but now they overflowed.

Moritz pulled her in close again and stroked her dark red hair. He'd never wanted this for his daughter. There had been a good reason why he'd wanted her safely married off to a man of means. It had been to protect her against the horrors he knew life could throw at an unprotected person. He barely remembered the attacks on their old village back in Lithuania but his parents had told him about them. How the Cossacks, sent by the Tsar of Russia to kill the Jews, had done so with smiles on their faces. How the children had been trampled under their horses' hooves, how they had shot the men and raped the women. Such had been the way of being a Jew in the old Russian Empire. And now this . . .

'Six died last night, Papa,' Rebekah said. 'That was just on my ward.'

He said nothing. What could he say? They both knew it could have been so much worse. The entire hospital could have been reduced to a smoking ruin.

'Come on, let's go home,' he said.

She put her arm through his and stepped carefully over a pile of wood that had once been a market trader's stall. The stalls outside Whitechapel Tube Station, on what had once been a patch of rough, unused ground, were still collectively known as 'the Waste'. And 'waste' was what both Becky and her father thought about as they began to walk back to Spitalfields. The waste caused by war in terms of businesses lost, homes destroyed, lives ended prematurely.

14

Becky got on well with her fellow nurses at the London Hospital. She had a lot of friends amongst the porters, the doctors and the laboratory staff too. But feeling as low as she did now, she knew that only close friends could really make her feel better. Little Rosie and brave, clever Bernie. Becky wondered where they were and what they were doing. She hoped they were both still alive.

Chapter 2

Although not an overtly religious woman, Bernie Lynch's mother Kitty had always believed in fate.

'If it's meant to be, it's meant to be,' was one of her favourite sayings. As well as, 'If God's already written it down, it will happen.'

Bernie didn't think like that, not usually. But when her editor told her to go to the East End and take photographs of the devastation down there, she couldn't help but remember her mother's words. Furthermore, Heinrich wasn't able to go with her and so she'd be alone.

She caught the Tube to Liverpool Street Station and walked through the old market and into Spitalfields. Men she didn't recognise were rolling beer barrels down into the cellar of the Ten Bells pub. All the young blokes she remembered from her schooldays had joined the Forces. She looked up at the clock on the spire of Christ Church and then at her watch: one p.m. The old clock was still working in spite of the bombing. Two days had passed since she'd seen Solly Adler in the basement of the Savoy. Two days and, more specifically, nights, punctuated by seemingly interminable air raids and sometimes crippling fear. And Bernie had already been feeling troubled.

When she'd first left home and gone to live with Heinrich she'd felt independent, powerful and free. Being away from home, especially travelling abroad, which she had done a lot before the outbreak of war, had exhilarated her in spite of her work involving the documentation of the rise of Nazism in Germany. Heinrich, once a German citizen himself, had often been in despair at that time but, Bernie had believed then, her love had pulled him through. Now she saw that it had to some extent, though only at the expense of his wife and children and her own family. Had such a price been worth paying?

Fournier Street didn't look so different. It had always been dark and dirty. Cleaned up, the old Huguenot houses here would have looked really elegant, Bernie reckoned, but that was never going to happen. Ten Bells Street would always be a poor place, full of struggling families, dirt and the smell of human excrement. If it survived this war.

Bernie took a picture of a car that had crashed into the side wall of the church. There was no one about and so she had no idea how that had happened. But the image was striking. Stranded in a sea of blown newspaper, dead mice and filth, the car looked like a great black beached whale with its head stoved in. She walked down the road and tried to pass old Mr Lamb's house but found that she couldn't.

Fred Lamb had been one of the last Huguenot weavers left in Spitalfields. His family had come to the area from France in the eighteenth century when the government there began persecuting Protestant Christians. The Huguenots had been accomplished silk weavers and their descendants had all continued the craft; Fred had been no exception. But someone had killed him back in 1937 when he had tried to stop a band of men robbing the house of the furrier next door. Those robbers had included Bernie's elder brother Joey and her younger brother Dermot. Bullied into taking part in the raid, Dermot had admitted his part in it while denying doing any harm to the weaver. But Joey had been another matter. He'd boasted that he'd killed Fred Lamb. Whether he'd been responsible for the weaver's death wasn't clear to her, but to avoid any possible trouble with the police, their dad, Patrick, had sent Joey away after the incident, and told him never to come back. To Bernie's knowledge, Joey wasn't even spoken of by the family nowadays. It was as if he'd died.

Moving onwards, looking up the street towards Brick Lane, Bernie could see that someone was sitting on the pavement outside her parents' flat. It didn't look like her mother, but it was a woman. As she drew nearer Bernie realised it was Rose's mum, Nell, and she was blind drunk and singing.

Becky brushed away from her bed the bits of plaster that had fallen from the ceiling during last night's raid and sat up. She'd managed to get about three hours' sleep, which was good considering the shift she'd had. She swung her legs out of bed and reached for her dressing gown. In spite of everything, her papa would be at work now and so if she wanted a cup of tea she'd have to go down to the kitchen and make it herself. That was provided the gas was still on.

Having a little more money than most people in the area had its advantages. Her papa had had the old kitchen range taken out and replaced by a modern gas stove back in the early thirties. Then it had been a godsend, but now, with the bombing and consequent disruption to gas supplies, it was a bit of a nightmare. Becky stood in front of it, willing it to turn back into the old coal-powered range. Tea-less, she wandered into the front parlour. It was then that she saw Bernie, out in the street.

'Becky?'

A tousled figure in a candlewick dressing gown, dark red hair awry, her face pale as the moon ... this was hardly the smart Nurse Shapiro Bernie had expected to see. But she was so glad to be reunited with her friend. The two girls hugged each other tightly as Nell Larkin shakily sat up.

'What the bleeding fuck is going on?'

Bernie looked at Becky who crouched down next to Nell and said, 'I think you might've taken a bit of a tumble, Mrs Larkin.'

There was debris in the street – guttering, some dustbin lids, a twisted bicycle – but there was also a strong smell of beer.

'I was pissed,' said the prone woman.

'You often are, Nelly,' Bernie said as she helped her to her feet.

Nell, face smeared with what looked like coal dust, peered at her and said, 'Bernadette?'

'That's me.'

'Oooh. Thought them was your long legs,' Nell shook her head, sending thick strands of black and grey hair flopping over her face. 'You wanna be careful, girl,' she said. 'If your mum was to see you, she'd give you a good hiding.'

Bernie brushed dirt off Nell's skirt. 'Don't worry about that now, Nelly ...'

'I don't judge, how can I?' she continued. 'But Kitty Lynch is a decent woman and she don't like her girl taking up with some married man. He got money, has he?'

Bernie just smiled.

'What time is it anyway?'

Becky said, 'It's a quarter-past one, Mrs Larkin.'

The woman put a hand up to her head. 'What was I doing?'

It was easy enough to guess. Becky, for whom drunk patients were nothing new, was always amazed by how resilient intoxicated people were, even in the middle of air raids. Less than a week ago an old man, minus his false leg, had been brought in, roaring drunk, from what remained of a destroyed street in Silvertown. When he eventually sobered up, he had to be told that both his wife and his dog had died in a raid he didn't even remember.

Nell Larkin grabbed Bernie by her coat collar. 'Here,' she said, 'you seen my Rosie?'

'No, Nelly, none of us have,' Bernie said.

'I heard you live up West so I thought you might've seen her.'

'Why? Do you think that Rosie's living in the West End?'

Nell waved a hand limply. 'Nah,' she said. 'Don't know where she is. But the West End's somewhere she might go.'

'Why?' Becky asked.

Nell shook her head. 'Blimey, who're you, Rebekah Shapiro? Snow White?'

'What?'

'It's where girls go to work on their backs,' the older woman said, matter-of-factly.

Bernie, who knew that Nell herself did just that, looked away.

'Make more money there than you do round here,' Nell said. Then she shook her head. 'But you have to be young ...'

'If anyone sees Rosie, I'm sure they'll tell you, Nelly,' Bernie said. 'Why wouldn't they?'

But Nell Larkin was wandering unsteadily back to her flat. Both Bernie and Becky watched to make sure she got there without falling over. Once she'd disappeared Becky said, 'Come on inside and we'll have a cuppa. You must tell me all your news ... '

It had been one of Kitty Lynch's younger sisters, Concepta, who had got her in. Thirty-five and unmarried, Con had been working at Tate and Lyle's sugar factory for fifteen years when she went to see the women's manageress, Miss Smith, about Kitty.

'Me sister needs a job,' Con told her without preamble. 'And now the men are all going off to fight ... '

'And why do you think I should take on another member of your family, Concepta Burke?' Miss Smith had said.

'Because you need a good worker for the Blue Room now Doris Chandler's in the family way,' Con said in her usual straightforward, almost downright cheeky, manner. 'And our Kitty's a hard grafter.'

Miss Smith had said nothing. But a week later she'd told Con that she'd see her sister. 'I'll make no promises, mind,' she'd said. Which was code for, if Kitty was up to standard looks-wise she'd take her. Because the other name for the Blue Room, which was where the sugar sacks were printed, was the Beauty Parlour. Every girl in there was attractive and every man who saw them at work felt happier with his lot in life – especially his job. Kitty had been surprised when Miss Smith had taken her on.

'Old bag like me,' she'd told her sister, 'about as glamorous as a dose of nits.'

Con had laughed because, in spite of being mother to six children and the wrong side of thirty-five, Kitty Lynch was still a good-looking woman. Careworn due to the worry of having a sick husband and two absent children, it was true that she was lined and she was grey, but those were things make-up and hair dye could fix. And her sister had fixed her very well.

But now she was 'in', Kitty found that she missed her home. Doing *schmutter* piecework for Mr Sassoon had been poorly paid and had hurt her eyes when she'd had to sew at night, but at least she'd been on hand to feed her son Dermot, who worked in the West India Dock. Now he fended for himself most of the time, poor lad. If it wasn't for the rest of the family she'd have been able to carry on looking after him. But with her husband Pat ailing, and down in Devon at his sister's along with the three youngest kids, she'd needed to earn more so as to be able to send a decent sum of money every week for their keep.

That said, at least they were away from the bombing, which had to be a good thing. It was bad enough she and Dermot had to endure it as well as, possibly, her eldest son Joey and her daughter Bernadette. She'd no idea where Joey was and, after what had happened with Fred Lamb, only a faint desire to find out. But she did worry about Bernie. Living somewhere up West with a married man, she'd shamed herself and the whole family, but Kitty still thought about her all the time. Bernie wasn't a bad girl and, when she'd first got her job with the *Evening News*, Kitty had been delighted. It had seemed that, for once, a member of the Lynch family might make something of themselves. But then the silly girl had fallen for that reporter, who was older than her own father, and put the kibosh on her future. Bernie still took photographs, still worked for the paper, so people said, but Kitty never read it and never would – until and unless the girl came to her senses.

Now on a tea break, she sat by herself as the other girls, most of whom were young enough to be her daughters, talked about their boyfriends. The young men were joining the Forces unless they were in reserved occupations like mining and dock work. This meant that Dermot was safely exempt, although Kitty knew he didn't want to be. A good Socialist like his father, Dermot was gagging to fight the Forces of Hitler's fascist Germany. It was only a matter of time before he volunteered and then she'd have none of her children with her. Kitty felt a painful squeeze of her heart at the thought.

'Here, Kitty, do you want a fag?'

Annie Hancock was nearer to Kitty's age than any of the others – a stunning blonde who, it was said, had been dumped by her husband for a younger woman.

Kitty smiled. She'd never smoked until she came to work at Tate's but she took the cigarette from Annie with a smile.

'Thanks, love.'

Annie sat down beside her.

'You all right, Kitty?'

'As I can be, yes,' she said. 'Just thinking about how our Dermot'll be joining up soon.'

Annie put a hand on her shoulder. Her elder brother had fought in the First World War and had come back with shell-shock. Kitty knew her workmate wouldn't tell her it would 'all be all right' like the other girls would, and Annie didn't. Instead they sat side by side and smoked and drank their tea in companionable silence.

'Does Mammy ever talk about me?' Bernie asked.

Becky stared down into her cup of tea and said, 'Not to me.'

Bernie shook her head. Her mother had always been very moral. Girls who got pregnant out of wedlock, girls who were free and easy with their favours and girls who went with married men, were all beyond the pale in Kitty's eyes. There were no exceptions made to this rule, not even for her own daughters. Becky decided to change the subject.

'So what brings you down here?' she asked her friend.

'I'm supposed to be taking pictures for the paper,' Bernie said. 'The East End: broken but not bowed, that sort of thing.'

'Well, it's very true,' Becky said. 'We are, as you can see, well and truly beaten up, but we can and will take it, because what other choice do we have?'

'Heine says every word's censored so as to remove the slightest hint that the Nazis could win. No stories about people fighting for their lives in the rubble of ... '

'So Heine is ... ?'

'My fella, yes,' Bernie said.

Becky nodded. Then she said, 'Do you remember Papa's friend who lived in Plaistow – Mr Kopoloff?'

'No, but ... '

Becky's father, so far as Bernie could recall, didn't really have any friends. There had been his sister, Becky's Aunt Rivka, but she'd died back in 1939.

'He used to live on Flower and Dean Street but then he moved to Plaistow, to be nearer the Royal Docks when he got a job at the Victoria. He came to see Papa yesterday, out of the blue. I heard them talking. Mr Kopoloff said twenty people died when the house at the end of his street took a direct hit. Not the people who lived there, they were sheltering some-where else, but people in another house across the road. The fire brigade put the bodies in the street and covered them with mats. Not a mark on them, Mr Kopoloff said.' Becky lowered her voice. 'We get them in the hospital all the time ... blast vic-tims. Just the power coming from these bombs can kill you.'

'That's what the government doesn't want talked about,' Bernie said.

'Exactly.' Becky shook her head. 'But people should be warned.'

'I know.'

They both fell silent. To talk about such things wasn't done. Not even between friends. Because who knew who else might be listening?

Bernie drank some tea and then she said, 'I saw Solly Adler the other night.'

'Oh.' Becky looked away very briefly, and then smiled. 'Where?'

'The Savoy Hotel, would you believe?' Bernie said.

'The Savoy!'

'There was a press briefing Heine had to go to, and I tagged along.'

'And Solly?'

Becky had been desperately in love with Solly Adler when she was a kid. If the truth be told, it had been her fixation on him that had put paid to her father's attempts to get her a well-off husband. She'd wanted Solly, and if she couldn't have him, she wouldn't have anyone. Even knowing that, at the time, Solly had been sweet on her friend Bernie, hadn't made Becky any more amenable to her father's plans.

'A group of Commies invaded the hotel, protesting about lack of shelters in the East End,' Bernie said. 'I didn't speak to him.'

But she'd wanted to. That was why she'd taken this assignment so willingly, risking laddering her nylons, and worse, in the rubble-strewn East End streets.

'Didn't you hear about the protest?' Bernie asked her friend.

'No. Being on nights, I don't hear very much these days.'

Bernie lit a fag and the girls sat in silence for a moment until Bernie said, 'Do you ever see our Dermot?'

25

'Yes. He wants to join up.'

In spite of being in contact with her brother, Bernie hadn't known this. 'I'll have to try and put him off,' she said.

'All the young blokes are going.'

'Yeah, I know, but if Dermot does Mammy'll be on her own here,' Bernie said. Then she added, 'Do you know how my daddy is?'

There was a telling pause before Becky said, 'Your mother says he's grand.'

'Which is what she always says when she doesn't want to give a straight answer,' Bernie said.

'I know.' Becky reached out to her friend and took her hand.

Mrs Muscat wasn't having it.

'If there ain't no water then you can't have a wash,' she told Rose. 'What we gonna put in the kettle for tea if you've took all the water?'

Rose knew her landlady was right. But she also knew that she stank. Night after night stuck down in that hot, stuffy basement at the Windmill, more often than not sleepless, was making her clothes and her skin smell sour. There was only so much Lily of the Valley you could splash on yourself to cover up the stink.

'Anyway, nobody don't care what you smell like so long as you take your clothes off,' Mrs Muscat said, to score a point.

And she was right. But Rose cared. When she was a child the local kids had called her 'Smelly Elly' on account of the fact her mum was never sober enough to wash her or her clothes. Even Bernie had called her that before she really got to know Rose. Being smelly also brought back lots of other bad memories. At fifteen she'd had a back-street abortion in a flat that smelled of stale sweat. The memory of the men who had raped her and got her pregnant, including her mum's then boyfriend, was still raw in her mind.

Rose went back into her room and flung on the dress she'd worn to come home in. Many of the Windmill girls had actually gone to live inside the theatre when the bombing began. But Rose's landlady had told her that if she left and didn't pay her rent, her things would be put out on the pavement and Mrs Muscat would find herself another tenant. Grabbing her handbag off the bed, Rose ran down into the street. If it hadn't been bombed to bits last night then she might be able to get a wash down at Westminster Public Baths on Marshall Street. It was only when she was standing outside the building and looking inside her purse that she realised she didn't have any money.

'Rosie Red?'

She turned to look at a woman of about fifty. Rose knew her vaguely but couldn't remember where from. Her confusion must have showed on her face because the woman put her out of her misery. Eventually.

'Maggie,' she said.

'Er ...' Rose felt her cheeks flush. This was bloody embarrassing!

'The Pony Club,' the woman said, and suddenly Rose knew who she was.

'Oh, yes,' she said, 'you ...'

'Yeah, well, best not spell it out in the street, eh?' the woman said.

'No.'

The Pony Club was a place where men could go either to ride women like horses, complete with saddles and bridles, or be ridden themselves. What satisfaction they derived from this, sexually, was obscure to most people except, as Tilly had once told Rose, 'public-school types'. They were, Tilly always

27

said, 'Kinky for kinky's sake – in my opinion.' Rose had met several girls who worked at the club.

'You going to get a wash?' Maggie said.

'I would if I had any money,' Rose said. She sighed. 'My own fault.'

'What you spend it on?'

'I couldn't tell you,' Rose said. 'I'm silly with money.'

Maggie, who, unlike little Rose, was tall and angular, and not a bit like a pony at all, laughed. 'We're all silly from time to time, girl,' she said. 'Blimey, I thought you were gonna say you'd spent all your money down Limehouse!'

Rumours had gone around for years about how the Chinese people in Limehouse smoked and sold opium. But Rose had never heard of anyone she knew actually buying it before she came to live in the West End. People in Soho were much more likely to take drugs than the folk she remembered from Spitalfields. Nobody there'd had the money for much beyond rent, food, booze and baccy.

'No,' Rose said. 'Not for me, that.'

'Nor me,' Maggie said. 'Mind you, I couldn't do me job without me gin.' Then she took Rose's arm. 'Come on,' she said, 'I'll stand you a strip wash and you can pay me back when one of your stage-door Johnnies gives you a couple of bob.'

A lot of people thought that the Windmill girls were easy lays for the men who hung around backstage after the shows, and some of them were. But not Rose. She'd had sex many times in her short life and, in her experience, it only ever brought misery.

Solly Adler had always lived with his mum and his brother Ben in a flat on Commercial Street next door to the Princess Alice pub. Whether he was still there or not, Bernie didn't know. She hadn't pressed Becky on the subject. But she'd had to go and have a look.

For a while she stood outside the Alice watching the coster-mongers go inside, counting the few coppers in their hands to see how much beer they could drink. Bernie hadn't seen her mother or her brother but she knew that her presence on the manor would get around to them. Although they weren't exactly 'mates', she knew that her mum always looked in on Nell Larkin and she'd most certainly pass on the news.

Unlike 'up West', in the East End lone women didn't go into pubs unless they were on the game or working behind the bar. They would only visit in crowds. Her mammy and her sisters used to go into the Ten Bells once or twice a year in a great big gang. But to go in alone was frowned upon. Women put a crimp in the pleasure men derived from getting drunk, fighting and swearing. But then Bernie looked down at her camera and realised it was her route in. Her editor had sent her to get photographs of the East End: images showing a little of the suffering being endured there, but a lot of the very high morale of the area's inhabitants. And where was morale at its highest? In the pub, of course.

Bernie opened the double outer doors and pushed through the yellowing blackout curtains into the bar. She was met by a wall of cigarette and pipe smoke, the sharp tang of stale beer and a cloud of free-floating snuff. The place was packed.

Frequented only by men, as far as she could see, the bar was a sea of brown clothing and blue smoke, with the odd stained apron as worn by traders from the Market. The costers or street traders were the rowdiest people there, probably because their livelihoods were so insecure. But then, wasn't everyone's these days? Bernie lit a cigarette and waited for her eyes to adjust to the gloom. Even what they drank was

29

dark – bitter or stout – and, although it was only midday, the whole place was already bathed in the jaundiced light of two weak gas lamps. It reminded her of the family flat on Fournier Street. Her daddy always wanted to turn the light up but Mammy was far too careful.

'For Christ's sake, Pat,' she'd yell at him, 'do you think we're made of money?'

Just the thought of her gentle, now very sick, daddy, made Bernie's eyes well up. When would she see him again? She swiftly had words with herself then, along the lines of 'pull yourself together'. People were already staring at her, and if she didn't either go and order a drink or else leave at once, the strange atmosphere would persist. She walked towards the bar, which was when she saw Solly Adler – with a woman.

'Sharon Begleiter? But she's years older than Solly!' Becky said.

'Large as life, drinking a port and lemon by the look of it,' Bernie said. She drew hard on her fag and then threw the dog-end to the ground. 'Canoodling in a corner they were.'

'Were they?'

'Yes.'

The girls had met again after Bernie had left the pub and started walking furiously back to Liverpool Street Station. Unable to get back to sleep after Bernie's visit, Becky had been on her way to see her mother's brother, her uncle Lou, who lived on Bishopsgate. He was a grumpy old man but then he did have leg ulcers. The girls literally bumped into each other. Becky could see immediately that Bernie had been crying.

'But then good luck to 'em, I say,' Bernie said. 'I mean, just because Sharon was horrible to me don't mean she's a bad person. She doesn't like me, that's all.'

'And she's a cow,' Becky said loyally.

Bernie looked away. Becky wanted to put a hand on her friend's shoulder for comfort, but she didn't dare.

'But she's the cow Solly likes,' Bernie said in a small voice.

She was supposed to be in love with this Heinrich, the reporter she was living with, but Becky knew Bernie and could tell that she was still in love with Solly. Becky herself hadn't seen Solly Adler for over a year, and now especially she was quite pleased about that. Comrade Adler, as he'd been known when he'd first joined the Communist Party, had a bad effect on both girls. There had even been a time when Becky and Bernie had almost fallen out over him. Never again.

Becky took her friend's arm under hers and began to walk her towards Bishopsgate.

'Come on,' she said. 'I'll buy you a cuppa at the station caff.'

For a moment Bernie didn't move, but then she smiled and squeezed her friend's hand in thanks.

Chapter 3

Sharon was blonde but she was no Bernie Lynch. She wasn't clever enough for that. But she was in love with Solly, and she was Jewish. He couldn't work out why his mum didn't like her.

'I do like Sharon,' Dolly told him as she put on her shoes and slipped her fags into her handbag. 'Why do you think I don't?'

He shrugged. 'I dunno.'

'Well, shut up about it, then! I'm off to work.'

Dolly Adler worked as a 'nippy', as the waitresses were called in Lyons Corner House restaurants. Pin-neat and well mannered, Dolly was proud to work at the chain's biggest Corner House, on Coventry Street, Piccadilly. So far, it hadn't been bombed. That didn't mean it wouldn't be, but she had other things on her mind, like the notion she had that her son was marrying a girl he didn't love. But what could she do about it?

Solly watched his mum walk down the street towards Aldgate East Tube Station and then settled back in his chair. Five more minutes and he'd have to get himself to work. The thought of it made him close his eyes in despair. A man of his age should be in the Forces, not pressing suits for some sweat-shop merchant. But as his mum was fond of saying, Solly had 'done his bit' when he'd gone to fight the fascist might of General Franco in Spain. That the Republicans had lost had been a bitter pill to swallow for everyone who had fought on their side. Solly had also lost a leg in that war, which made his gesture of support seem even more futile.

Slowly, he got out of his chair and picked up the salt-beef beigel his mum had left for him on the sideboard. It hadn't been so bad when he'd been driving for Mr Sassoon, but he'd had to give that up on account of his leg. Driving made the stump ache and, at the end of a long day, that had meant he could hardly walk. Solly limped towards the door. At least at work he'd see Sharon. And when she showed off her engagement ring to all the other girls, he'd feel like a man for a little while.

Solly made his way down Fashion Street towards Brick Lane; fag in one hand, beigel in the other. Some of the sweat-shop girls outside old Monty Richman's gaff winked at him; one even called him 'gorgeous'. He had been once. Before the Spanish Civil War, when he'd swept Bernie Lynch into his arms and kissed her after they'd defended Cable Street from Mosley's fascists together. Twenty-four, tall, dark and dan-gerous, he'd been a proper catch then! Sharon still thought he was. But Solly knew better. In spite of the winks and the cat-calls from the *schmutter* girls, he knew he was all washed up. He'd seen what he was in the eyes of Bernie Lynch, living it up with her posh lover at the Savoy. Solly Adler was nothing.

Aggie knew she should be at school, but she didn't like it. The country kids made fun of her because she was from London and she just got into trouble all the time for getting into fights. Even if her daddy didn't understand, Auntie Mary did.

'If you're gonna look at the bats then at least clean beneath the jars,' her aunt said to her crossly.

Hastily wiping an old cloth under one of the many jars containing preserved bats, twelve-year-old Aggie Lynch looked closely at the dead creatures and wondered where their souls had gone. Did animals even have souls? It wasn't something she felt any of the teachers at Ilfracombe Grammar School would know. All they seemed to care about was how you looked and whether you attended their Church of England assembly in the morning, which she didn't. Instead, and against her father's wishes, she went to work with her auntie Mary, who felt sorry for her.

Everyone knew that her daddy was dying. Her seventeen-year-old brother, called 'Little' Paddy to distinguish him from his father, had told her that even before they left London. The three youngest Lynch children, Aggie, Paddy and Marie, had done all their crying then. Now there was just looking after Daddy, which Marie did full-time, and making life as easy as possible for Auntie Mary.

Patrick Lynch and his sister Mary had never been close as children and when she'd married a man from Devon and gone to live in Ilfracombe they'd become even more distant. Mary couldn't have children and so her life had revolved around her husband, who had been a fisherman, until his death in 1934. So, although she would never tell them this, not wanting them to feel she was vulnerable in any way, she had been very glad when Patrick and the children came down to Devon when the war began. Apart from anything else, the money Little Paddy gave her from his job on Mr Pickard's farm helped to supplement her own meagre earnings from cleaning jobs at some of the local hotels and Ilfracombe Museum. Kitty paid Pat's and the younger kids' expenses.

Aggie picked up another jar of dead bats. 'Why did Mr Grove Palmer put animals in jars?' she asked.

'I don't know, you'll have to ask him,' her aunt said.

Ilfracombe Museum had been set up by an explorer called Mervyn Grove Palmer in 1932, mainly to house his anthropological specimens, which came principally from South America. He was currently the curator of the museum but was rarely to be seen when Auntie Mary was cleaning.

'I wonder where he found the kitten,' Aggie continued. 'I mean it's not usual for a cat to have two heads, is it?'

'No. The Church would say it's an abomination, but Mr GP is the boss here and so we have a cat with two heads in a jar. Not to mention . . . ' Auntie Mary lowered her voice ' . . . idols.'

Aggie shuddered. Mr Grove Palmer had spent a lot of time in the jungles of Mexico and had returned with a huge number of the weird things the Maya there had once worshipped. Luckily, when the Spaniards had arrived, they'd all been forcibly converted to Catholicism.

Aggie heard running footsteps before she saw anyone. Mary, too busy mopping the floor and whistling, didn't hear anything until sixteen-year-old Marie came flying into the exhibition gallery.

As soon as Aggie saw that her sister's face was white with fear, she said, 'Is it Dad?'

In between gasps for air, Marie said, 'I've called Dr Renwick!'

Aggie put her hands up to her face and wept.

Sleep didn't come easily to Becky after such a heavy shift at the London. Another night spent in the basement trying to keep dust and debris off from the seriously ill – while still more patients pressed in on them. It was a miracle that, so far, the hospital hadn't taken a direct hit.

Becky was just on the brink of dropping off when she heard a very strange sound coming from downstairs. It was a ringing noise which, after a few moments, she recognised as her father's only rarely used telephone. Assuming it was one of his customers calling about a fitting, she closed her eyes. But then suddenly her father was in her bedroom doorway.

'Rebekah!' he shouted. 'It's the telephone! It's for you!'

'For me?' she said. 'Is it the hospital?'

Oh, God, did they want her to put in an extra shift? She couldn't! She was exhausted!

'No, no, no! It's young Patrick Lynch,' said Moritz. 'You must speak to him quickly! Come!'

If Little Paddy was calling then Becky feared it could only be about one thing. She ran downstairs and picked up the telephone receiver, which had been left hanging from the wall.

'Paddy?' she said.

She heard him choke on a sob.

'Oh, Paddy!'

'It's me dad,' she heard him say. 'Doctor reckons he ain't got long.'

It was for just this reason the Lynches had been given the Shapiros' number. And yet, even knowing that, the shock made Becky sink to her knees. Apart from her papa, her uncle Pat was the most important man in her life.

'Paddy . . . '

'Can you tell Der and Mammy? They need to come at once,' Paddy said.

'Of course.'

He hesitated for a moment and then he said, 'And our Bernie.'

Becky shut her eyes.

'I know she done wrong according to Mammy but she needs to be here. You understand that, don't you, Becky?'

'You know I do, Paddy,' she said.

When she put the receiver down, Becky wiped her eyes. She had too much to do to indulge herself in useless tears. Both Auntie Kitty and Dermot would be at work now; she needed to get a move on.

Normally the smell of rum would have made him smile. But not when it was accompanied by the sight of so many shattered barrels. The Import Dock hadn't taken any direct hits but it had been knocked about. Dermot Lynch looked up at the vast hull of the ship that had just docked and scratched his head. Before any new cargo could be warehoused, the guv'nors would need to come down and make an inventory of the damage and then the splintered barrels would have to be taken out and stacked up outside. So far, the foreman, Artie Cross, hadn't told any of the blokes what to do and so the dockers hung around in groups, talking about what they'd seen and heard of the bombing the night before and smoking. All except for Dermot.

None of the other geezers had so much as breathed over him since that terrible night back in 1937 when Artie and a group of his 'royalty', as his group of hard-core docker brothers were called, had robbed a furrier's warehouse on Fournier Street. Joey and Dermot had been among them – Dermot very much against his wishes. Fred Lamb, one of the Lynches' neighbours, had died trying to defend the place.

Joey Lynch had privately admitted to killing Lamb but neither his father nor Dermot had believed him. Artie Cross had done it, they were sure, and the only reason Dermot was still employed at the Import Dock was because he and his father had sworn not to grass up the foreman in return for Dermot continuing to be taken on. But the shock of the incident had affected him badly and now he lived for the day when he could join the Forces and get off the dock. Even if it meant being killed by a ruddy Nazi. But then maybe that wasn't such a bad thing anyway.

It had been months since he'd seen his old schoolfriend Chrissy Dolan, mainly because Dermot was avoiding him. He didn't want to, but if the other dockers saw him with Chrissy he knew things could get even worse for him at work. When he'd first left school, Chrissy had got a good job as a window dresser in Swan and Edgar's department store up West. But then he'd been dismissed for having a romantic liaison with another man and now was reduced to working as a cleaner in a Limehouse brothel. And everyone knew – what he'd done and why he'd done it. Artie and his mob hated 'poofs'. They had always taunted Dermot for his 'poofiness'. It had hurt all the more because, although he'd never say it to a soul, not even to Chrissy, he now realised it was true.

'Oi! Lynch!'

He looked around. Christ! Was someone actually talking to him?

'What?'

'Some lady asking to see ya.'

Harry Sims was one of Artie's closest allies. He hadn't so much as looked at Dermot since the night Fred Lamb died. Now he smirked and said, 'Can't think why.'

Dermot ignored the jibe. 'Where is she?' he asked.

Sims nodded to the left. 'Dock office,' he said.

It seemed to Dermot as if every docker on the Import watched him walk away.

*

Mary had heard that sound before. A thick, wheezy rattle was the only way she could describe it. But she knew what it meant. Her Matthew had done it for the last two days of his life. Fortunately, Pat was sleeping now and, although breathing was hard for him, the laudanum that Dr Renwick had given him had eased his pain. How they were going to pay him for it was anyone's guess but Renwick was a good sort and money hadn't been mentioned.

Mary stroked her brother's head. Pat had been the only member of the family who had wished her well when she'd gone off with a Protestant fisherman from Devon. Her da and her mammy were hard, tough people with few sympathies for anyone outside their immediate circle. Her brothers and sisters were the same – except for Patrick. He'd always found room in his heart for anyone who behaved kindly towards others and, although he'd only ever met him once, Pat had liked Matthew.

Her youngest nephew came running in then, panting.

'Did you get through?' Mary asked.

The lad had gone to the George and Dragon at the top of the street to use their telephone. It had been Matthew's local and the landlord was always happy to help Mary out whenever he could. She had a notion he was a little sweet on her.

Little Paddy nodded. 'Becky said she'd tell Ma and Der and ... and our Bernie too,' he said. 'Did I do wrong, Auntie Mary?'

The boy sat down beside her and she took his hand.

'No, you didn't, Paddy,' she said. 'Your daddy loves Bernie and I know he will want to see her.'

'Mammy'll go bonkers.'

'So let her.' Mary ruffled his pale red, sun-bleached hair. Working in the fields was making a man out of this boy. 'This is about your daddy.'

39

'I know.'

Marie came in with a glass containing a dark, cloudy liquid, which she gave to Mary.

'Betsy sent this,' she said. 'Says it's cider.'

Betsy was a barmaid at the George and Dragon. Childless, like Mary, she sometimes popped by for a chat or a drink or both.

Mary took a draught and then smiled. 'Scrumpy,' she said.

'Looks horrible.'

'But tastes like a dream.' She finished half the pint in one go and then put the glass down on the bare-boarded floor. Mary and Paddy had moved Pat's bed down into the parlour weeks ago when his illness had started to get worse. He had emphysema, which meant, as Mary saw it, that his lungs were falling apart. There was no cure and so there was only one end in view, which Pat had almost reached.

'Hopefully your Bernie's posh man'll bring your mammy and Dermot here in his car. If he's got a car,' Mary said. 'Otherwise it'll be the train to Exeter, provided Paddington ain't been bombed.'

Marie lay down on the bed next to her father and took his hand. 'You must hang on, Daddy,' she said. 'Mammy, Dermot and Bernie are coming. They'll be here soon, I know they will.'

Becky had left telling Auntie Kitty to Dermot. Then she'd come home and telephoned the number she'd found for the *London Evening News* in the previous night's paper. But a very well-spoken lady in the photographic office had told her: 'Miss Lynch has taken a day's leave.'

Becky didn't have Bernie's home telephone number, if indeed she and Mr Simpson even had a phone (as she suspected they did). But she did have her friend's address. It was in Pimlico, which was over near Westminster, some-where Becky couldn't remember ever having visited. She told her father what she was doing and then got a trolley bus as far as Holborn. Sitting on the top deck, Becky could see the normal business of the city going on all around: men in bowler hats walking quickly to their places of business, groups of young typists stepping gingerly down glass-strewn streets, hardware shops and cafés with windows taped with crosses, designed to protect against the blast from bombs and incendiaries. It was normal and yet not normal. Although the expressions on people's faces looked determined, they were also afraid.

From Holborn to Victoria, she walked. All the buses were packed and many streets were closed due to unexploded bombs – or UXBs as they were known. Becky didn't have a clue where this Dolphin Square place was, except that it was somewhere near Victoria Station. All too aware of how having had no sleep today would affect her when she went on shift that evening, she asked a station newspaper vendor for directions.

'You wanna go south towards the river, love,' he said around the fag at the corner of his mouth. 'Chichester Street's where it is. Dirty great big buildings they are. You got rich mates, do you?'

It looked like something you might find in America. There were thirteen blocks, or 'houses' as Becky later learned they were called, making up the complex of buildings known as Dolphin Square. Set in sad-looking gardens, the houses at the front, nearest the river, had taken some bomb damage, but those farther back appeared to be intact. Bernie lived in Rodney House, which was farthest away from the Thames.

Even knocked about, it was easy to see that Dolphin Square

was posh. A man in a uniform of some sort had challenged Becky as soon as she entered the complex. She felt this wasn't surprising; the other women she saw coming and going were dressed in expensively tailored costumes and elaborate hats. The only people who looked like her were girls in the black-and-white uniforms worn by servants.

'I've come to see Mr Heinrich Simpson,' she said to the commissionaire. 'I have an urgent message for his ... er ... '

How was she supposed to refer to Bernie? She felt herself blush.

'His assistant, Miss Lynch?' the man asked.

'Um, yes,' she said. 'His ... '

He smiled at her. 'Rodney House, third floor. You may use the lift provided, miss.'

Even before she got to the door of the flat, Becky found herself shaking. What was she going to say if Bernie didn't answer the door? She'd never met Heinrich Simpson. Did she just ask for Bernie and ... then what?

She knocked and for a long time heard nothing except for vague sounds of music coming from somewhere. She thought it sounded like jazz. When Bernie finally opened the door Becky realised it was jazz – probably. Trumpet music anyway.

'Becky!'

She was wearing some sort of silk robe, which could have been a dressing gown, and smoking a cigarette.

Tired, foot-sore and already in mourning for the man she had always called 'Uncle Pat', Becky burst into tears and blurted out, 'It's your dad!'

'What you doing?' Kitty asked.

Dermot threw his pyjamas into a valise on top of his tobacco tin and said, 'I'm coming with you.'

'To Devon?' She shook her head. 'No. You need to go to work. Your daddy's my responsibility. I'll nurse him.'

It took Dermot a few moments to realise she either hadn't taken in what was happening, or she wouldn't.

'Mammy . . .'

'I'll get a train from Paddington to Exeter and then a bus to Ilfracombe. I'll be gone a week . . .'

'Mammy.'

'At the most.' She turned to him and smiled, one hand on her suitcase. 'Promise.'

Dermot knew the only way to get her out of acting this charade was just to say it.

'Mammy, he's dying.'

For a moment Kitty looked confused and then she said, 'No . . .'

'Paddy told Becky Shapiro he's on laudanum.'

'Yes, well, they give it for all . . .'

'They give it to the dying,' Dermot said. 'If you won't believe me then ask Becky, she's a nurse.' He went over to his mother and took her hands. 'Mammy, Daddy can't breathe. When he left for Devon, he was struggling, but now he can't breathe at all.'

'No . . .'

She tried to pull her hands away from his but Dermot held onto her, tight.

'I'm coming with you because he's my daddy,' he said. 'He's your husband but he's my daddy and I need to say goodbye to him. We both do.'

The dam burst then and she cried. Of course, Kitty had known that Pat was dying. When she'd told Miss Smith she couldn't work for a while, she knew that her manager knew too. It was why the stern mistress of the Blue Room had briefly put her hand on Kitty's shoulder. She didn't show emotion for any reason. Except death.

Some of the girls took all their stage make-up off between shows, but not Rose. Apart from being expensive, stage make-up always smeared and melted under the lights but, if you knew what you were doing, it was easy enough to repair. Naked, she sat looking at herself in the mirror while other girls around her chatted, smoked and got ready to go out together for the afternoon. Rose often went with them, but not today. She was hot after the show, which was why she hadn't put her clothes on after her set, and she felt unaccountably glum. She did sometimes, although usually that happened only when she had spent time thinking about her mum and her friends back in Spitalfields. And today she hadn't.

Everyone but a girl called Mavis left the dressing room. Rose offered her a drink of brandy from a bottle she'd been given by a grateful punter, but the other girl declined. Rose drank some anyway. Since the Blitz had started she'd found herself needing a 'little nip' more and more. Not that she was anything like her mother, she hoped.

A knock on the dressing-room door followed by an immediate entrance meant that it was probably Kenneth the stage doorman. Fortysomething, he'd lost a leg in the Great War, for which the rest of the Windmill staff were very sorry, but he did also, Rose felt, sometimes use his misfortune to get the things he wanted. These included fags, booze and sneaky peeks at the girls when they were sitting around in the buff.

Kenneth, smiling, put a bottle down in front of Rose. It was champagne.

'From some bloke outside,' he said. 'There's a label on it.'

Rose looked briefly at the label, which read: *With great admiration from Mr Lance Pym.* Then she gave the bottle back to Kenneth.

'He can have it back,' she said. 'I don't want it.'

'Thought you liked a little drop now and then, Rosie Red,' Kenneth said with a toothy smile. Rose thought he looked a bit like the music-hall star George Formby when he smiled. That and the way he seemed to leer into her heart-shaped face made her cringe.

'No,' she said.

She could feel him looking at her naked body and she shuffled uncomfortably in her chair. Of course he'd seen her like this before, he'd seen all of the girls naked. But that still didn't mean any of them liked it.

When he'd gone, Mavis said to her, 'He gives me the creeps.'

'Ignore him,' Rose replied.

'Oh, I do,' Mavis said. 'And if he gets all uppity, I've always got my Sammy I can get onto him.'

Sammy was Mavis's boyfriend or rather sugar daddy. At least sixty, he owned a milliner's shop in Stoke Newington.

'Why don't you have a fella, Rosie?' she asked. 'The punters really like you. You could get a fella just like that.' She clicked her fingers.

Rose shrugged. She didn't want to go into it. She imagined that maybe sex could be all right if you loved the man, but to her it was associated purely with violence – and loss. What, she often wondered, would the baby she'd had ripped out of her when she was fifteen be like now? And would she ever get over the guilt she felt about it?

Because Rose didn't answer, Mavis said, 'But don't worry if you're the other way. I mean, look at Suzy . . . she's one of them and we all love her like a sister.'

'I'm not a lesbian,' Rose said.

But Mavis just smiled. If you didn't have a beau then you had to be a lesbian according to some of the girls. But it didn't matter. Rose turned back towards her own image in the mirror and suddenly wondered what Dermot Lynch might be doing. Was he still working in the docks or had he joined up?

'Mammy, it makes sense,' Dermot said as he took his mother's hands and led her away from the smartly dressed couple at the front door. 'Sit down, have a cuppa and think about it.'

'I will not!' Kitty Lynch said. She pulled her hands away and turned her back on him. 'You can tell them people to go.'

Bernie Lynch wasn't the sort of girl who wept easily but Dermot could see that his sister was close to tears now. He heard Heinrich Simpson say to her, 'Let's go.'

'No! Please don't,' Dermot said. 'Mammy'll change her mind . . .'

'I bloody won't!'

When Becky had told Bernie that her dad was gravely ill, Heinrich Simpson had dropped everything so that he could help her. He had not only volunteered to drive Bernie down to Ilfracombe to see her father, but also to take her mother and brother as well. And this was the thanks he got from Kitty Lynch.

Suddenly furious with what he saw as her foolish stubbornness, Dermot said, 'Oh, for the love of God, Mammy, trains and railway stations are being bombed every night!'

'Not Paddington!'

'No, but maybe it'll get its share tonight,' he said.

'So go in that fancy car if you want . . .'

'Oh, no. If you won't go in the car, I won't either,' he said.

'But not because I feel my sister's "bad" or Mr Simpson's some sort of rapist! They fell in love, Mammy. They didn't want ...'

'How do you know so much about it?' she snapped.

Bernie put a warning hand on Dermot's shoulder but he shrugged it off.

'Because I go to see them, Mammy,' he said. 'There, I've told you! I go to see them because Bernie is my sister and I love her, and Mr Simpson is a straight-up geezer who treats her nice! And, yes, I did go behind your back and I'm *not sorry*.'

Kitty turned to face him. 'She's living in bleeding sin with a married man, don't you—'

'Oh, for the love of God, we could all be dead tomorrow, Mammy! Christ Almighty ...'

'Watch your mouth!'

Dermot got down on his knees to her. 'Mammy ...'

'No! Get up, you look bleeding stupid!'

Dermot stood and looked at his sister and her man, standing on the threshold, and said, 'Well, all right then, Mammy. Have it your own way, I'm going with them.'

'Good. God alone knows where your man is getting his petrol from ...'

Bernie moved across the threshold and said, 'Don't you worry about that.'

'Get out!'

Dermot held his breath.

'No,' Bernie persevered. 'And do you want to know why, Mammy?'

'From a bloody brass? I don't think so.'

'Well, you're going to hear it anyway,' Bernie said. 'How can you be so bleeding selfish, is what I want to know?'

'Selfish? Me?' Kitty's face was as red as a pillar box. 'You bloody little cow!'

Dermot moved, ready to step between them should one or other woman go for a punch.

'Yeah, selfish,' Bernie said. 'Because you're making it about you and me and your belief that God gives a tupp'ny damn about all this, when what it's actually about is Daddy. Daddy's dying and ...' she began to cry '... you ain't going to stop me seeing him! You can kill me after, but you ain't stopping me from going to him!'

Heinrich Simpson walked over and took her in his arms.

'Bernie ...'

The sound of his sister's sobbing made Dermot's heart feel as if it would break. But his mother simply turned her back and glared into a corner of the room while Dermot looked at Heinrich apologetically.

'I'm sorry for this, Mr Simpson ...'

Heinrich shrugged. 'Bring your things and let's go,' he said. 'The quicker we get out of London the better.'

Chapter 4

The 'sleep before death' was what her mammy had called it. Mary didn't know what its real name was but she recognised it. Only the knowledge that Pat would hang on until the rest of his family arrived prevented her from falling into despair. She could hear the other three, Paddy, Marie and Aggie, talking quietly in the back yard. It wasn't easy being in a room with a dying man even if he was your father.

It had started to get dark about an hour ago and so Mary lit the gas lamp farthest away from where her brother lay sleeping. Although Ilfracombe itself hadn't been bombed, Exeter, just fifty miles away, had on 7 August. No one had been killed, but it made a person think. As the light faded, soon enemy bombers would be flying in over the Channel with their sights set most probably on London. If only Mary could be sure that Kitty and the others were on their way.

Where on earth were they? Bernie had been out of the country when she'd accompanied Heinrich to Germany, but she'd never been west of Hammersmith in her life. She looked over her shoulder at Dermot, who was looking out of the back window of the car. What seemed to be huge fireworks were exploding above something quite distant, that she assumed to be London.

She looked at Heinrich. 'Where are we?'

They'd just gone through a town that had been entirely blacked out. Heinrich had been forced to drive slowly through the gloom but now that they appeared to be in open country the car had started to speed up again.

'Just gone through Windsor,' he said.

'Where the castle is?'

'Yes.'

Bernie hadn't seen it, but then how could she?

'Docks are copping it again,' Dermot said. 'If you look, you can see that most of the bombing's in just one place.'

Bernie didn't look, because she couldn't bear to. Her mother, although hopefully far from the docks by this time, was probably still at or near Paddington Station. Although she saw it in herself, Bernie hated her mother's stubbornness. Nobody had told Kitty she'd have to be civil or even polite if she travelled in the car with them, but she just wouldn't. Bernie was 'living in sin', for God's sake! In Kitty's eyes her daughter was a fallen woman and a lost cause. Didn't her mother know there was a war on – that they could all lose their lives at any moment? What did such considerations matter now? If there even was a God, He had well and truly abandoned them.

'Have you any idea how long it'll be before we get to Ilfracombe?' Bernie asked.

Heinrich shook his head. 'No. It's a long way yet. I'll be honest with you, I may have to stop for a rest at some point. Most people do when they go down to the West Country.'

'So Mammy may get there before us?'

'Depends on what the trains are doing,' he said. 'If she left Paddington before the bombing started, maybe. But the time-tables are useless at the moment. Trains run when they can.'

Everything ran when it could – trains, buses, the Underground. Everywhere you went it seemed as if people were struggling to get somewhere or do something that was being made almost impossible by the bombing.

Bernie's first photographic assignment for the *London Evening News* had been a trip to Berlin with Heinrich. As a native German, he'd been able to put what she saw in context for her by speaking to anyone brave enough to let their views be known to the foreign press. As a Jew and a German he had been prepared for the brutality of the Nazi regime – its rise had forced him to leave his home country after all. But what they had seen in Berlin had marked Bernie. The city's Jews, or those that remained, were huddled into frightened groups, at constant risk from the Nazi thugs who roamed the streets night and day. It was only Heinrich's British passport that had saved him from becoming a target too and she remembered how he'd almost worn it as a badge. She also remembered thinking how much her daddy would have hated to see fascist bullies on the streets, their hated symbol, the swastika, even flying from on top of Christmas trees. Her daddy had been a staunch Socialist all his life and she knew that when Britain had declared war on Germany he had been upset, but he had also been certain it had been the right thing to do. Dermot had told her he'd said, 'Whatever the cost, we have to beat 'em. Fascism is evil and the only way to deal with evil is to smash it into the ground.'

Pat Lynch had never been a violent man but he was some-one who knew that sometimes you had to fight for the right thing. Bernie looked out into the blackness of the night and hoped that Heinrich wouldn't see her crying.

Tommy and Trisha the Tap-Dancing Twins were enough to try the patience of a saint. They were only kids but still, their antics in the confined basement of the Windmill Theatre, and their endless chatter, were getting on everyone's nerves – Tilly's most of all. It wasn't easy as it was, keeping one's make-up pristine in a hot basement during a bombing raid, but the more dance-based antics the Twins performed, the more drag-queen Tilly heated up.

'Blimey,' she said to Rose, 'chiffon's a bloody trial in a confined space!'

Rose smiled. Tilly, or Herbert to use her non-drag name, used silent-star Gloria Swanson as her model of feminine allure. This meant a lot of chiffon was required, which in such quantities could be stifling.

'I wish they'd just pipe down!' Tilly said as she sat beside Rose and lit a cigar. 'Why do they have to be so bloody active?'

'Because they're kids.' Rose squeezed Tilly's arm. "They're full of energy but they're trapped down here.'

'You'd think the mother'd have a word,' said Tilly as she tipped her head towards a thin, sour-looking woman standing in front of the basement door, smoking.

'I don't think they can do any wrong in her eyes,' Rose said.

'Bloody stage mothers! All frustrated thesps, the lot of 'em.'

Some of the 'turns' that were on between the Windmill Girls' *tableaux* were easier to like than others. Kids, as in teenage acts, were not that common, especially now the bombing had started. Most of London's children had been evacuated to the countryside. Rose liked an old man who called himself the Genie of the Lamp, a magician who performed the most breathtaking illusions while completely drunk. Currently passed out underneath the stairs, he was probably dealing with the bombing better than most.

Apart from the continually tapping twins, most of the Windmill Girls and the other turns sat in groups, drinking, smoking and gossiping. One of the few exceptions to this was Kenneth. He sat on his own, apparently reading a dog-eared paperback book. But Rose could see his eyes were actually on the girls. Instinctively, she moved closer to Tilly who said, 'Oh, you cheeky mare, I think you just touched me bum!'

'Tea's up!'

Becky didn't usually get the chance to leave her patients for a moment once they were all down in the cellar. But, sadly, there had been a lot of deaths that day and so, not for the best reason in the world, Becky was able to go and make everyone a cuppa. Getting thirty-one cups of tea made in the confined space of an old store cupboard wasn't easy. But the looks of appreciation on the faces of the patients and other members of staff made her smile.

One lady who had just gone into labour with twins said, 'Oh, bring it here, love, I'm gasping!'

Becky put the cup and saucer into her hands just as something loud happened above their heads.

'Fucking Nazis!' the woman said, and then closed her eyes briefly as her next contraction took hold.

The nurse who was caring for her said, 'Enough of that language, please, Mrs Sims.'

'Sorry.' Once her contraction had passed, the woman in labour took a sip of her tea. 'That's better. You ain't got a fag, have you?'

The nurse, a young woman from up West somewhere,

reached into her pocket and produced one. 'Here you are,' she said. 'But there's no more where that came from. I'm almost out.'

'Thank you, nurse.'

Becky passed amongst the trolleys and the wheelchairs, distributing tea.

'Thank you so much, Nurse Shapiro,' a foreign voice said.

Becky looked up into the face of Dr Rajesh Desai.

'Not a problem, doctor.'

'But requires effort in very cramped surroundings,' he replied. 'And is appreciated.'

'Thank you.'

She walked away, aware that the other doctors, who hadn't even acknowledged her action, were looking on. Dr Desai was the only Indian doctor at the Royal London. In fact, he was the only Asian member of staff, full-stop. Tall and slim, he had neat black hair and eyes that smiled when he spoke. Becky liked him even though she knew some of the other nurses didn't. A rumour had gone around when he first arrived that the young man had said something he shouldn't have to Sister Moore, though Becky didn't know whether that was true or not. Sister Moore was one of those people who imagined no man could resist her. In fact, Bridie, one of the longest-serving of the long-suffering hospital cleaners, had once told Becky that Sister M was usually upset with any new doctor if he *didn't* try it on with her.

'She teases the men, that one,' Bridie had said. 'I'll not say as she follows through and allows them, you know, liberties. But she does play with fire, that I do know. I'd lay good money she came on to Dr Desai and he rebuffed her.'

Becky took tea to the next patient.

'Thank you, nurse.'

Rita was only sixteen but looked much younger. Black-eyed and stick-thin, the girl was the youngest patient anyone had ever seen with the 'Barking Cough'. Becky wondered how long she'd been working at the Cape Asbestos plant, but Rita wouldn't say. A lot of poor families took their kids out of school early just to make ends meet. Whether their employers were informed the children were underage or not wasn't known and probably wasn't even thought about much. But there were many young victims as well as adult ones. After just a couple of sips from her cup, Rita began to cough and splutter and so Becky took the tea away and sat her up straight. As she tapped the girl's back to help her bring up the mucus that was drowning her lungs, she said, 'Get as much out as you can, Rita, there's a good girl.'

What did come out was threaded with blood and Becky thought about Pat Lynch. Paddy had said he was dying and Becky had wished she could see 'Uncle' Pat one more time. But she couldn't because she had too much to do for the people in her care. And Uncle Pat, better than anyone, would under-stand that, she knew.

Rita lay back down, her face the colour of ash. After a while she began to make snuffling noises as sleep overtook her. As the whole building shook in response to blast from a nearby explosion, Becky took the young girl's hand.

Life wasn't fair. That a girl like this should be dying because her lungs were clogged with something everyone had said was safe, wasn't right. That Uncle Pat was dying because the air in the East End was poison to him, wasn't right either. The lives of ordinary people had been bad before the war; now they were almost unbearable. And yet . . .

And yet Bernie had her Heinrich, who was a kind man, if a little old. Their lovely flat in Pimlico showed all the signs of a couple setting up home together for good. So on some level, Bernie and Heinrich had to feel hope. Why didn't Becky?

*

Dermot sat down on a lump of rock sticking out of the ground and smoked a cigarette.

'Where did you say this is again?' he asked Heinrich.

None of them knew exactly what the time was because looking at a watch was difficult in the pitch dark.

'Exmoor,' Heinrich said.

'Middle of nowhere.'

'I know. But I had to stop or I was going to fall asleep.'

'It's all right, mate,' Dermot said. 'I am grateful, you know. And if Bernie's finally asleep, we can only thank God for that.'

'Indeed.'

Bernie had tried to stay awake but, already exhausted by her argument with her mother, grief for her father and the journey so far, she'd finally dropped off just before they'd reached Taunton.

'It's not too far now,' Heinrich said. 'But it's all moorland until we reach the coast and I need to be properly awake for it.'

'Gives me the creeps, I have to say,' Dermot told him.

He heard Heinrich laugh. 'There's nothing but ponies to worry about here,' he said. 'And ditches, of course, which is why I need to be alert. There is a story that the devil built a bridge on Exmoor long ago ...'

'How do you know that?' Dermot asked.

Heinrich knew so much! All about Germany, about writing, he could drive, and now it seemed he knew about Exmoor too.

'I'm a reporter,' he said. 'It's my job to find things out. Before the war, when I first came to this country, I had to take any job that I could. I worked for a few months on a newspaper in Exeter. People were always coming in to report strange things happening on Exmoor. Unexplained lights were very common and there were stories about people drowning in peat bogs ...'

Dermot shuddered. It sounded like some of the stories

his grandparents had told about Ireland when he had been a child. Tales of fairies and pookas and changelings. Things that went bump in the night and the chilling scream of the banshee, signalling death.

'Dermot,' Heinrich continued, 'you know I love your sister very much, don't you? I want to take care of her. I'd give her anything.'

'I know,' he said, 'but you're also married and so I can see Mammy's point of view too.'

'I do intend to get a divorce.'

'With our Bernie named?'

Even if the female half of a couple had committed adultery, it was generally the husband who took the blame. But that meant a woman's name had to be cited in court – as his partner in adultery. Sometimes this was the woman the man had fallen in love with; sometimes it was a friend, acquaintance or even a prostitute, paid for her services in exchange for having her name used as co-respondent. Being cited in a divorce case was a serious matter that could result in a woman being dismissed from her employment.

'I will take care of her, Dermot.'

'If she loses her job she'll never be happy again, you do know that, don't you?' he said. 'You've seen how we live, it took guts for Bernie to get out of Spitalfields. She's always been ambitious. You can't take her job away from her. It ain't fair.'

But Heinrich said nothing more. Neither of them did. And when they got back in the car that silence persisted.

Although she'd managed to get a seat by the window, Kitty still had to sit next to a small boy with a heavy cold. His mother, a tiny, drawn woman probably in her thirties, kept on wiping his nose and apologising.

'I'm sorry,' she said, 'he's not been well ...'

Kitty just smiled and said, 'Don't worry, love. Had six of me own, so I know how it is.'

The train had left Paddington on time but had quickly ground to a halt. And, although the bombing seemed to be concentrated on the docks, incendiary devices were giving the West End fire crews a run for their money. Kitty had no idea where they were now, somewhere to the west of Paddington but still in London. As the ground shook under the train tracks she heard the people around her gasp in fear. Kitty herself was afraid, every raid was terrifying, but her mind was distracted by her greater need to get to Pat while she still could.

She should've taken Mr Simpson's offer of a lift and gone with Bernadette and Dermot. But her stupid pride just hadn't let her. Right from the start she'd been against Bernadette taking that job with the *Evening News*. Going abroad with a strange man, things had been bound to happen! And they had. Now the girl was living in sin with a married man older than her own father and doomed to the role of the 'other woman' for all time. It wasn't what Kitty had wanted for her eldest girl. She'd wanted a nice boy for her, a boy Bernie's own age, Catholic, preferably Irish, with both of them virgins on their wedding day. She'd wanted Bernadette's wedding to be the one Kitty herself never had, the one where the bride wasn't pregnant or her father's face red with shame. Kitty had been five months gone with Joey when she'd married Pat. Such a long time ago!

She felt her eyes sting with tears and was glad that the train carriage was in darkness so no one could see. Dermot had shouted at her to face up to the truth about her husband, but Kitty already knew it. Pat was dying. He'd had emphysema for years. He'd carried on working for at least a decade with it. But the disease only had one outcome and that was death.

How would she live without her husband? She'd *coped* without him ever since he and the children had gone to Devon, but that was very different from living with the knowledge that he was no longer in the world. Kitty looked out of the carriage window at the blacked-out houses that lined the railway track, lit from behind by the fires the Nazis had rained down, and continued to rain down, on the city. She'd be lucky to get to Reading by dawn at this rate, let alone Devon. If Pat had died before she got there . . .

No, she couldn't think like that. Kitty took a cigarette out of her handbag and lit up. Thinking like that would do her no good, she had to pull herself together!

It was then that she noticed her skirt felt wet and, as she looked around to discover why, saw that the little boy sitting beside her was shaking.

'What . . . '

'I'm so sorry, Mrs,' his tiny mother said, 'he has a problem with his, you know, his *waterworks.*'

Suddenly and explosively, Kitty burst out laughing. God Almighty, she was travelling on a train, in a bombing raid, to somewhere she'd never been before in her life – and now she was covered in a little boy's piss!

The woman had no eyes! Nell was scared but she screwed up her courage and looked closer. You could see through the woman! Nell had to get out! Why had she come to such a place? Church it was, but it was also full of the dead who as everyone knew were unclean and, if they walked, only meant people harm.

Nell jumped to her feet and began to half stagger, half run across the crypt of Christ Church while everyone else looked at her as if she was mad. Some old coster said, 'Where you going? You do know there's bombs going off out there?'

But Nell didn't care. Rather bombs than ghosts. She could still see the woman, floating now up by the ceiling, smiling down at her. When she got to the door leading on to the churchyard, Nell opened it and hurled herself through into a world of noise, smoke and fire. Across Commercial Street, firemen trained long bucking hoses into Spitalfields Market, yelling at each other, hanging on for dear life. Something cracked nearby and Nell watched part of the back of what had been Fred Lamb's house collapse into its back yard. She ran through the graveyard and into Fournier Street. If she could just get back to the flat, Nell knew she'd be all right. That was until she saw the woman with no eyes following close behind her.

Nell didn't hear herself scream, but it was the sound that attracted Moritz Shapiro's attention. When Rebekah was at work, he didn't go into the shelter. Being in there on his own made him start to go crazy. And so he stayed in the house, usually as on this occasion in his chair by the fire in the front parlour. He reasoned that if he was going to die, then he was going to die in comfort. When he heard a woman's screams he got up and walked out into the street where he suddenly found himself with his arms around Nell Larkin.

'Help me! Help me!' she said.

Strangely, she didn't smell of drink but she was terrified.

'Mrs Larkin, you should be in the shelter ...'

'I went,' she said, 'but it was full of the dead ...' She looked behind her and pointed at some point in the air '... like her!'

'Her?'

'That church is full of ghosts, Mr Shapiro,' she said. 'I can't go back there! I won't!'

It was said by many that Nell Larkin was a gypsy and they were known to be fey. But whether this was sheer superstition on her part or an hallucination as years and years of drinking caught up with her, Moritz didn't know.

'No one will make you go back to the church,' he said. 'Come to my house and let me make you tea. Come on.'

He enfolded her frail body in his own thin arms and walked her up the steps and into his house. Outside incendiary bombs began to fizz and ignite as the woman with no eyes continued to laugh.

He was smiling. His skin was grey and his voice no more than a whisper, but Bernie's daddy was smiling at her.

'Hello, sweetheart,' he wheezed. 'What you doing down here?'

Bernie wrapped her arms around him. It had been such a long time since she'd done that and he was so thin!

'We came to see you, Daddy,' she said. 'Me and Dermot. And Mammy's on her way.'

He nodded. Did he realise how weird it was that his wife wasn't with his children? If he did, then he didn't say anything.

'You come with your fella?' he asked his daughter.

Bernie looked at Dermot who shrugged as if to say: *You have to tell the truth, especially now.*

'Yes, Daddy,' she said. 'Heinrich's out in the back yard with Auntie Mary.'

Auntie Mary – who knew just what it was like to be frozen out by the Lynch family.

'Heinrich drove us,' Dermot said. 'All through the night.'

'That's nice,' Pat said.

'Mammy's . . .'

'I know your mum'll be here in her own time and under her own steam,' Pat said. Then he closed his eyes and sank back into sleep.

According to Auntie Mary it had been a miracle he'd woken

61

up at all. Last night she had feared he was on the point of death. But as soon as Bernie and Dermot had walked through the door he'd opened his eyes.

Dermot put a hand on his sister's shoulder and said, 'Come on, let's go out the back.'

Mary's yard was small but it was full of potted plants which, in the summer months, were a riot of colour. Now autumn was coming they were more muted. But it was still a restful place to be, especially since Mary had set out chairs and a small table with a jug of scrumpy on it. As Bernie and Dermot walked into the yard, Heinrich and Little Paddy stood up.

'How is he?' Paddy asked, his face a pale mask of anxiety.

'He's holding on.' Dermot took his cap off and sat down.

'You both need a good drink,' Mary said as she poured out two large glasses of scrumpy. 'Heinrich here's just been telling me about your journey.' She handed the glasses to Bernie and Dermot. 'Across Exmoor at night! You wouldn't get many round here as would do that. All sorts of weird things supposed to happen on Exmoor.'

'We had to get to Daddy,' Bernie said.

Mary nodded. 'And your mother ... ?'

'On her way,' Dermot said. 'Train to Exeter.'

Nobody said anything until Aggie, full of the honesty of youth, said, 'She ain't half daft sometimes.'

'Agg!'

She waved Marie away.

'Because Bernie lives with Mr Simpson, Mammy won't get in his car,' she said. 'I know. You try to keep things from me, but I know. Mam's ridiculous.'

'Aggie!'

'Well, she is, Bernie,' Aggie said. 'You've got out of the East End and good on you, I say. And if you're in love ... '

Mary put a hand on Aggie's arm and said, 'That's enough now.'

The young girl fell moodily silent. She had always looked up to Bernie and just because her sister had gone to live with a married man, it hadn't changed Aggie's mind.

'When Mrs Lynch gets here, I'll go,' Heinrich said to Mary. 'Is there a pub maybe that has rooms?'

''Course,' Mary said. 'I'll sort that out for you.'

Bernie looked at her lover and smiled. He was so kind and caring. He had no reason to give ground to her mother at all, but he was so decent, he just did these things automatically. It was all part of the way he was. He loved her so much, she knew she could never reciprocate with the same intensity. She also knew that, even now, with her father dying, her thoughts would inevitably turn towards Solly Adler.

Patrick Lynch never did regain consciousness – not even when Kitty finally arrived later on that night. By the following morning he was dead, eased out of this world with his family at his bedside. Three days later, his body was laid to rest in the local municipal cemetery.

All the children cried as well as Mary. But not Kitty. It was as if the fact that her husband hadn't woken up to say goodbye had turned her to stone. And, as soon as he was in the ground, she left to go back to London without a word. It seemed to Bernie, by the way Kitty looked at her and the fact she didn't address so much as one word to her eldest daughter, that her mother blamed her for the loss of Pat's last words. When Heinrich drove them back to London the day after the funeral, Bernie and Dermot held each other in the back of the car the whole way.

Chapter 5

10 May 1941

'So what d'ya reckon then, Sol?' Wolfie Silverman said. 'They coming tonight or not?'

It seemed as if the Luftwaffe had been bombing London forever. Every night since 7 September 1940 they'd come. The city was exhausted. There was no reason to think that this night would be any different.

'Yeah,' Solly said as he scanned the skies from the roof of Christ Church. Down below he could see people, many of whom he knew, scuttling around in the rubble-strewn street, trying either to get home or else near a shelter before nightfall. Mrs Simon the tobacconist's wife was pushing an old pram full of, knowing her, booze as well as food; the old matchmaker Mrs Rabinowicz was trailing one of her precious fox-fur scarves in the mud; and Hyman Salzedo, the local madman, was riding his bicycle through the piles of horse shit and broken guttering on Fournier Street. It was like watching the last days of one of those old villages back in Poland his mum had told him about, the ones where the Cossacks used to arrive from time to time to kill all the Jews.

Wolfie shuffled his large bottom on the dubious ridge tiles that ran down the middle of Christ Church's roof. The poor old place was in a sorry state, not improved by the recent pounding it had taken via blast from nearby explosions. But it was a good vantage point from which to watch for fires. Armed with buckets of water and sand plus a stirrup pump, the two young men had heeded the call for a fire-watch put out by the vicar. Although Solly couldn't be called up to the Forces on account of his false leg, Wolfie was gagging to go and have a pop at the 'Jerries'. In the meantime, he, like Solly, wanted to be useful.

'When you getting married?' Wolfie asked his mate.

'Sharon and her mum are doing all that,' Solly said.

'You must have a date.'

'Not that I've been told,' he said.

The light was fading over the city, turning everything pale yellow, reminding them that soon it would be summer. As if anyone cared.

'What about your mum?' Wolfie said. 'She's gotta be pleased?'

Solly didn't say anything. Both he and Wolfie knew that Dolly Adler didn't like Sharon Begleiter. For a start, the young woman was older than Solly, and to make matters worse she was a gossip with a taste for some sort of mythical high life she couldn't afford. Dolly Adler knew her soon-to-be daughter-in-law would tire of Solly as soon as his looks began to fade. She also knew that he was still in love with that Irish girl he'd never even walked out with, Bernadette Lynch, with whom he'd shared just one kiss as he was going off to fight in Spain.

Down in the churchyard they saw the vicar wave to them.

They waved back. The poor old sod hadn't slept properly for months, trying to protect his blackened, broken-down church. Apart from Wolfie and Solly there were few people hereabouts prepared to help him; few people, Wolfie sometimes felt, who still believed in God. The *frummers* did, but then they'd already been through so much back in Poland and Russia that if their faith was going to give way, it would have done so already. Wolfie didn't understand them any more than he understood the Christians who still attended church every Sunday, albeit in dwindling numbers. How could anyone believe in a caring God with all this going on?

It had taken a while, but the relentless bombing had finally, or so it seemed, broken the Windmill Girls. Taking her make-up off after the last show of the day, Rose realised that in spite of the fact that the dressing room was full, you could have heard a pin drop. She didn't feel much like talking herself and so she understood why all the other girls were silent. Another night spent down in that hot, smelly old basement was enough to send anyone round the bend. They all dreaded it.

Rose smeared Vaseline over her face and began to wipe away the thick foundation on her cheeks using a tissue. It was horrible stuff, clay-like and claggy when cool, running away in rivers when hot. What it did to a girl's skin was any-one's guess. But then what they put in their mouths was a bit of an unknown too, these days. The Ministry of Food was recommending whale meat as a substitute for regular meat and had even, so some of the other girls said, issued recipes. Apparently, before you could use it, you had to soak it in vin-egar to get rid of the rank fishy taste. Rose had never tasted it and didn't want to.

'Champers! I've got champers!'

All the girls, including Rose, turned around to see Tilly the drag queen burst in carrying a case full of bottles. She put it down on the floor and the girls ran over to have a look.

'Oooh, Tilly darling, what kind is it?'

'Can we have a cheeky sip now?'

'Champers? Lovely!'

But Tilly put herself between the girls and the drink. Resplendent in green satin and black lace, she held up one gloved hand and said, 'Not now, ladies! This is for later. Can't have you lot falling down the stairs when the siren goes, can we?'

'Oh, Tilly!'

'Spoilsport!'

Rose smiled. A lot of the girls came from posh or at least middle-class families and had some idea about and experience of champagne. Rose had only ever had it twice – once on her birthday and once after her first show. Tilly had been the supplier on both those occasions too. Even back then she was getting what came to be known as Dodgy Cru from a well-known member of a Maltese crime family.

One girl said, 'Is it from Maltese Michael or is it real?'

Tilly mugged being offended then said, 'Yes, it is from Mr Messina, if you must know, but it's also a hundred per cent kosher. The fact the bottles don't have labels is on account of ... '

'Them being pinched!' one of the other girls yelled.

They all laughed.

'Yes, well, I'm taking them down to the basement now and when the sirens go you can all get as tiddly as tits. But for now, get your mitts off!'

As she walked past Rose, Tilly whispered, 'I've kept a bottle just for you and me, girl.' And then she winked.

*

'Dermot!'

He took off his cap and smiled. 'Hello, Becky,' he said. 'You on your way to work?'

'Yes,' she said. 'Is Auntie Kitty in?'

'Yes,' he said. 'You want to come indoors?'

'I haven't got time now,' she said. 'But Papa says that if you both want to come into our shelter later on, you're welcome.'

'I know but . . . ' He shrugged. 'You know how Mammy is.'

She did. Ever since Uncle Pat had died, Kitty Lynch had lived a very different type of life. Working all the hours God gave, she'd also taken to going out drinking with the other Tate and Lyle girls. Dermot was due to join the Forces in just over a week.

'You know I'll keep an eye on her when you go,' Becky told him.

'Yes, I do. But . . . '

His younger brother Little Paddy was already in basic training down in Wiltshire and Becky knew that Dermot was keen to join him. But she also knew he was worried about his mother.

'Mrs Larkin comes over every night now,' Becky said. 'She's already in ours.'

What she didn't say was that Rose's mother probably only came over for her father's kosher wine, for which she seemed to have developed a taste. But then Papa wasn't averse to sharing a glass or two with her these days. Although Becky had begged him many times to leave the capital and go and stay with his cousin Stanley in Essex, he wouldn't shift. He said he was too old and tired to move. He certainly didn't have much work to detain him but Becky realised this was about much more than work. It was about her. If she left the Royal London and got a job in a provincial hospital, her father would go with

68

her. But she didn't want to leave. In spite of everything, she loved what she did and where she did it.

'I'd come,' Dermot said, 'you know I would. But I can't leave Mammy on her own.'

'I understand.' She touched his arm. 'Take care, Dermot.'

He watched her walk away down the street through the gathering dusk. He didn't want to go back to the flat and listen to his mother's endless drunken complaints. Most of them revolved around Bernie and her 'immoral' lifestyle. Sometimes she'd even speculate that Marie, hundreds of miles away in Devon, would one day go the same way. Back in 1939 the government had revived the old idea of getting women to work on the land and, by the end of 1941, a Women's Land Army was to be established. Marie had told her mother she was keen to join. Kitty had responded with horror. The thought of her daughter grubbing around in the soil amongst a load of, no doubt, randy farmers' boys was more than she could bear.

'She'll be picking spuds one day and holding a baby the next,' she'd told Dermot just before he'd left the flat that evening to get some peace.

Dermot lit a fag and looked up at Christ Church at the end of the street. Solly Adler and his mate Wolfie Silverman were fire-watching on the roof. Solly always looked so miserable these days, Dermot wondered whether he had some sort of death-wish. He had no idea whether his sister Bernie was still sweet on the man but felt instinctively that Solly still thought about her.

'Der?'

He looked down and saw his old school-mate Chrissy Dolan. Dermot hadn't seen him since before Pat had died. In fact, if he were honest with himself, Dermot had wondered whether

69

the little lad was dead too. Living as he did in Limehouse, so close to the docks, Chrissy's gaff was vulnerable.

'Chrissy!' Dermot shook his hand, which appeared to make Chrissy feel a bit uncomfortable.

God, the boy looked terrible! His face was covered in smuts, clothes torn and filthy. His boots looked as if they were about to fall apart. Even his usually bright red hair was dulled by debris and dust.

'What's going on?' Dermot asked.

'We got bombed out,' Chrissy said. 'No one was hurt 'cos we was all down the shelter, but Mrs Smith-Brown has buggered off.'

'Where?'

The lad shrugged.

Mrs Smith-Brown was the madam of a cheap Limehouse brothel specialising in what she herself called 'old whores'. She'd given Chrissy a job as a cleaner and prostitutes' maid when no one else would look at him after his 'immoral behaviour' at his first place of employment. He'd been rejected by his own family and shunned by all his friends including, seemingly, Dermot. But they had been best friends right from very young when they went to school together. And although he'd not seen Dermot for ages, Chrissy hadn't known where else to go.

'Can I kip at yours?' Chrissy asked. 'I know it's a lot to ask. I've been wandering about all day, not knowing what to do.'

Dermot hesitated for moment but then he put a hand on his shoulder. This was after all his best mate and he'd missed him. ''Course you can,' he said. 'But I've just decided I'm going over to the Shapiros' shelter when the sirens go and I suggest you come with me.'

Dermot hadn't been able to face another night spent on his own with Kitty.

'All right.'

Chrissy was visibly relieved.

'Come on,' Dermot said, 'let's get some grub inside you before the Luftwaffe turn up.'

Heinrich had his brief. Frank Fitzhugh, editor of the *News*, wasn't a man who took his duty to his readers lightly. But there were regulations now about what the press could and couldn't reveal to the public and, with only four pages of newsprint available to him, Fitzhugh knew he had to try and say something worthwhile without breaking the law.

'We need quotes from the people on the ground,' the editor said. 'Costers, vicars, fire-watchers – the man in the street.'

'The East End salt of the earth,' Heinrich added, in a slightly sarcastic tone.

'That's it.' But Fitzhugh had the grace to look away at the same time as he sanctioned the cliché. The East End especially had been pounded by bombing nightly since September of the previous year and, although the official line was that Cockneys could 'take it', both men knew that, even if that had once seemed to be true, it couldn't go on for much longer.

Heinrich sat down. The two men were in Fitzhugh's wood-panelled office at the paper's headquarters in Blackfriars. Carmelite House, home of the *News*, had been the first press office in London to install a telephone.

'You know I'll be hard pressed to find anyone willing to talk on the record, don't you, Frank?' Heinrich said as he lit a cigarette.

Fitzhugh didn't look at him.

'They're all losing their minds in the East End,' Heinrich continued. He suspected that Bernie's mother was close to breaking point, and Walter Katz, the old man he'd known

71

back in Germany and who now owned a shop on Brick Lane, was beginning to show signs that he too was losing his grip. Refusing to go into a shelter, he would wander the streets during the bombing, sobbing.

'We can't say that,' Fitzhugh said.

'We should.'

'But we can't. Provided we all survive the night, I'd like you to get over there tomorrow morning and put together a nice, morale-boosting piece for me,' Fitzhugh said. 'Miss Lynch can accompany you. I can't use too many of her pictures these days, they're too hard-hitting, but she's still got the best photographic eye of anyone I know. Tell her we want portraits of people smiling through adversity, preferably while raising a cup of Rosie Lee.'

'She won't like that.'

'I know.' Fitzhugh looked him in the eye. 'But it's what is required. Not pictures of people crying over their broken possessions or, worse, the dead ... '

He was referring to a series of pictures Bernie had taken after a bombing raid in Silvertown back in 1940. A family of eight had all died instantly from the effects of bomb blast while they sat around their kitchen table. Not one of them had sustained any visible injury. Fitzhugh had been shocked by these images and refused to publish them in spite of Bernie's argument that the public needed to know how dangerous blast could be. They had to avoid it by getting to deep shelters. The subtext so far as she was concerned was that more of these needed to be constructed in poor and deprived areas where houses had not been built on substantial cellars or basements. But the government didn't want that kind of blunt, frightening truth being propagated by the press.

'Go in the morning,' Fitzhugh instructed. 'Light's fading

now and we should all be getting home.' He raised an eyebrow. 'Unless you want to stay here, of course?'

A lot of the hacks went down into the subterranean print hall. It could be quite jolly, especially if said hacks were well oiled with alcohol. The printers were a belligerent lot, but they also had a salty sense of humour that could be entertaining. However, the reporter clearly had better company waiting for him at home.

'No, thanks,' he said. 'I'd rather get back.'

Frank, who knew what Bernie was to Heinrich, just smiled.

'Did you really think they wasn't coming tonight, Mr Shapiro?' Nell Larkin asked as she braced herself against the side of the Anderson shelter. Somewhere, really close by, a terrible noise like the roar of a dragon split the air.

Moritz Shapiro passed her a mug of kosher wine.

'I don't know ... I hoped at least,' he said. Then he muttered to himself, 'Silly old *schlemiel*.'

Dermot Lynch and his friend Chrissy Dolan had joined them this time, but not Kitty Lynch. She was drinking alone in her scullery and not even Nell could shift her. She'd tried. She'd called her neighbour an 'old drunk' and told her to 'Stop fucking well doing what I do!' but to no avail. Kitty seemed determined to destroy herself now her husband was dead and two of her kids had gone. It was her business, of course, but Nell knew it was a road to nowhere, whatever the reason for taking up drink.

She looked at Dermot Lynch, sitting there with the little ginger poof who'd been his friend all the way through school. Nell wouldn't have been surprised if Dermot was an 'iron' himself. Her Rosie had stepped out with the boy once or twice and he'd never touched her, so it was possible. Not that Nell

73

cared about such things; she'd known a few poofs in her life and had always found them kind and gentlemanly.

She hoped that wherever Rosie was, men were treating her right, like gentlemen should. But she doubted it. The girl was probably on the game somewhere by this time, that or on the rob, or else dead. Nell didn't like to think about it too much. Contrary to what she knew many of her neighbours thought, she loved her daughter. She also felt guilty for many of the bad things that had happened to Rose. She'd got pregnant at fifteen because Nell had been too drunk to help her push her stepfather Len Tobin and his mates away. Then she'd become a thief in order to help her mother escape eviction. It all came down to the bad effects of drink. But when Mr Shapiro offered Nell some more wine she took it, because, she told herself, by the sound of the bombing outside, the world was about to come to an end.

Chapter 6

'Where'd you get *this*?'

A girl called Harriet held up her half-filled champagne saucer and pulled a face sidelong at Rose.

'Never you mind,' Tilly said.

'It tastes like ...'

'Don't matter what it tastes like, girl, it'll get you tiddly!' Tilly turned to Rose then and whispered, 'Bloody posh tart! They're all the same.'

Rose smiled. Quite a few of the Windmill Girls were 'posh'. It struck her as odd. Posh girls didn't usually need to work.

'Anyway, what do you think of it, Rosie Red?' Tilly asked.

The champagne did taste a bit strange, although Rose was no connoisseur. She'd had it a couple of times and was sure it had tasted better then. But it was fizzy, even if there was a sort of oily film on it, and Tilly had got it for them specially. Not that they didn't deserve it. Rose couldn't remember when the bombing had actually started; sometimes it felt as if it had been going on all her life.

She knocked back what remained in her glass and said, 'It's nice. Thank you, Tilly. Can I have some more?'

A large, ring-bedecked hand picked up the bottle and refilled Rose's saucer. 'There you go, darling.'

'Ta.'

Unlike Harriet, most of the other girls seemed to like the champagne and, as the bombs rained down up above, the bottles quickly emptied down below. Only creepy Kenneth didn't seem to feel the need to indulge. But then people said he always had a hip-flask full of brandy on him, which helped him through the bombing. He was sitting at the back of the basement in a corner on his own. Rose saw his body move slightly as the walls shook when a bomb dropped. Looking at her, as he often did, he smiled but she didn't smile back. Instead, she swilled down her next glass of champagne and then asked Tilly for more.

'Did you bring your heart pills down with you?' Becky said to the thin old man wearing nothing but a pair of pyjama trousers.

'You what?' He cupped a hand around his ear. 'Can't hear you!'

Given that the city they lived in had been bombed every night for almost six months, it was a wonder anyone could still hear anything. The elderly were particularly at risk.

'Your heart pills, Mr Yates,' Becky yelled. 'Did you bring them down from the ward with you?'

'Me heart pills? Got 'em here,' the old man said as he showed her a small brown bottle of tablets. 'Do you think I'm silly or something?'

'No.'

'Well ... good.'

He walked away. But then at least he could walk, unlike most of the other men on his ward. Male Surgical seemed to be stacked up with either amputees or amputees-in-waiting. This was usually because of injuries sustained during the bombing or due to the collapse of unstable buildings. Becky replaced the drip that she'd carried from the ward over Mr Hynes's bed and checked to see if he was showing any signs of coming round from his anaesthetic. He was breathing evenly but was still asleep. His lips moved as if he were speaking in his dreams and so she knew it wouldn't be long before he became conscious and aware of the excruciating pain that accompanied any amputation. A shot of laudanum would make him more comfortable but it wouldn't take the pain away. Becky checked to make sure she had the syringe ready.

She breathed deeply. Even during the winter it had been hot down in the basement. Now summer was coming it was becoming unbearable. One of the doctors arrived to check on Mr Hynes and Becky joined Nurse Ann Shiner at the bedside of a dying patient.

'You all right?' she asked.

Ann had sat at the bedside of Mr West for most of the afternoon. The doctors had thought he might pull through after his operation but he'd got an infection and had first slipped into delirium, then a coma.

Ann shook her head. 'I just wish there was something we could do,' she said. 'Dr Rayner cut out as much of the infection as he could find, but it can't have been enough.'

Becky squeezed her shoulder. The doctors sometimes talked about an infection-killing drug called penicillin. It had first been discovered back in the 1920s but had only been put to limited use at the time. Now there was a war on, research into it and possible other valuable new treatments had all but ceased.

'Part of a chimney fell on him,' Ann continued. 'Severed his leg. I hate this war.'

Becky did too. And now that lots of its other cities besides London were under bombardment every night, she didn't even feel hopeful that Britain could win anymore. She knew how tired she was, and it had to be the same for the country's Armed Forces. The Germans, on the other hand, were like a tireless machine rather than a nation.

One of the Tilley lamps sputtered and so she went to find some paraffin for it. As she passed one of the beds she heard Dr Rayner declare a boy of about Dermot Lynch's age dead. With the top of his head wrapped in a dense, blood-soaked bandage, the youngster almost looked as if he was asleep. She'd only just managed to find the paraffin when she heard one of the mainly female porters shout, 'Casualty coming through!'

God Almighty, another body in the already crowded basement! Becky couldn't see any space anywhere. One man and a tiny woman, probably half Becky's size, carried the stretcher, which looked to be heavy.

One of the senior doctors called out, 'Put him by the stairs!'

'All right.'

The pair turned the stretcher around. As they were doing this, Becky saw something fall from it onto the floor. The female porter said, 'Oh, blast it!'

When she picked it up to put it back, Becky saw what it was: a false leg.

Moritz looked at the two boys and he knew. They were the same, the little homosexual boy and young Dermot. Had he always known this? He probably had, but he'd ignored it.

Wasn't his business. But if Dermot Lynch was going into the Forces, then it could be a problem. And although the boy and his rackety crew of siblings were not the kind of people Moritz had wanted as friends for his daughter, he knew that Becky loved all the Lynches and so he wished them well.

The ground shook and flashes of eerie white light burst through the gaps between the door and its frame. Moritz had heard that Reuben Salzedo the *mohel* was as deaf as a post now because of the bombing. All his family, except the idiot boy Hyman, had gone up North somewhere to stay with relatives. Then there was Mrs Rabinowicz who had got stuck in the doorway of the Lippmann sisters' Anderson shelter in Wentworth Street. Four hours she'd been there, caught between her fat back and her enormous belly, screaming in fear and pain. And to think that he'd considered inviting her to use his shelter!

A lull in the explosions outside allowed him to say, 'You know, Dermot, your mother is always welcome to join us.'

The young man smiled at him. 'I know,' he said. 'And I do appreciate it, Mr Shapiro, but Mam just can't do with being under the ground. She's too frightened.'

And probably too drunk, Moritz thought. But he didn't say anything. The poor woman had all but fallen to pieces since the death of her husband. She worked and that was to her credit; however, her life outside the job had collapsed. There was only so much a person could take. Although it was never spoken of, Moritz knew that the loss of her eldest boy had to be preying on her mind too. Although he was never one to listen to gossip, even Moritz Shapiro was aware of the local fascination with Joey Lynch. Had he really killed Fred Lamb? His father Pat, it was said, hadn't believed it, but then that was only natural. But if the boy was innocent, where was he? At Joey's age, Moritz reckoned, he had to be in the Forces. But was he?

It was said, admittedly by mad Hyman Salzedo, that the Rebbetzin Cohen, who could talk for England, had told Suss the jeweller that Joey Lynch had been spotted selling knocked-off cigarettes in Stratford. But who knew? And Moritz wasn't about to go and see Suss to find out more. Before the war, his Rebekah had been engaged to marry Suss's son, Chaim. It would have been a good match had Rebekah had even the slightest feeling for the young man. Back then she'd been besotted with that Communist, Solly Adler. A bad lot, according to Moritz, but what could one do against teenage passions? Although the Adler boy and Rebekah had never walked out together, he'd felt duty-bound to call off his daughter's engagement to Chaim. He loved Rebekah too much to make her do something her whole soul rebelled against. Did he regret that now the Nazis were carpet bombing his city, preparing to invade his country and, so people said, kill all its Jews?

Of course he did, in a way. Suss senior was now safe in Canada with his wife. Money could buy you that kind of security. But in another way Moritz was content. Although tired all the time and much thinner now than she'd ever been, Rebekah was happy and fulfilled in her work at the Royal London. She hadn't spoken about the Adler man for years – or indeed any other man. She had a profession that could last her a lifetime and people she had nursed were grateful to her, but ...

Moritz looked up as some of the earth that covered the Anderson drifted down into Mrs Larkin's drink. If the Nazis did invade, at least two of them in this shelter would be as good as dead. Nell Larkin was a gypsy and, if stories coming out of Germany were correct, they too were being targeted by Hitler and his thugs.

Moritz put his hand out to Nell and said, 'Come, give me your glass, it's got dirt in it.'

'Oh, it's all right . . .'

'No, no,' he said. 'Wine I have more of and you are welcome to it. But never let it be said that Moritz Shapiro let a guest drink from a dirty glass.'

Nell smiled. 'You know, Mr Shapiro,' she said, 'you're the nicest man I've ever met.'

What was this stuff? Rose peered, albeit through a thick haze of drunkenness, at her glass and then looked over to where Tilly was snoring her head off in one of the old armchairs Mr Van Damm had put down in the basement. Over by the door, a group of girls were attempting to dance, but in reality they were just falling about giggling. Rose felt a bit sick. She didn't usually drink to excess, but Tilly had been so pleased with herself for getting hold of actual champagne, if that was what it had been, that Rose had felt duty-bound to drink it.

The ventriloquist known as Captain Glasshouse and his doll Private Crafty were sprawled out on the floor, apparently fighting. Rose could accept that something like that might just be a fancy of hers, but then again maybe not. 'Vents', as they were known, were a queer bunch. Some of them only ever talked to their dolls, or else through them.

'Rosie?'

At first she thought it was Mr Talent, the One-Man Band, but then she saw that he was taking a pee behind the old piano someone had dumped in the basement years ago.

'Rosie.'

She felt her head turn. She also felt how sick it made her feel when she did it.

'What?' she said to the doorman.

He was dark and had a big bulbous nose and, even in her drunken state, Rose could see that he was sweating. She didn't like Kenneth. He was creepy, all the girls said so.

'I see old Tilly's out for the count,' he said.

Tilly had passed out ... sometime. Rose couldn't remember much about the night. She could hear noise from outside. Explosions, shouting. Feel the grit and dirt in the air all around her. She wanted to say something but couldn't think what. Then a massive 'whoosh' seemed to suck all of the air out of the basement and she heard Kenneth say, 'That's right, you lean on me. I'll make sure no harm comes to you.'

Leaning on the window-frame, Bernie looked out across a London that was in complete blackness except for random flashes of light and what looked like sulphur as the German Luftwaffe rained death down on the East End, the docks and the City.

As soon as Heinrich had got in they'd gone to bed. They'd made love to the sound of the air-raid sirens, which had felt both wrong and defiant at the same time. Dermot had told her that their mother rarely left the flat when the sirens went these days. Since Daddy had died, Mammy seemed to have lost much of her desire to live. And Bernie could understand that. Pat Lynch had been the kindly glue that had held his family together. Now he was gone, maybe it was inevitable that they were scattered all around the country.

Heinrich brought her a cigarette. His wife and children had gone to Henley-on-Thames in Oxfordshire when the bombing had started back in September 1940. Bernie was glad they were safe even if Heinrich's wife, Adrienne, hated her. Bernie could understand that. If someone had taken her husband and the father of her children away from her, she'd hate that person too.

'Are you going to be all right to go down to the East End in the morning?' Heinrich asked.

Fitzhugh wanted a 'happy' East End story about chirpy Cockneys. Bernie briefly closed her eyes.

'If we're still alive and there's anything left to see, I thought we'd start down by the river at Limehouse,' Heinrich said.

'It's as good as anywhere.'

Dermot's old friend Chrissy Dolan lived down in Limehouse. Bernie wondered how he was doing, whether he'd been bombed out or just beaten up by local 'hard' sorts who didn't like 'irons'. The world was a sick place and sometimes she felt as if the war was a punishment for that. Whether it had been sent by God she wasn't sure. It had been a long time since she'd thought about such things.

'I'd like to take some real pictures too,' she said as she looked back out of the window again, smoking. 'I know Fitzhugh has to toe the government line with what he publishes but I want photographs for my own portfolio.'

'I know.'

'So that one day I can look back and see how it really was.' She turned to face him. 'How I remember it, and so as to show people how badly we were treated.'

'We?'

'People like my family,' she said. 'Expected just to get on with it, to be brave and uncomplaining. Expected to try and survive without enough food or shelter . . . '

'Ah, your friend Solly and his protests . . . '

'What of it? He's right,' she said. 'People round here have no idea. What do any of the lot in these flats know about not being able to get a wash when you're covered in soot and rubble? What do they know about going hungry and being cold and—'

'What do you know about it, Bernie?'

'I grew up there,' she said. 'It's my home.'

'Yes, but this is your home now, isn't it?'

She didn't reply. Heinrich went into the living room.

'I'm going to make myself a Martini,' he said. 'Do you want one?'

'No.'

His words had hit home and, just briefly, she hated him for it, because he was right. She'd been born in the East End, but she hadn't suffered with her family and friends since the bombing had started. She'd been here in this comfortable flat in Pimlico with its stylish furniture and Dry Martinis. There was even a clean and comfortable shelter if she chose to use it. How in all conscience could someone like Bernie speak for the poor and displaced of the battered East End?

She couldn't but she knew that she wanted to. She knew too that she'd give almost anything to be with Solly Adler at this moment.

He was unconscious.

'What happened to him?' Becky asked the female stretcher bearer who had brought him in.

'I don't know,' the porter said. 'I just pick 'em up.'

Solly Adler was covered in blood but it wasn't easy to see where it was coming from. Was it even his?

The woman's male companion said, 'We found him outside the church on Commercial Street.'

'Christ Church?'

'I dunno what it's called. Some other bloke was beside him, dead. Don't know as he's got long either, to tell you the truth, poor bastard.'

Becky looked around to see whether any of the doctors was free. But all of them were treating patients.

She bent down over Solly's body and said, 'Hold on, I'll get someone to you!'

She ran. There had to be other doctors out in the corridors. There had to be!

The night before was all a blank to Rose, though she thought for some reason she had been sitting with Kenneth. Noises still came from outside – loud bangs, voices, the sound of masonry hitting the ground – but when she shook herself awake, Kenneth had gone. Beside her, as before, Tilly lay with a smile on her face but the girls were no longer dancing and Mr Talent had his head on his drum, snoring.

Although her vision was clearer than it had been, Rose still felt nauseous. She also ached, as if she'd fallen over. She rubbed her left hip and then moved her legs to get the circulation going again. There was a very good reason why she normally didn't drink and this was it. How could anyone want to feel sick and unwell? Also, whenever people got drunk around her, it always reminded Rose of the man she'd lived with all through her childhood, Len Tobin. He'd been an alcoholic who had literally sold her mum – and Rose – for booze. She still hated him for that and always would.

Rose shifted position and that was when she felt the liquid beneath her. Fearing that she'd either sat in a puddle of booze or wet herself, she moved until she could see what was wrong. It was then that she realised she wasn't wearing her knickers anymore. When had she taken them off and why? Rose's heart began to pound. She lowered her head to smell the liquid she'd been sitting on and it was then she found out it was neither pee nor booze. Rose rooted about inside her handbag and took out a handkerchief with which she mopped up the puddle. Trembling with fear, she hid the hanky in the sleeve

85

of her cardigan and then, suddenly, retched and vomited all over her shoes.

'Compound fracture. Can you see the clavicle sticking out of the skin?'

A small piece of red-tinged white bone stuck out of Solly's skin, near his shoulder joint.

'Usually indicates a fall when it's in the outer third like that,' Dr Pierce said. He palpated the unconscious man's chest. 'Couple of broken ribs too if I'm not mistaken. And that looks like a burn on his face.'

Although almost eighty years old, Dr Horace Pierce had come back to work at the London Hospital in 1940. He managed to do at least three night shifts a week. Becky, for one, was extremely grateful for it. When all the other doctors had been up to their elbows in patients, sometimes literally, Dr Pierce and his ever-present cigarette had been free.

'While he's unconscious like this, I might actually try to slip the clavicle back in,' he said. 'Can you hold his head still for me, please, nurse?'

Becky positioned herself at Solly's head, while Dr Pierce ground out his cigarette on the floor.

'On three. One, two . . .'

Becky looked away.

'Three.'

It would have been amazing if Solly had just woken up at that point, but he didn't. She saw his eyelids twitch, but that was all.

The doctor harrumphed in what could have been satisfaction or dismay. Then he said, 'Poor chap appears to have taken a heavy fall. May wake up, may not. I must move on.'

He went to leave and then he said, 'Oh, nurse, strap up his

shoulder, will you? His breathing seems all right so he'll probably come round. Poor sod'll be in all kinds of bother if he's not strapped up. And cover that burn. God knows someone should deal with that, but who? All right?'

'Yes, doctor.'

Without access in the basement to a convenient medical supplies cupboard, nurses carried things like bandages and cotton wool in the pockets of their uniforms. She took a roll of crepe out of her apron and began to unwind it.

She hadn't seen Solly for over a year. Word was that he was engaged to Sharon Begleiter, which seemed strange to Becky. Sharon wasn't in the least bit political and she was hardly the brightest button in the box either. But then maybe Becky was simply comparing Sharon to Bernie, who was not only the brightest, but the very best, button there was.

Chapter 7

Bernie hadn't been able to sleep. Between worrying about her mum and her brother in the East End and the conversation she'd had with Heinrich, it had been impossible.

After he'd made himself a Martini, Heinrich had sat down opposite her and said, 'You know that if the Nazis get here, you will have to go.'

She'd known immediately what he had meant. She'd seen the Jews of Berlin with the yellow stars on their jackets. She'd seen how the Nazis casually pushed and kicked them in the street. She'd even photographed a kid throwing dirt at an old Jewish woman as she tried to do her shopping.

'Adrienne and the kids will go to Canada,' he'd continued. Sad and bitter already, his wife might also be obliged to leave her own country. 'I should have organised this before but . . .'

He'd shrugged.

Bernie had said, 'I'm sorry.'

There had been no light save for the flashes from the

explosions that threatened to turn London to dust. As usual, they had neither used lights nor drawn their blackout curtains. Maybe it was because their jobs necessitated seeing and experiencing as much as they could. Also, Bernie hated to be cooped up. A big part of the reason why she'd always wanted to travel was because she'd felt stifled by her family's small flat on Fournier Street. Her dad had understood. She missed him so much!

Heinrich had told her, 'It's not your fault.'

He'd taken her hand then and she had kissed him. But when the kiss had come to an end, he'd said, 'I say all this because I'm not sure this country can take anymore. The Germans could invade any time now. And when they do, you and I will not be able to know one another.'

She'd wanted to say that would never happen, that she'd stand by him whatever, but she hadn't. She also knew he had been grateful for that. Because everything he was saying made sense.

They'd gone to bed then and made love. Afterwards, Heinrich had slept, but not Bernie. Now she was preparing to leave the flat, not for good, not yet, but to go to the East End. She needed to go alone. Even in Pimlico she could taste brick dust in the air, see flames and smell blood on the rancid early-morning air. How much worse would it become the nearer she drew to her former home?

There was no water and she stank. When Rose groaned about it, Mrs Muscat lost her temper.

'Fucking hell, Rose!' she said. 'This water thing again? People died last night! People died, for God's sake! And here you are, wanting a fucking wash! Find a puddle, go down the river, stink like the rest of us!'

Rose knew her landlady was right. In the scheme of things, stinking was nothing. But she also knew that she stank in a particular kind of way. She smelled of *him*.

Kenneth hadn't said a word to her when they'd all emerged from the Windmill basement that morning. But he had looked at her. Rose thought she'd seen him smirk, but she couldn't be sure. She couldn't be certain about anything except for that smell, which she knew of old. Men came inside you and then you were marked by that smell. It was something she'd hoped never to experience again.

She slumped down on her dusty bed. She'd smelled like this, on and off, ever since she was ten. That had been when Len Tobin had first taken a shine to her and then raped her whenever Nell was too drunk to care. Rose had been lucky not to have got pregnant until she was fifteen. But there'd been no baby. Nell had taken her to an old girl she knew down Canning Town and she'd dealt with that. Rose had nearly died. Just the memory of what she'd been through made her shake. What if she was pregnant again now? This time she didn't even have her mum to help her.

However, she could remember what Nell had done the morning after her fifteen-year-old daughter had been raped by Tobin and the load of drunks he'd brought home with him. And although drinking loads of gin and having a hot bath hadn't worked that time, maybe it would now? Not that she could have a bath any time soon.

Rose went downstairs into her landlady's parlour. Mrs Muscat was bent over that terrible old table covered in the figurines of saints she liked so much, trying to wipe thick dust off their weird, painted faces. As she leaned forward, Rose could see her varicose veins travelling right up her legs towards her bloomers.

'Mrs Muscat . . .'

The old woman turned sharply, one hand going up to press her chest.

'Blimey, you gave me a turn!' she said.

'Sorry.'

'What do you want?'

'Do you have any gin?' Rose asked.

Mrs Muscat's fat face settled into a grimace. 'What you want that for? 'Ere, you're not up the stick, are you?'

'No.' But Rose found she had to look away.

'Because I can't have no screaming kids about the place.'

'No.'

There was a silence, which the old woman only broke after what appeared to be a period of reflection. She took a bottle down from the mantelpiece and gave it to Rose.

'But then,' she said, 'your nerves probably have taken a bashing, I know mine have. Go on, have a swig.'

God, she remembered that taste! Vile when she was fifteen, vile now! Rose pulled a face. The old woman laughed. 'Oh, I've always liked a drop of gin meself,' she said. Then she looked cautiously from side to side before she continued, 'I've used it a coupla times too . . .'

'I'm not . . .'

'I know you're not, dear,' she said. But then she winked. 'Can't be too careful though, can we?'

'Wolfie Silverman's mum came to see me.'

Becky sat down beside Dolly Adler and put a cup of tea into the woman's hands. Aware that her uniform was covered in blood, she folded her apron over the worst bits.

'They was fire-watching on the roof of Christ Church,' Dolly continued. 'As they've been doing for months. Bertha

91

Silverman told me there was hardly a scratch on her Wolfie.'
She looked up. 'What do you think happened?'

'We won't know until Solly wakes up,' Becky said.

'When'll that be?'

'We don't know.'

Since he'd been back on the ward, Becky had managed to clean Solly up as best she could. But a doctor had been called to dress the burn on his face properly. He had been of the opinion that it would probably leave a considerable scar. There was also concern about Solly's continued unconsciousness. If, as Dolly Adler thought, the two young men had fallen from the roof of the church then he was lucky to be alive at all. But what damage had been done to his brain, if any, still wasn't clear. Until he woke up, if he ever did, it wasn't possible to know.

'My boy was beautiful, you know, nurse,' Dolly said. 'Then he went to war in Spain and lost his leg – and now this.'

Becky put a hand on her shoulder.

'You know my Ben's fighting in North Africa?' Dolly said.

'I'd heard, yes.'

'So I could lose 'em both!' She began to cry.

Becky should have gone off shift five hours ago, but she couldn't leave Solly. Red-eyed and exhausted as she was, she couldn't even imagine what the mother of a child in such a state was going through. She put a protective arm around Mrs Adler. Years ago, she'd met Dolly in the home of one of the expectant mothers she used to clean and wash for, not that Solly's mother seemed to recognise her now. But it didn't matter.

Not knowing what to say, Becky let Dolly cry. Some of the doctors looked a bit disapproving, but they'd have to put up with it. There was no way Becky was going to tell the poor woman to stop. With her elder son fighting in North Africa and now her younger one possibly with brain damage, Dolly Adler was entitled to cry her heart out.

When she'd finished, she squeezed Becky's hand and said, 'Thanks for putting up with me, love.'

'I wish I could do more.'

'You're looking after my boy, that's enough for me,' Dolly said. She lit a cigarette and then looked back at her son. 'Looks like he's just asleep, don't he?'

'Well, he is . . .'

'Yeah, but not really, is he? I mean if he fell on his head then . . .'

Dolly began crying again. This time it was less of a sob, more of a howl, and this time everyone looked at her.

'Oh, Christ!' she screamed. 'What am I gonna tell his fiancée?'

Becky was going to try and take her outside the ward but, as she stood up, she glanced at Solly. Which was when she saw his eyes open.

Uncle Pat's chair. It seemed almost wrong to sit in it, but Chrissy couldn't help himself. The battered old wing chair, nicked off the site of the Old Nichol slum that used to be at the top of Brick Lane so it was said, still smelled of him. Fags and beer. Uncle Pat had been the best of men and Chrissy knew that, poor and dark and battered though it was, the Lynches' flat was a place where he could always be himself.

When they'd come up out of Mr Shapiro's shelter that morning, he and Dermot had found Auntie Kitty getting ready for work. An elaborately tied turban on her head, she'd stepped out into the shattered street in spotless high heels, carrying a leather handbag that gleamed in the weak May sunshine. Dermot had told her that Chrissy had nowhere to go and

Auntie Kitty had first looked at him with what looked like cold eyes and then said, 'Well, you'd better come and live here then, Chrissy.'

'But I ain't got a job,' he'd protested, feeling both relieved and guilty at the same time.

All she'd said to that was, 'Keep the place nice and we'll all get along like a house on fire.'

He'd black-leaded the range as soon as she'd gone, even before Dermot had left for the docks. He'd be going in the army in a week's time, something Chrissy knew he'd never do.

He'd been born with what his mother had always called a 'weak heart', which had meant he'd never been able to participate in sport. His mum had not allowed it and he'd not really wanted to do it either. Sport meant getting out of breath, which always made him ill. Dermot had been the only boy at school who had understood. Like the girls in their class, he had always encouraged Chrissy to draw and paint and make things instead of struggling to keep up on the football field. Chrissy's dad had called him a 'poof', and, when his mum had died, his dad and his brothers had given the fragile boy a bad time. If it hadn't been for Dermot he would have died of loneliness. But then, Chrissy suspected why Dermot understood him so well, even though they'd never spoken of it. Not really.

Chrissy got up out of Uncle Pat's chair and began making the beds. He was fluffing up Dermot's one, sad little pillow when he heard a knock at the door. He hoped it wasn't his dad or one of his brothers. In Spitalfields everyone knew everyone else and it was very possible that someone had told the old man his youngest was back on the manor. Chrissy put the pillow down and went to the street door where he saw Dermot's sister Bernadette, looking anxious but even more glamorous than her mother had. There was a large camera slung around her neck.

She looked surprised to see him. 'Chrissy!'

'Hello, Bernie,' he said.

'What you doing here?'

He told her over a cup of tea.

'So Mammy and Dermot are all right?'

She sat on the pile of old cushions to one side of the range where her little sisters used to sit in the winter. They'd called it The Nook.

'Yes,' Chrissy said. 'Although it was just me and Der as went to Mr Shapiro's shelter last night.'

'Not Mammy?'

'Der said she wouldn't go.'

Chrissy knew that Kitty wouldn't leave the flat when raids were on. Dermot had told him she preferred to sit in the dark at home and drink alone. She'd been like that ever since Pat had died. She just went to work at Tate's, came home and drank. It wasn't right, but it also wasn't his place to tell Bernadette about it.

'She was always a stubborn woman,' Bernie said.

Chrissy smiled. 'So why you down here then?' he asked her.

Bernie picked up her camera. 'Supposed to be here with a reporter getting a story about how tough the East End is,' she said.

'It is!'

'I know. But it's also bleeding,' Bernie said. 'After eight months of bombing every night, it's a bloody wonder it ain't bled to death.'

He smiled. She was right. It was also amusing Chrissy the way her accent became more 'East End' the longer she talked to him.

'I want people to know the truth,' Bernie said. 'I want them to see the bravery here, which is what the government and all that lot want, but I want them to see the suffering too. I want them to understand that us down here don't just exist to be courageous or to "take it" all the time. You know, Chrissy, that I live up West now?'

He did, and he knew why, but didn't say anything about that.

'We get raids, but it's not like it is here,' Bernie continued. 'They have staff to look after the shelters where I live. Even with a war on, it ain't like it is here. The way they talk about us . . . ' She shook her head. 'As if "the cockney" is some sort of special breed built for suffering. I hate it. I hate them. Even though they don't know no better, I still hate them.'

'So where's your reporter then?' Chrissy asked.

She smiled. 'He ain't turned up,' she said. 'Still in his pit.'

'Oh.'

'Don't matter.' She shook back her long blonde hair. 'I'll get what I need and then I'll go back.'

'Up West?'

'Yeah,' she said. 'Up West.'

But there was a sadness in her eyes when she said it that told Chrissy she didn't really want to leave.

'All brass and no knickers' was how Tilly described the Salisbury on St Martin's Lane. On the face of it just another Victorian London pub, the Salisbury was also where the 'gay set' would meet. The dim lighting and the cosy little bars made it a good meeting venue for men and women who pre-ferred their own sex. And although nowhere was really safe from the prying eyes of the legal establishment, the Salisbury was one of those places where people could, to a certain extent, be themselves.

Already tipsy, Rose pushed through the ornate double doors and walked into the dark, fuggy atmosphere inside. Huge mirrors etched with patterns of vines and flowers forced her to look at her own slightly flushed face and note the anxiety in the darkness of her eyes.

'Oi! Rosie *palone*!'

She recognised the voice. She'd come to see Tilly, if she was about, but Rose couldn't see her.

'Over here, you daft cow!'

A man dressed in a tweed suit and wearing a trilby hat had replaced the glamorous 'Tilly de Mer' of Windmill Theatre fame. Rose wasn't used to seeing her friend in civvies; she'd almost forgotten that Tilly, as Herbert, spent a great deal of his time toiling over ledgers in an office in Jermyn Street not far from the pub.

Rose walked over to a table at the back of the bar where Tilly sat with two other men. One of them was burly and had a broken nose, like a boxer's, while the other was not much more than a boy, all doe eyes and with a red feather boa round his neck. As the girl approached them Tilly said to her friends, 'Come on, budge up! Rosie love, do you wanna drink?'

'No, thanks.'

Rose sat down next to the 'boxer' and smiled. She'd wanted to speak to Tilly alone, but it seemed like that wasn't going to be possible any time soon.

'This here's Reg,' Tilly said, introducing her to the battered-looking man.

'Hello, darlin'.'

She shook his hand, which entirely engulfed hers.

'Takes photographs and writes a bit,' Tilly said, and then turned to the boy. 'Pedro. Spanish. Can't speak a word of English but has the best basket this side of the Pyrenees.'

Not that long ago, Rose would have blushed at the way Tilly referred to the boy's genitals in this fashion, but now she just said, 'Oh.'

'So what's happening, daughter?' Tilly asked her.

'What?'

'Don't normally see you up here in the light of day.'

'Shocking raid last night,' Reg said as he puffed on a Woodbine. 'My poor old mum nearly cacked herself.'

'Blimey, I didn't know Lil was still with us,' Tilly said.

Reg smiled. 'She likes to see me girls,' he said. 'I think sometimes it's what keeps her going.'

'Well, it certainly keeps you going,' Tilly said, and then moving close to Rose he whispered, 'Reg here specialises in "artistic" photography, plus a little bit of popular "literature".'

'You could sit for me any time you like, love,' Reg said to Rose.

Tilly waved this off dismissively. 'She's a bleedin' Windmill Girl, Reg!' she said. 'What's she want to go being in one of your mucky books for! Christ . . . '

'Tilly, can I have a word?' Rose asked. 'In private?'

Tilly looked confused for a moment and then, adjusting her trilby hat, said, ''Course, love.' She stood up and walked towards the little bar known as The Snug. ''Scuse us, gents.' She took Rose's arm. 'Why don't you step into my office?'

'Bernadette?'

Bernie turned around and saw a small woman dressed in a brown raincoat. She was pushing a pram laden down with a wireless set.

Bernie said, 'Yes?'

'Don't you remember me?' the woman said. 'Dervla Connor as was, now Chitty. You and me was in the same class.'

Dervla Connor had been known as a bit of a glamour-puss at school, and in consequence Bernie had given her a wide berth. Glamour girls were not usually keen on other girls who failed to be impressed by them, and Dervla had been no exception. She'd also made fun of Bernie for hanging around with Becky and Rose. *Can't get yourself a decent Catholic friend, can you, Bernie Lynch?* she used to say. Bernie had always ignored her – until now.

'Dervla,' she said, and smiled. God, but Dervla Connor, as was, had not aged well at all! With huge dark circles underneath her eyes and her once shining brown hair snagged up underneath an old beret, she was barely recognisable as the queen bee who had once condescended to Bernie.

'What you doing round here?' Dervla asked. 'I heard you moved up West.'

And, knowing her, she probably knew why as well.

'I'm taking photographs,' Bernie said. 'For the *Evening News*. What are you doing?'

Bernie had been walking down Brune Street and had just passed the Soup Kitchen for the Jewish Poor when she'd come upon Dervla. Women with stout arms told destitute men to 'Wait! Wait!' while they prepared big cauldrons full of unidentified gruel. Bernie had photographed an old man in the queue who'd told her about his career as a prize fighter back in the old days. He'd been called Israel.

'Been bombed out,' Dervla said.

'I'm sorry.'

The Connors had lived in a tenement on Frying Pan Alley. All ten of them squashed into two rooms at the top of a staircase that was always threatening to collapse.

'Yeah, well, we're all alive,' Dervla said. 'Ain't got nothing much except for the wireless but ... ' She shrugged.

'Where you off to?' Bernie asked.

'Me mum's sister's got a place on Cannon Street Road.'

'You're all going there?'

'Me, Mum, our Declan and our Tina,' she said. 'And my Ernie when he gets off his shift.'

So Dervla must have married Ernie Chitty, Bernie thought. He had been a very popular boy at school. He'd gone into the docks at the same time as her brother Joey.

Dervla leaned forward and whispered, 'I'm expecting.'

'Oh, that's . . . '

'So good job we was all down the shelter, weren't it?'

'Yes.'

'Not like some,' she continued. Then frowned. 'Here,' she said, 'you knew them Commie boys, didn't ya?'

'I knew some of them,' Bernie said. Her dad had been in the party. 'Which ones did you mean?'

'That Solly Adler and his big mate – Wolfie,' Dervla said.

'What about them?'

'Dead, one of 'em, or so I heard . . . '

Bernie began to feel dizzy. Although usually sure-footed despite the jagged rubble beneath her feet, she now lost her footing and turned her ankle. 'Ow!'

'Fire-watching up Christ Church,' Dervla said. 'Fell off the roof. Here, you all right, Bernie?'

'Yes, yes . . . ' She made an effort to stand up straight. 'Fine.'

'Yes,' Dervla said as she began to walk on, pushing her wireless before her. 'Took 'em down the London, so I heard. 'It's where your mate Rebekah works, ain't it?'

Tilly hung onto the back of Rose's head until she'd finished being sick. They were outside the Salisbury, lurking in St Martin's Court; she'd had to rush Rose outside as soon as she'd started retching. As she began to recover, Tilly said, 'Oh, blimey, don't tell me you're up the stick!'

Rose fanned her face. 'I had a lot of gin so that I won't be,' she said.

'All that's gin?'

'Yes.'

'Bloody waste.' Tilly shook her head. 'Anyway, thought you said you never liked the beast with two backs. What's gone on?'

Rose stood up and sighed. 'Tilly, if I tell you, you must promise not to tell anyone else.'

'Oh, Jesus.'

A man with a very straight back, wearing a dark suit and a bowler hat, passed them by and Tilly put her arm around Rose's shoulders. When the man was out of earshot, Tilly said, 'Copper, you mark my words. Come to give us fairies grief. Now what's going on?'

Rose breathed in. The sickness had come on her suddenly. She wasn't used to hard drink and, because the liquor had been gin, the bad memories it had brought back had contributed to her feeling unwell.

'You know when we all drank that champagne last night?' she said. 'When the raid was ... '

'Oh, Gawd blimey, I never had a sudden straight moment, did I?' Tilly paled.

'No, no, not you,' Rose said. She moved close to her friend and whispered, 'But I think that maybe Kenneth ... '

'What? Kenneth Zear the doorman?'

'All I can remember is being with him, his voice ... Everyone else had passed out,' Rose said.

'Yes, well, Maltese Michael don't muck about when he buys knock-off booze ... '

'When I woke up I was . . . I was sore and . . . ' Rose lowered her voice still further. 'Wet.'

'Wet? Well, maybe you pissed your drawers . . . '

'No!'

'Wouldn't be the first time a girl's wet herself when she's had one over the eight. I know I have . . . '

'Tilly, it smelled,' Rose said. 'Of men.'

Tilly wrinkled up her nose. Rose had said once before that she'd been pregnant as a kid, so she had to know what she was talking about. But Kenneth Zear was such a timid, mousy sort. Admittedly he did look at the girls, but then what red-blooded straight man didn't? Even Tilly wasn't always averse to the sight of a naked female breast.

'You're saying he raped you?'

Rose didn't answer for a moment and then she said, 'He took advantage of me when I was asleep.'

'And pie-eyed.'

The girl looked down at the grey London pavement. 'What am I going to do?'

'You? Nothing,' Tilly said. 'You can rely on me to sort out that toerag Kenneth – and to see you right if there's any need. Don't worry, Rosie. It'll all work out fine, I promise you.'

Chapter 8

Like Becky, Dr Pierce was supposed to have gone home hours ago.

'I'm glad I stayed to see you come back to us,' he said to Solly Adler as he shone a light into his eyes.

'It hurts,' the patient mumbled.

'What does?'

'Everything.'

Becky, at the end of the bed, her back touching the curtains Dr Pierce had pulled around Solly's bed, looked on anxiously.

The doctor moved Solly's head from side to side. 'That hurt?'

'A bit.'

'Do you remember what happened?'

When the doctor touched his face, Solly winced. Although his burns had been dressed they were obviously still raw underneath the iodine-soaked gauze.

'I was on the roof of Christ Church and then I was here,' he said. Then looked straight at Becky and said, 'Do you know what happened to my pal, nurse? Called Wolfie Silverman.'

Did it hurt more that he didn't recognise her or that he was clearly in for a terrible shock when he found out about Wolfie? That Becky was even thinking these things made her feel ashamed.

Dr Pierce said, 'The man who was found with you is dead, Mr Adler.'

Solly didn't have much of a colour anyway but now his face turned grey with shock. Why had the doctor broken the news to him when he was clearly still so ill? And so baldly and brutally too?

'Oh.'

'I'm sorry you have to know but better now than later, so you can start to get used to it, eh?' Pierce said.

Solly looked down at his hands. 'Yeah. I suppose.'

The doctor took his pulse and then lit a cigarette. Solly watched him write some case notes.

As Solly had woken up, his mother shrieked with joy. Even before Becky could find a doctor Dolly had been all over her son, stroking his hair, kissing his face. Solly himself just kept on saying 'Ma! Ma!' and looking confused. He was still in shock, Becky realised.

Dr Pierce sat down in the chair next to the patient's bed.

'Now, I believe your mother has gone to fetch your fiancée who is, I'm told, anxious to see you, Mr Adler,' he said. 'But you must understand, you've suffered some injuries that will take time to heal. You've broken your collarbone, which is why nurse here bandaged you up. You've bruised and broken ribs, you've sustained considerable burns to your face and, although you are now back in the land of the living, you were unconscious for many hours. You will have to be closely monitored before we can send you home. Do you understand?'

Most of the doctors were upper- or, at the very least,

middle-class. Even amiable old buffers like Pierce tended to talk down to their patients. It still grated. Becky thought it was probably especially hard for a Communist like Solly to be spoken to in patronising terms. But all he said was, 'Yes, doctor.'

'And when your fiancée does come to visit you, I need to stress that absolutely no cuddling and canoodling can take place. Happy as I'm sure you are to be alive, you must take things easy for a good long while.'

'I will.'

The doctor looked at Becky. 'Nurse, do we have Mr Adler's prosthetic leg?'

'Yes, doctor. I, er, put it underneath the bed.'

'Good show.' Dr Pierce smiled at her. Then turning back to Solly again, he said, 'Once you feel more like yourself you can put that back on again. Until then, the nurses will aid you with toileting and bed bathing. Any questions?'

Solly shook his head. Dr Pierce put a hand on his shoulder and said, 'Jolly good. Soon have you right as rain.'

Then he left.

For a little while Becky just stood, not knowing what to say or do. Sitting immobile, Solly Adler looked down at his hands as if hypnotised. It was only when she moved to draw back the curtains that he spoke to her.

'Don't!'

'Oh, I . . . '

'I can't face it,' he said.

'That's all right.' She picked up the water jug from his bed-side table and said, 'Would you like me to . . . '

'No!'

Becky visibly jumped. Then she saw he was looking embarrassed by his outburst. He said, 'Sorry.'

'It's . . .' She walked towards him.

'If you'd known my mate Wolfie,' he said. 'What a laugh he was, what a *mensch* . . .'

She sat down lightly on the side of the bed. Should she tell him or not? Eventually it just came out.

'I did know him,' she said. 'He was a kind man.'

Solly looked at her, his eyes narrowed. Where his face had been burned, one eye was bloodshot and watery-looking and she got the impression he couldn't see out of it very well.

'How'd you know Wolfie?' he asked.

'We were all at the Battle of Cable Street together,' Becky said. 'When Mosley's fascists wanted to march through the East End . . .'

'. . . and the Jews and the Irish and the Communists stopped them! Yeah,' he said. 'I was there. Donkey's years ago now, before Spain, before this lot . . .'

'I'm Rebekah Shapiro,' she said. 'Daughter of Moritz Shapiro from Fournier Street.' She paused briefly and then added, 'My best friend is Bernadette Lynch.'

That got Solly's attention. Not that he said anything. He just looked at her as if she'd told him he was about to die.

Sometimes it took a moment for Bernie to remember that she didn't have to go everywhere on foot, on the bus or by Tube. Now she had money she could do things much more comfortably, even if there was a war on. Even if, when she thought about Heinrich and what he'd said to her last night, she knew it could all fall apart in a second. The Nazis could be in London any time now, any time . . .

'Taxi!'

She waved a hand into the flow of traffic on Bishopsgate, outside Liverpool Street Station, and a cab pulled over. A bloke of about forty stuck his head out of the driver's window and said, 'Where to, miss?'

As she got in the back, Bernie said, 'The London Hospital, please.'

'Okey-dokey.'

It wasn't far away, only in Whitechapel, but the journey there seemed to take forever. Whether this was because she was anxious to get to the hospital so that she could see whether Solly Adler was really alive or not, or because of all the diversions the cabbie had to take to avoid falling buildings, UXBs and other hazards, Bernie didn't know. But in the back of that cab she did at least have time to think.

As soon as Dervla had mentioned Solly's name, Bernie felt as if she'd been punched in the stomach. To hear that he was possibly fighting for his life had been almost too much for her to bear. And yet, why was that? She'd never walked out with the man, she'd only ever danced with him once, after what became known as the Battle of Cable Street back in 1936 when she'd been little more than a kid. Then there'd been that parting kiss everyone on the manor had talked about for months, the one that had made her mum so angry. It had happened, again back in '36, just before Solly had left England to go and fight in the Spanish Civil War on behalf of the Republican side. Right in the middle of her street she'd been when he'd kissed her on the mouth. He'd called her his girl then. He'd also said that he'd write to her, which had been a lie. Then when he'd come home, wounded and surely in need of 'his girl', he'd ignored her. She didn't know why. And after that Heinrich had come along and she'd gone to Germany with him to take photographs, which was what she'd always wanted to do . . .

The cab passed Bevis Marks Synagogue, the old Sephardic

temple on the street that shared its name. Battered but still standing, it reminded Bernie of her mother. The last time she'd seen Kitty, she'd stood straight-backed at the head of Pat's coffin during his wake. She'd not said a word. Not just to Bernie but to anyone.

Her mother was a stubborn woman and yet Bernie ached for her. In truth she'd probably loved her father more, but she had always sought Kitty's approval. She'd always wanted her mother to be proud of her.

Chrissy Dolan had told her that her mammy was working and she was fine. But the fact that she wouldn't go to Mr Shapiro's shelter with Dermot was worrying. Why not? Did she have some sort of death wish? Did she want to be with her darling Patrick again? Even if she didn't manage to find Solly at the London, Bernie could at least see if Becky was on duty and ask her if she knew anything about Mammy. She felt there was more to this than grief. What, she didn't know.

When they finally hit the Whitechapel Road, a burst water-main was pumping what looked like grey sludge high into the air. The cabbie swore as he struggled to find a way around. Bernie wondered how much longer this could continue without the city grinding to a standstill. Already few people could actually remember what a night without a raid felt like. Babies had been born, old and young people had died, and future generations been conceived, to the background noise of explosions. There would be a price to pay for that, beyond the obvious casualties of war, at some point, but what would it be? A generation left deranged? Or would they not, as Heinrich believed, live long enough to find out?

She looked out of the window at the tough and tired people of London, struggling to climb mountains of rubble just to get to work or else back home, and suddenly noticed that tears were running down her face.

'Whatever you do, make sure you hold on tight to your wotsit and don't let anyone see it.'

Rose clung on to the little piece of gauze she held over her pubis and said, 'Yes, Mr Van Damm.'

'And try not to look so constipated,' the impresario continued. 'You're supposed to be a bloody goddess!'

The new tableau they were rehearsing involved Rose standing naked inside a papier-mâché shell to recreate the famous 'Birth of Venus' by Botticelli. At least she'd been told it was famous. Apparently, in the original, Venus had long blonde hair, which she held over her 'privates'; all black-haired Rose had was a bit of chiffon.

Vivian Van Damm shook his head then said, 'Take five, everyone.'

As Rose stepped down from the stage she heard him tell one of the ASMs to: 'Get the bloody girl a blonde wig, pronto.'

Rose walked to the dressing room and sat down in front of her mirror. Two lots of alcohol – the champagne last night and then the gin from Mrs Muscat this morning – were not doing her face many favours. Her eyes looked black and sagging and her cheeks were still a little bloated, although thank God no longer hot. She took a swig of water from the cracked jug Tilly had insisted she place on her dressing table and sighed.

A new act, a magician called the Great Mysterio, was trying out during the matinee and, as well as being Venus, Rose had been asked to help him with his act. All she had to do was lie down in a box and be sawn in half. She'd seen it done before and knew it was just a trick, but that didn't mean she necessarily felt like doing it. Mysterio had a bit of a cocaine habit it was said, and indeed did always seem to perk up very dramatically before rehearsals and then almost fall asleep later. But he put on a good show and even did something with a disembodied head – although no one, so far, had seen that.

Vera, the girl who was going to close the show that afternoon, came into the dressing room wearing nothing but a tin hat.

'God, that flag's heavy,' she said as she slumped down in the chair beside Rose.

'What flag?'

'The one I'm supposed to wave at the end of the show,' she said. 'The old Union Jack, darling.'

'Oh.'

'Must keep the punters' spirits up.' Vera picked up a packet of cigarettes from the dressing table and lit up. 'Although after last night I don't see how that's possible,' she continued. 'Some people are saying it was the biggest raid yet.' Then she laughed. 'Not that we'd know, eh?'

Vera had been very greedy with Tilly's champers, like most of the girls. Like Rose herself. The difference was that Vera was happy about it.

The nurse, that nice Shapiro girl, left them alone with Solly.

Dolly sat down on her son's bed and waited for him to wake up. Sharon stood at the foot, her eyes like saucers.

When Dolly looked over at her, she said, 'What's happened to him?'

Solly's mum had never taken to Sharon. Beyond blonde hair (out of a bottle) and a certain swagger some would call sexy, Dolly didn't know what her son saw in the young woman.

'I told you,' she said, 'he's broke a few bones and he's got some burns.'

'On his face ... I never knew they was on his face ... '

'So his face is burned – so what?'

Solly began to stir. Dolly took hold of one of his hands and squeezed it. 'Hello, son,' she said.

He opened his eyes and smiled at her.

'Hello, Mum.'

'I brought Sharon with me,' Dolly said. 'Been going on about coming to see ya, she has, ever since I told her you was all right.'

'Mum, Wolfie ... ' He frowned.

It had to have hit him hard. Solly and Wolfie had grown up together. And although the poor boy's body couldn't be buried within the Jewish religion's stipulated twenty-four hours from death, Bertha, his mother, had let it be known that Wolfie's funeral would take place the following day. But Dolly didn't want her son to know that, because then he'd insist upon attending and there was no way his doctor would allow it.

'I don't know why these things happen, love,' she said. 'You both come off the roof somehow, yet he died and you survived.'

Out of the corner of her eye, Dolly could see that Sharon was trembling. Far from being anxious to see her injured fiancé, Sharon Begleiter had done nothing but moan about how she hated hospitals all the way over. Her old dad had died in the London admittedly, but Dolly couldn't help but think her son's fiancée was being a bit over-dramatic.

'How ... How you feeling, love?'

Finally she spoke – for what that was worth, to Dolly's way of thinking.

Solly looked up and said, 'Sharon.'

'Hello,' she said.

Dolly watched her force a smile. Yes, Solly didn't look his usual handsome self, but what else did the silly bitch expect? The boy had fallen off a church roof, she was lucky he was even alive!

'Hello.'

And yet her son was no fool. Dolly could see in his eyes that he knew exactly what Sharon was thinking. His mother was disgusted with the silly mare. Wrestling against the bad feeling she'd always nursed towards Sharon, Dolly stood up and said, 'Why don't you come and sit here, Sharon love? Be close to your intended.'

But Sharon Begleiter didn't move.

Bernie saw her down the end of a corridor so long it seemed to go on forever.

'Becky!' she yelled, sounding, she thought, like the street urchin she had once been.

The petite figure in the nurse's uniform turned to face her.

Bernie waved; she saw her friend smile and then run full pelt down that endless grey corridor like her life depended on it. Bernie held her arms open and, when Becky flew into her embrace, she sighed. There was precious little comfort to be had in wartime, but the love of a good friend was hard to beat.

'What are you doing here?' Becky asked.

Should Bernie tell her that she'd come to find out whether Solly Adler was alive, or should she lie?

'I came to take some photographs for the paper,' she said.

'In the hospital?'

'All over. The plucky old East End *schtick*, you know ...'

Becky shook her head. 'That we can "take it" ... As if we're a different species.'

They laughed together. When Bernie felt Becky's hand

rest warmly on her shoulder she couldn't hold in how she felt anymore.

'Becky ... ' She felt tears come into her dark blue eyes. 'Oh ... '

Her friend put an arm around her shoulders. 'Bern? What is it? What's the matter?'

She felt as if she was about to pass out. God, did this mean that she still in some way loved Solly Adler? And if she did, what did that say about her love affair with Heinrich? Confused and hurting, Bernie blurted out, 'Becky, is Solly Adler here in the hospital?'

A silence stretched between them. In spite of the sounds of trolleys clattering down at the other end of the corridor, feet running on a staircase and distant voices in conversation, a silence that went back years made itself felt. Becky too had loved Solly and, although Bernie knew he never, ever reciprocated her feelings, she understood that her friend's emotions had been badly bruised. Attempting to backtrack, Bernie said, 'Not that it's my business ... '

'I'll take you to him,' Becky cut in.

'Oh, no, no, it's ... '

'He is alive,' she said. 'I left him with his mum and that Sharon ... '

Bernie put her arms around her friend and said, 'I don't want to see him. Well, I do, but I don't need to. I just need to know he's alive.'

Although Becky hesitated for a moment, she went on to give Bernie a reassuring hug. 'Solly will be all right,' she heard her friend whisper. 'I promise you.'

She couldn't take it. The wooden leg she'd been able to adjust to because, even with that, Solly had still walked tall. Burned and broken in a hospital bed, though, he looked like an old, dying man. In fact, he looked like her dad had and Sharon couldn't stand that. Her old man had been a nothing. Now Solly, the hero of the Spanish War, the handsomest man on the manor, the man she had agreed to marry, was about to go the same way.

Dolly, the old witch, had tried to get her to sit next to him. But Sharon couldn't. She'd had to run, she'd *had* to. She couldn't marry *him*. She'd only ever walked out with Solly Adler to impress the other girls at her uncle's *schmutter* factory. Years ago, when he'd been young and eye-catching, everyone had wanted him. But that had been back in the bloody Dark Ages. Now all the girls wanted blokes who were in the Forces and that was never going to be Solly. Christ, he'd had this accident while he was fire-watching, for God's sake. Brave warriors didn't do menial stuff like that, did they?

But if she didn't marry Solly, who was she going to marry? At nearer forty than thirty, Sharon had a reputation to try and kill off too. In her twenties she'd put it about a bit. Luckily, she'd never got 'caught', but then she'd made the boys she'd gone with take great care. Now, she'd be lucky even to get in the family way at her age. And, so far, Solly didn't seem that keen to oblige. She'd given him chances but he'd always had too much pain in his leg or been too tired. And she knew why. Everybody did. He was still holding a candle for that Bernadette Lynch, that rough old slag who lived, it was said, with some rich Yiddisher bloke up West. Well, as far as Sharon was concerned, she was now welcome to him.

Her mum'd have a fit if she called the wedding off now, but what else could Sharon do? The change in him beneath that bandage on his face was probably horrible – and would his injuries mean she'd now have to keep him? Unlike that saint

Rebekah Shapiro, Sharon knew she couldn't do that. But then she'd be back to square one, wouldn't she?

She sat down on the steps outside the hospital's front entrance and lit a cigarette. All three of Sharon's sisters had been married for years. Even her youngest sister, Essie. She was only twenty-one and already in the family way. It wasn't as if Sharon wasn't attractive to men – she was. She had a good body which, in the past, she'd freely shared. But then maybe that was the problem; maybe blokes just didn't take her seriously unless they were desperate. Like Solly. Who else but a tart would actually marry a broken man like that?

Some people reckoned that if the Germans invaded England, or if their allies the Japanese began threatening the USA, then the Americans would join the war. Sharon wondered whether that would mean American troops would come to London. She went to the pictures whenever she could and loved all the Hollywood films. Her favourite stars were Errol Flynn and Clark Gable. They were real men.

Solly Adler was asleep again when Becky went back onto the ward. Dolly was still with him, holding his hand, but Sharon Begleiter had gone.

Becky put a hand on Dolly's shoulder. 'Everything all right, Mrs Adler?' she said.

When she looked up, Becky could see that Dolly had tears in her eyes.

'You know your son's going to be all right, don't you?' Becky said. 'Dr Pierce is looking after him and he's a really fine doctor.'

'I know, it's not that . . . '

'Why don't you come with me and have a cup of tea?' Becky said. 'I'm going off shift now. Come on. Let's go to Bloom's.'

'Oh, no, I couldn't . . . '

'My friend Nurse Lloyd is taking over from me and I know she'll take really good care of your son,' Becky continued. 'Come on.' She took Dolly's hand. 'My treat.'

The matinee over, there was still two hours to go until the early-evening performance, a time during which the performers at the Windmill usually wound down by either sleeping, reading or having a few drinks. First-timer the Great Mysterio had been very happy with his magic show's first debut and was celebrating with a bottle of brandy and a box of cigars.

'That young Rose was absolutely marvellous,' he said to Tilly as she passed, dressed as Herbert, on her way out. 'A natural.'

Tilly smiled. Little Rosie Red was a particular favourite of hers too. She'd found her one night sleeping rough in St James's Park. And, although Tilly didn't know Rose's whole story, she did know that the girl had been running away from a bad situation. This had involved rape and Rose had confided that it had put her off 'intimate relations' for life. And so if Rose had been assaulted by Kenneth Zear, Tilly wanted to make sure that, at the very least, it never happened again.

Ferreting away in the drawer of his desk in the booth behind the stage door, Kenneth looked up as Tilly approached and said, 'You off out, Till?'

'In a bit,' she said. She made sure that the corridor was clear and then entered Kenneth's booth. It was a cramped little space for one person, let alone two. Tilly saw Kenneth's heavy-lidded grey eyes widen in surprise.

'Wanted to have a chat,' she said.

'A chat? What about?'

Kenneth Zear lived with his mum, so he said, although

some of the girls reckoned she had probably passed away years ago. If she hadn't, then she had to be very thin as he never, so far as anyone could tell, did any shopping for the old girl. Mr Talent the One-Man Band was the only person Kenneth had ever had a drink with and he was of the opinion the doorman was 'dodgy', which in Mr Talent Speak could mean anything from shoplifting up to and including murder. What Tilly had heard a lot of, however, were the comments that most of the Windmill girls made about Kenneth being 'creepy'. He'd lurk around dressing-room doors, sometimes letting himself in without knocking and then staring at the girls in their various states of undress. And although Tilly couldn't be certain that what Rose had intuited had actually happened, she knew that the girl wasn't usually a liar. She'd been more upset today than Tilly had ever seen her before.

'About last night,' she said.

'What about it? I must say, that champagne you got . . . '

'I'm not talking about that,' Tilly said. 'I'm talking about you and young Rose.'

'Me and Rose?' laughed Kenneth. 'What do you mean? She's a little kid.'

'Yes, ain't she?' Tilly said. 'Which is why I was a bit disturbed to hear that you took advantage of her last night.'

'Took advantage . . . ' Kenneth's cheeks were red; his jowls wobbled as he tried to make himself laugh. 'Don't be so damn' silly! Me? Why, Tilly, I take . . . '

She pushed him up against the back wall and leaned one tweed-clad knee into his groin.

'When little Rose got up this morning, she was sore, she was confused and she smelled of spunk.'

'Well, all the girls were drunk, thanks to you. Gawd knows what went on. That vent was very dodgy, if you ask me!'

He was referring to a ventriloquist known as 'Uncle Pippin'; Tilly knew for a fact that he was most definitely a lover of men.

Tilly ignored the sweating hulk in front of her. 'Rose saw you,' she said. 'Saw your face leering over at her ... she smelled you.'

'She can't prove ...'

'Maybe not, but you ever touch her again and I'll fucking skin you alive!'

Several emotions passed across the doorman's face then. Derision featured among them but his feelings condensed down mostly to fear. Tilly articulated for him exactly how she felt.

'Because I know that you know never to make an enemy of a drag queen,' she said with a threatening smile. 'Remember, you have to be tough to be a bloke in a dress in a world run by blokes in suits and bowler hats. Touch her again and *I will make you pay.*'

And then, to reinforce her point, she kneed Kenneth in the groin.

'Aaagghh!'

He doubled over and, while he was down, Tilly whispered in his ear, 'You just pray you ain't got her pregnant because, if you have, you'll be made to pay in more than blood, you twisted little bastard!'

'I said to her, "You come over here and sit next to Solly," and she just upped and left,' Dolly said.

Becky watched Solly's mum move around the lemon slices in her tea with a spoon.

'I mean, what am I supposed to make of that?'

Out in the street the two old sisters from Frostic Walk began yelling at each other in Yiddish again. They had a pickle shop and were probably rowing about how much vinegar to use or some such detail. The only word Becky could understand from either of their tirades was 'nufke', which meant 'whore'.

'I'll be honest with you, nurse,' Dolly carried on, 'I never understood it when our Solly got together with that woman. When he come back from Spain I thought he'd pick up with that girl you used to go about with – Bernadette.'

Becky said nothing. If Solly had kept his promise to write to Bernie and not ignored her when he came home, maybe that might have happened. But as it was, he had locked himself away inside his own grief and bitterness for years. It was something for which Bernie was not to blame.

'I know she's a *shiksa*, but if he really loved her I wouldn't have stopped him! And if her mother'd've objected, I'd've had it out with her.'

Becky doubted this last statement. Knowing Auntie Kitty, she would have slammed her door shut in Dolly Adler's face.

'Things don't always go to plan,' Dolly continued, oblivious. 'I know that. I was supposed to get married myself a few years ago, but my intended, a very nice gentleman from Ilford, died.'

Becky remembered that Ben, if not Solly, was said to have been greatly relieved when the old man died. Apparently he'd been very boring – but he'd had money, which had since gone not to the Adlers, but to the old man's sister.

'It was probably just the shock that made Sharon behave like that,' Becky said. 'We see it a lot when relatives come to visit patients for the first time. Sharon needs to get used to things.'

'I thought she'd be happy just to see him alive,' Dolly said. 'I know I was.'

And so was Becky when she first saw him. Sharon Begleiter

was, and always had been, a nasty piece of work. She'd got Bernie sacked from her first job at Zvi Sassoon's sweatshop because she was jealous of her, and the woman's habit of spreading spiteful gossip was poisonous. A lot of people, including Becky, had wondered what someone like Solly had seen in Sharon. Those who could bring themselves to be honest about their thoughts admitted it was probably to do with sex. Old Mrs Michael, who still managed to do the Shapiros' washing once a week, had told Becky that Sharon Begleiter: 'Never wears knickers, like a nice girl does. Always ready to *schtup* the first man she sees, that one!'

But Becky didn't really know Sharon, just like she didn't know Dolly. Years ago she'd had the biggest crush on Solly anyone could imagine, but that was all over now. She'd still got a jolt when she'd seen him brought in, but that had passed. Shame it hadn't for Bernie. As she'd watched her friend walk out of the hospital and onto the Whitechapel Road that afternoon, Becky had felt so sad for her. Bernie's head was bowed as if weighed down and her eyes had been full of tears.

Becky had tried to comfort her, but it had been impossible. Bernie just cried and cried until eventually she'd admitted: 'I don't think I'll ever get over him, Becky. Not ever.'

Which at least meant she knew what the problem was. And Becky felt for her, but she also felt for Heinrich too. She'd only met him a couple of times but often enough to know that he was hopelessly in love with Bernie. Just the look in his eyes when he watched her told Becky all she needed to know. Bernie had to have more in common with him than with Solly, surely?

Dolly Adler said, "Course, I played it down for Solly. Told him Sharon had to go, quick like.'

Knowing Solly, he wouldn't have been taken in, but Becky kept that thought to herself. Instead she said, 'Nurse Lloyd ... my friend Iris ... she'll look after him, don't you worry, Mrs Adler.'

'Oh, I don't worry about him being in hospital, love,' Dolly said. 'I know you lot'll put him back together again. I just wonder about his head, you know?'

'His head?'

'Well, losing his best mate Wolfie is going to carry on hitting him hard for a very long time. They was like brothers. And if Sharon's gonna play up now ...' She shook her head and then looked at her watch. 'Better get home, both of us,' she said. 'They'll be coming over again tonight, bleedin' bastards.'

But that night the Luftwaffe didn't come. Becky, her father, Rose's mum, Chrissy Dolan and Dermot Lynch all made their way down to the Shapiros' Anderson shelter but nothing happened. Nor did it happen the next night or the night after that.

Unbeknown to everyone in Spitalfields and beyond, the first phase of the Nazi attack on Britain had come to an end. Now other fronts in the conflict would open up, bringing new sorrows, new friendships and the re-emergence of some faces from the past, both loved and hated.

Chapter 9

Christmas Eve 1941

The pastry, if it could indeed be called that, looked like an unappetising grey handkerchief. Kitty considered the small bowl of mincemeat she was about to smear onto it and said, 'Well, I hope you lot ain't going to be hungry tomorrow. Four ounces of mincemeat – what am I supposed to do with that?'

Marie, who was attempting to dress up a branch she'd found in Christ Church graveyard to resemble a Christmas tree, said, 'Don't you know there's a war on!'

'Blimey!'

Kitty folded the pastry over the mincemeat, put it on a baking tray and slipped it into the range. Aggie, warming herself in The Nook, said, 'I wish Auntie Mary could be here.'

The two girls had come back from Devon to London in June when it seemed that the bombing had come to an end. Both had gone straight into war work, Marie driving ambulances and Aggie in a bomb factory in Dagenham. But Aggie, at least, missed the countryside as well as her Auntie Mary. Being with his sister after her dad died had, in a way, kept Patrick Lynch alive for a little longer in the girl's mind.

'Travelling's hard,' Kitty said. 'You should know that. Anyway, Mary's got friends in Devon, she'll be fine.'

'Not the same as family,' Aggie said.

Kitty didn't answer. Marie, who knew much more about how her mother was thinking and feeling these days, put a finger to her lips to silence her little sister. There was almost nothing for Christmas dinner beyond a few potatoes and parsnips. Marie knew that as soon as she and Aggie either went out or went to bed, their mother would be drinking. Dermot, who was on his last leave home before going abroad to fight, had already gone out with his army pals. In the old days the whole family had gone to Midnight Mass together on Christmas Eve, but that hadn't happened for the last two years.

'Is Mrs Larkin coming for dinner tomorrow?' Aggie asked.

Kitty sighed. 'She is,' she said. 'She'll bring nothing and eat something as usual.'

'She's poor,' Marie said.

Her mother glared at her. 'We're all poor,' she said.

'Not like that.'

'Like ...'

A knock on the door caused Kitty to look away. 'Aggie, answer that,' she said.

The youngest Lynch girl placed the family's battered old Star of Bethlehem at the top of the Christmas 'branch' her sister had been dressing and went to the street door. When she opened it she saw Moritz Shapiro holding out a large paper bag.

'Ah, Agatha,' he said, 'I wonder if you would give these to your mother for me, please?'

Kitty called out, 'Come in, Mr Shapiro.'

'Oh, er . . . '

Aggie stood to one side to let him in. Becky's father had aged a lot since the dark days of the Blitz. Now, not only was his hair white, but his back was bent and his fingers clawed.

'I have something here for our lunch tomorrow,' he said. 'It's not much but . . . '

'Oh, anything is welcome, you know that, Mr Shapiro,' Kitty said.

In the past Moritz hadn't ever taken the Lynches up on their offer of Christmas dinner. He'd even forbidden Becky from going. Christmas was not their custom, he had always said. But things had changed since the start of the war. People looked out for each other as never before, especially when it came to sharing food.

Moritz opened the bag and took out five fat sausages. 'They're only Viennas,' he said. 'And there's not one, I don't think, for each of us . . . '

'Oh, you dear man!' Kitty nearly cried. 'Gawd blimey, I don't care what they're called, they're meat and it's Christmas!'

'Beef to be precise,' he said.

'Beef!'

'And kosher, I hope you don't mind . . . '

Kitty laughed. 'Mind? Christ, if I didn't think it'd upset you, I'd kiss you, Mr Shapiro!'

'Oh.'

She laughed. 'Look, come on and sit down and warm yourself by the range, Mr S. Here, you can have my Patrick's old chair.'

He knew that was an honour and so he sat down in the battered old chair with a smile.

'How many will we be tomorrow, Mrs Lynch?' he asked.

'There's the two girls, you and me, our Dermot, your Becky, Chrissy Dolan and Nelly next door, so eight,' she said. 'Just over half a banger each.'

'It's not a lot. I wish I could have got more.' Moritz shrugged.

Kitty smiled. 'We've got spuds, some parsnips, and I'm going to make some stuffing balls from a coupla crusts I managed to hide from this lot,' she said. 'And there'll be a drink. My Pat'd come back and haunt me if I didn't have a drop of the good stuff in.'

'Becky is coming, isn't she, Mr Shapiro?' Aggie asked.

'Oh, yes,' said Moritz. 'She would be with me now, but she's gone to visit one of her patients. Not far away, she told me. I don't like her going out in the blackout but it seems we no longer have raids for the time being, so what can I do?'

'Let's hope it stays that way,' Kitty said.

The whole room went silent then. Everyone agreed with her but no one dared to say so in case they were tempting fate.

Charlie's dad had 'contacts', which was why he was drunk before they even got to the pub. And he had fags. Outside the Coach and Horses on Greek Street, he distributed them to his mates.

Dermot shook his hand. 'Ta,' he said. Sixty Woodbines were not to be sniffed at.

'So's we can have a good night and have some snout to offer the girls,' Charlie said with a wink.

Larry, the third member of their group, just stared. 'Where'd you get all this snout from, Charlie?' he asked.

He tapped the side of his nose. 'Ask no questions, you'll get no lies,' he said.

Dermot shook his head. Charlie, like himself, came from the East End of London where the black market was a separate economy. Blokes with contacts in the docks and on the railway, like Charlie's dad, could get hold of all sorts of things people wanted, and you didn't have to have a ration book to get them. Just a bit of spare cash. Poor old Larry, on the other hand, was a country boy, from Devizes in Wiltshire, and he, to quote Charlie, 'didn't know his arse from his elbow'.

'And when the Yanks come over, there'll be even more,' Charlie continued. 'No rationing over there. They'll be loaded.'

'Which means what for us?' Dermot said. 'Even if they're loaded, they won't just give their stuff to us, will they?'

'No, but if it's there for the taking . . . '

Charlie's dad had always been a tea-leaf.

'Anyway,' he said, 'let's get some beer inside us before we go and see these girls.'

He opened the door to the pub and walked inside, closely followed by Larry. But Dermot lingered a little longer in the darkness of the street. Like Charlie Bush, who he'd known a bit from back home, and Larry, who reminded him of the farmers' boys he'd met in Devon, Dermot had joined the Wiltshire Regiment back in the summer. In the New Year they were going to set sail for the Middle East, although none of them knew where to exactly. As far as anyone could tell, given the censorship that was being applied to British news, the Nazis and the Allies were both holding their own in that theatre of war. But Dermot was anxious and knew that his family were anxious too. Little Paddy had been out there somewhere for almost eight months and so far their mother had only received one letter from him. And she was drinking. If he or Paddy died on top of the loss of their dad, their mammy'd drink herself to death.

Another group of squaddies pushed past him and went into the pub. He heard Charlie roar, 'Come on, Der, you bastard!'

Dermot smiled. The two lads were good mates. They'd helped

each other through the horrors of basic training via a mixture of good humour, rude banter and the occasional act of disobedience. Now trained infantrymen, they were going to have to be, well, 'men' ... But what did that mean? Dermot hoped he wouldn't have to kill but knew that wasn't realistic and that he could do it if he had to. The enemy did, after all, threaten everyone's way of life, including his. But being a 'man', quite apart from 'playing the soldier', wasn't easy. It meant coming on 'beanos' like this – spending a night out boozing with the boys followed by a trip to the famous Windmill Theatre to see the naked girls. No doubt Charlie would make a right old racket when he saw a girl in the buff. Larry wouldn't know where to put himself. And Dermot? Well, as he looked into the darkened shop-doorways that lined Greek Street, Dermot saw much more attractive prospects for a memorable night out. But he turned away from them and, with a sigh, went into the pub.

The tea was strong and it had been served to her in what was obviously one of Mrs Adler's best teacups.

'It's ever so nice of you to pay us a visit, nurse,' Dolly Adler said as she sat down next to Becky. 'It's lovely to have a bit of company, ain't it, Solly?'

Solly Adler, seated in a large, brown-upholstered wing chair by the fire, smiled back at her. 'Yes, it is.'

'You know, we used to have a right old blow-out at Christmas before the war,' Dolly continued. 'There was Solly, me and our Ben, and we used to have Mrs Llewellyn come over. Then for a coupla years my friend Mr Green joined us. Always had a good joint of meat, plenty of spuds and a plum pud with custard, we did.'

'Sounds lovely,' Becky said.

She'd seen Mrs Adler talking to one of the costers on Crispin

127

Street. Once Becky had seen goods change hands, she'd gone up to her and said hello. It was then that Dolly had invited her to come round: 'Christmas Eve, if you like, for a cuppa and a bit of sherry ... if I can organise it!'

And so here Becky was, in the Adlers' flat on Commercial Street, drinking tea but with no sign, as yet, of sherry. Solly looked better. Occasionally, he got up and walked about; his broken bones had healed months ago. But his poor face still looked sore. The burned skin hadn't healed well, making one side look uneven, red and raw. The damage dragged his left eye downwards.

'This year it's short commons,' Mrs Adler sighed. She shook her head regretfully. 'If Sharon hadn't managed to get them Viennas off her uncle, I don't know what we'd be noshing tomorrow.'

The last thing Becky had heard about Sharon Begleiter was Dolly Adler's misgivings over her as a future daughter-in-law. And now there she was, standing in the doorway to the scullery kitchen.

'Hello, Nurse Shapiro,' she said.

'Hello, Miss Begleiter.'

Although Sharon's greeting sounded perfectly pleasant, their visitor could see the dislike in her eyes. Sharon had always known about Becky's friendship with Bernie. Sharon herself didn't have any real female friends. But now she was in the living room, she put her arm around Solly's shoulders, just to let Becky know that he was hers. She must have decided she could 'cope' with him after all.

'We're just having a quiet day here all together, aren't we?' Sharon said.

'Just the three of us.' Dolly added, 'You doing anything tomorrow, nurse?'

'Papa never used to allow us to celebrate Christmas but since the war started he's got to know more people. We'll be with our neighbours the Lynches tomorrow.'

'Oh? What – Bernadette Lynch's family?'

Of course Sharon knew it was Bernie's family!

'Yes.'

'Oh.'

Becky saw Solly look away.

'So is Bernadette coming . . . '

Sharon knew she wasn't. Everyone knew that Kitty wouldn't allow it.

'No, she has other plans,' Becky said.

'Is she engaged . . . '

'So when are you getting married, Miss Begleiter?' Becky cut in, to stop the needling questions. God, this woman was an evil cow! She knew what Bernie's situation was, the same as everyone else on the manor did. She was living with a married man, and increasingly these days living off him. Ever since Bernie had presented her editor with those terrible photographs of what was *really* going on in the East End, back in May, new commissions for her had been few and far between. Her boss had, according to Bernie, lost his mind when he saw her shot of a bombed-out house on Hanbury Street. Firemen were shown removing a corpse and an Indian woman, who'd lived there for years, was screaming her heart out and tearing her face with her fingernails.

'We're after a spring wedding, ain't we, Solly?' Sharon said.

'Yes.'

'God willing,' Dolly said.

'When the Yanks get here people reckon we'll be able to get all sorts of things we ain't had for ages,' Sharon said.

'Maybe.'

Becky was sceptical. A lot of people seemed to think that once the Americans came over, all their troubles would be in the past. To hear some of them talk, it was as if the Yanks would arrive carrying armfuls of nylons, chocolate and chewing gum, to hand out to whoever asked.

'I mean, I know there's a war on but I still want to have the best wedding dress I can get, don't I?' Sharon said. 'What every girl dreams of, ain't it?'

Becky didn't say anything and neither did Dolly, whose eye she caught. Her face hollowed by constant tension, Dolly looked genuinely sad. It seemed things were still not right in the Adler household and maybe they never would be.

Chrissy came in just after Mr Shapiro left and went straight to his bed. The two girls stayed up for a bit longer but then they went to their beds too. Alone in front of the range, Kitty organised the youngsters' meagre Christmas stockings underneath the one-branch tree. It was all stuff she'd made. After unpicking an old cardigan that had once been Pat's, she'd made socks for the two boys and Mr Shapiro, and gloves for Marie, Aggie and Becky. She'd found a pad of paper for Chrissy to use for sketching on the street – probably used to belong to some poor soul who'd been bombed out. She'd managed to blag some tobacco from the girls at Tate's for Nell Larkin who was down to smoking dried leaves.

Kitty took out the bottle of whisky she'd hidden behind the girls' Nook and drank a long swig. It burned the back of her throat and for a moment made her heave. Gin was her usual drink but that was nowhere to be had and she'd been obliged to do some things she hadn't liked to get this whisky. No more, in reality, than turning a blind eye to small amounts of precious sugar being liberated from the plant, but she still didn't feel good about it. She also knew she should have got something for her compliance that would have benefitted the whole family. But then as long as she didn't drink it all, the whisky could be everyone's Christmas drink.

Kitty looked through the grille at the flames leaping up inside the range and felt bad. Pat would've hated the way she carried on these days. He'd always liked a drink, but he'd never been a drunk, he'd never needed alcohol. She did. To deal with the hole his death had opened up in her life, to deal with Joey and Bernadette going to the bad. One a thief and possibly a murderer, the other a whore. How had that happened? Hadn't she brought them up properly, to work hard and fear God?

Kitty had another swig and held the bottle up to her one dim gaslight to see how much she'd drunk. It wasn't that much. There was still well over half remaining. That'd do for a drink at Christmas. And then she began to cry, thinking of what Pat would say. He'd be disgusted by such a small amount of drink in the flat. He'd put his cap on and go out to find some more. But she couldn't go out, not now, not in the darkness all on her own. Kitty took another swig from the bottle and lay down on the floor.

'You've got snout, what you looking at that for?'

Charlie couldn't see that it wasn't the cigarettes Dermot was looking at but the girl selling them. He knew her and she knew him.

'I'll see you in there,' he told Charlie.

'Suit yourself.'

He and Larry disappeared into the auditorium. Alone with the cigarette girl, Dermot said, 'What you ... '

'I work here,' Rose said. 'You won't tell anyone, will you, Der?'

He didn't know what to say. In many ways she still looked exactly like the old Rose he remembered from his youth, albeit with her hair done and a bit more make-up. But in this sort of place ... He comforted himself with the fact she was only selling fags.

'Where you been?' he said.

'Here.'

She cast her eyes down, which made him wonder whether she was telling the truth.

'Selling fags?'

'Yeah.' She looked up. 'You'd better get in or the show'll start and you'll miss it.'

He took one of her hands. 'I can't leave you like this,' he said.

'You have to,' she said. Then she leaned towards him. 'I'm a thief, don't forget. A criminal ... '

He shook his head. 'No one even remembers that now,' he said.

A bell sounded to tell people to take their seats.

'Look,' he said, 'can I meet you after? Will you still be here?'

'I will, but ... '

'But what?' He began to run towards the auditorium.

'All right, I'll see you,' said Rose. 'At the stage door.'

Going out to the privy in the middle of the night was always a risk. There was only one and you could find yourself meeting all sorts out there on a dark night, even people who didn't live in your house. Chrissy Dolan took a candle with him when he let himself out of the Lynches' flat and walked up the steps into the back yard. He didn't feel well. Lying to Dermot and the others about what he did was making him anxious. But, although he'd tried, Chrissy hadn't been able to obtain employment since he'd returned to Spitalfields. He'd done most of the housework in the flat for months, but he hadn't earned a penny until he'd gone back down Limehouse and sold brief moments of sexual relief to men whose proclivities were usually hidden even from themselves. Chrissy hated himself and them.

He was just about to open the privy door when he heard someone moan. Holding his candle low and peering into the darkness, he eventually managed to make out a figure lying on the ground. As he got closer he saw that it was Kitty.

'Auntie Kitty?'

Oh, Jesus, and there was an empty bottle beside her.

'Auntie Kitty?'

She opened her mouth first and Chrissy got a faceful of whisky fumes. Then she opened her eyes.

'Chrissy?' she said. 'Wha—'

'You're outside, Auntie,' he said. 'Must've taken a tumble as you went to the privy.'

'Did I?'

As he raised her to her feet she said, 'Ooohh!'

'Is the world going round, Auntie Kitty?'

'I am a little bit dizzy, yes,' she said.

She was so drunk. But then if that whisky bottle had been full and now it was empty ...

'Do you want me to take you to the privy now, Auntie?' Chrissie asked.

He could do with going himself but felt that her need might be greater.

But she said, 'Nah! Nah, you go ...'

He couldn't just release her, though, or she'd collapse like a pile of books. First he tried to prop her up against the side of the privy, but she just slipped down to the ground. Then he tried laying her back down on the ground, but she said this made her feel sick. Something else she said also caught Chrissy's attention and it was this: 'I'm a bad woman really. You know, years ago I burned the letter a man my daughter loved sent her from Spain. Now my Pat's dead, I know I done wrong. To be without those we love is bloody hell!'

Then Kitty collapsed in the doorway to the privy. But Chrissy thought about what she'd said and it made him disinclined to pick her up again. She'd been talking about Bernie and Solly Adler. Bernie had loved him once, long ago.

Charlie and Larry were waiting for him at the bottom of the alley so he couldn't be long. In a way Dermot wanted them to push off and leave him alone with Rose. All they wanted to do now was get even more tanked up and talk about girls' tits. He didn't want to do that but it was what was expected.

'So where you living?' he asked Rose.

Wrapped up in a thick, winter coat and long scarf, she looked like a little dumpling. Clearly she wasn't starving, not like in the old days.

'I've a room here in Soho,' she said. 'Although I'm moving soon.'

'Oh? Where you off to?'

'I'm going to share with another girl – Tilly,' she said.

'That's nice. So where . . . '

'Oh, I don't want no one knowing,' Rose said.

'I won't tell no one,' Dermot said. 'I'm just glad to see you. We've all been worried.'

'I'm all right.'

''Specially your mum.'

Rose looked away.

'You know she's still in your old flat, don't you?' Dermot said. 'And Len's long gone.'

Len Tobin, her mother's pimp and sometime lover, had been

on his way out when Rose had left Spitalfields. But she was surprised to hear her mum was still in the flat. Rose had stolen money from the Jewish matchmaker Mrs Rabinowicz to pay her mum's rent. Surely the old woman had wanted it back?

'What happened?' she asked. 'About that money I nicked?'

'It was all right,' Dermot reassured her. His father had spoken to Mr Shapiro who had sorted the old girl out somehow. 'Everyone'd love to see you, Rose. Especially Becky and Bernie.'

And she wanted to see them. But she couldn't.

'Oh, no,' she said. 'I've got me life here now, Der.'

'What, as a cigarette girl!'

'I weren't always a cigarette girl,' Rose said. 'I used to be on the stage, in the *tableaux*, right at the front. I was Venus once, I . . .'

She'd been so keen to make him realise that she'd made something of herself, that she wasn't 'just' a cigarette girl, she'd forgotten completely why she'd actually taken a more lowly form of employment. As soon as it was out of her mouth, she knew he'd ask.

'So if you was a Windmill Girl then why you just on the fags now?'

From the other end of the alleyway, Charlie called, 'Oi! Private Lynch! What you doing down there!'

This was followed by a laugh.

Dermot ignored his mates. He had a look on his face that Rose didn't like, though she didn't know why. Dermot had always been the kindest of men, just like his dad.

'Well?' he said. 'There's something you're not telling me here, isn't there?'

Which was when Rose drew her scarf to one side, opened her coat and showed him her swelling stomach underneath.

For a moment he just stared and then he said, 'So the father . . .'

135

'There isn't one,' Rose replied. 'Or rather, there was but he's gone now. Mr Van Damm sacked him when he found out I was in the family way by him. Won't never see him again.'

There had been rumours that Rose had got in the family way once before back when they were kids. If she had, why had she taken the risk again? But then that was a stupid question even if Dermot didn't actually speak it out loud.

'I'm going to live with Tilly,' Rose said. 'She'll look after me.'

'Yes, but the baby won't have a father.'

'Well, no, but ...'

'Der!'

Angered by the interruption, he called out, 'You lot go on. I've got to talk to her, she's me cousin ...'

'Oh, right,' he heard Charlie say. 'Cousin, is it?' He laughed. 'All right, mate, we believe ya!'

'I'll see you Boxing Day, yeah?' Dermot said. 'Down the Ten Bells.'

He heard Charlie laugh. 'All right, mate. 'Never been one to get in the way of a geezer's *cousin*!'

Both men walked away, in Charlie's case very unsteadily. Dermot felt duty-bound to explain this and said, 'My mate, he's had a few ...'

'More than a few,' Rose said.

They looked at each other and then she said, 'Does Mum really want to see me?'

'I promise you, she does.'

Rose looked down at the ground and then said, 'Will you come for a drink with me, Dermot? I know a place.'

Lily Law had been busy that night and so the party wasn't as lively as it could have been.

Doris held court on the sofa, spreading the bad news as well as her own hilarious take on the situation. The boys at her feet laughed but there was an edge to their mirth. Getting picked up by 'Lily' was something that could happen to any of them at any time. Tilly filled their glasses with some Irish stuff that was supposed to be almost a hundred per cent proof. She'd got it from a bloke in her office whose gran had come from County Cavan.

'That redhead with the gammy arm got picked up with a viscount of my acquaintance,' Doris said. 'I was trolling along the Strand when I saw them. Little red on her knees, the toff with his hands on his fly buttons. Then along comes Lily with her torch, nicked the both of them. 'Course, the viscount'll get off, he always does, but how that little red queen'll make out in a prison cell with only one good arm, I don't know. Full of drunks and pervs ... she'll have a night to remember and no mistake!'

Tilly's flat wasn't much more than a room with a sink. Luckily for her, the other tenants were also either drag queens or 'girls' on the game up at what was known as the 'Meat Rack' on Piccadilly Circus. In the darkness of the blackout, men with a need for sex with other men would come and pick a 'girl' from the Rack, then disappear into a back alley where 'congress' would be achieved and money would change hands.

'Is little Rosie Red coming?' a 'girl' called Mary asked.

'Yes, love,' Tilly said. 'I don't know where she's got to. Said she was going to have a few words with an old friend, but she's taking her time.'

'How you gonna manage with Rosie and the baby, Til?' another rent boy asked.

'We'll get by,' Tilly said. 'I got a cot the other day off this bloke I know down Berwick Street. It's in the coal cellar at the moment. And me cousin Edie's knitting.'

'You'll need more than a cot and some booties,' Doris said.

Tilly topped up her glass. 'I know that,' she said. 'Mr

Talent's making a pushchair and Rosie's been collecting material to make nappies out of for months. It's like this war, we all need to pull together.'

'Kid'll still be a bastard,' someone murmured.

Tilly sat down on the floor and took a swig from the bottle of – whatever it was. She coughed. 'Christ Almighty, what is this?' Then, collecting her thoughts, she said, 'Well, I've told her I'll marry her if she wants. But she don't want so I dunno what else I can do. This kid won't be the first to be had out of wedlock and it won't be the last.'

'My bloke ... you know, the one what's in the Home Guard? He reckons that when the Yanks get here with their Hollywood smiles and their big muscles ...'

'Can't wait!' someone breathed.

' ... women'll be throwing their knickers at them. There'll be Yank kids as far as the eye can see!'

A knock on the door brought conversation to a halt.

'Come in!' Tilly yelled. 'The water's fine!'

Rose put her head round the door first, followed by a very attractive man with jet black curls.

Tilly leaped to her feet. 'Rosie Red!'

Rose walked in. 'I hope you don't mind, I brought me friend,' she said.

The young man walked in. Tall and dark-eyed, he was also clearly clocking all the boys in the room.

'This is Dermot.'

Tilly held out a hand, to be either shaken or kissed, she didn't really mind which. Dermot shook it vigorously.

'Hello, pal,' he said.

'Hello, mate,' Tilly countered, thinking all the while that she'd not seen a boy so beautiful and yet so in denial of his true nature for a very long time.

Chapter 10

Christmas Day

The girls were good kids really. Marie and Aggie had already lit the range and were boiling potatoes and making stuffing balls when Kitty staggered out of her bedroom.

'Merry Christmas, Mammy!' Aggie yelled. She had a hat made out of a sheet of newspaper on her head and a big smile on her face.

'Yeah, and to you, love,' Kitty said as she climbed into Pat's old chair, clutching her sore head.

'Mammy, do you know how we cook them Viennese sausages?' Marie asked.

Kitty tried to think through the fog of her hangover. 'Mr Shapiro said they need to be boiled,' she said. 'Like pudd'ns.'

'How long for?'

'I don't know!' she snapped.

The girls looked at each other and then went back to their tasks in silence.

After a few moments Kitty said, 'When did Dermot get in?'

Again the girls looked at each other and then Marie said, 'He ain't back.'

'Ain't back?'

'No. He went out drinking with his mates from the army,' Marie said. 'I expect he's sleeping it off at Charlie Bush's place.'

'Well, when he does get in he won't be needing none of my whisky,' Kitty said. And then she looked around the room to see whether she could locate her bottle. It appeared to have disappeared.

'What you looking for?'

Chrissy closed the door into the yard behind him and wiped his face on the towel hanging from the back door.

'Me whisky,' Kitty said. 'Can't find it.'

'Oh.'

Chrissy appeared to be deep in thought for a moment and then he said, 'I'm really sorry, Aggie, but I've left me snout outside in the privy. Do you mind going out and getting it for me?'

Aggie loved the boy she called her 'other brother' and was always keen to do anything she could to make him happy.

'All right,' she said. 'Back in a mo'.'

As soon as she had closed the back door behind her, Chrissy looked across at Marie, who nodded.

He walked over to Kitty and said, 'You drank it, Auntie Kitty.'

She looked up at him through watery, bloodshot eyes. 'Drank what?'

'The whisky,' he said. 'You drank it all.'

Outraged, she pushed herself out of the chair and looked him straight in the eyes. 'No, I never! Who says?'

'I had to go to the khazi last night and you were laying in the yard with an empty bottle at your side,' Chrissy said.

For a moment her eyes moved from side to side as she struggled to recall what might have happened, then she said, 'Nah. I dropped it. Or you lot had it or ... '

'Auntie Kitty, you were as drunk as a sack,' Chrissy said. 'I had to carry you back indoors.'

Marie picked up something from the floor and then held it up. 'You drank all of this, Mammy,' she said. 'No one else, you.'

Feeling dizzy again, Kitty sat back down in Pat's chair. 'How'd you know?' she asked her daughter. 'You went to bed ... '

'Chrissy told me and anyway we know you drink,' Marie said. 'Only Aggie don't ... '

'What don't Aggie know?' the girl said as she came back in from the yard. 'Your snout ain't out there, Chrissy.'

'Oh.'

They all fell silent for a moment until Aggie said, 'But, yes, I do know about Mammy's drinking.' She looked at her mother. 'You been doing it for months.' She turned to Chrissy. 'What's she done now?'

'Drank all the Christmas whisky.'

Aggie shook her head.

Kitty began to cry. 'Oh, God Almighty, what do we do about a Christmas drink now?' she wailed.

'We don't have one,' Marie said simply.

'Yeah, but Mr Shapiro and Becky are coming, and Nelly ... '

'You should've thought of that before you drank yourself into a stupor,' her daughter continued.

Aggie said, 'Marie ... '

'No, Ag, she has to know!' Marie said. 'She can't go on like this! The fact we ain't got no Christmas drink is down to you, Mammy! So if you want to find us some more booze from somewhere, I suggest you go out and look for it. Me and

Aggie's cooking the dinner and I think Chrissy should have a bit of a rest after being up with you half the night, don't you?'

Kitty wanted to die. She didn't know whether to curl up in Pat's chair and weep, go back to bed or run out into the street. In the end she went to bed.

When she'd gone, Chrissy said, 'I'm sorry I had to tell you, Marie.'

'You done the right thing,' she said.

Aggie put the potatoes into the oven. 'Mammy's so unhappy,' she said. 'Now that Daddy's gone.'

'We all are!'

'Yeah, but ...' She shrugged then said, 'Going to make the beds.'

Marie put a hand on her sister's shoulder and said, 'It'll be all right in the end. Promise.'

Aggie smiled.

Once she'd gone Marie walked over to Chrissy and said, 'So what you going to say to Mammy about Bernie and Solly Adler's letter?'

He'd told her what her mother had said in the middle of the night, before Marie started cooking.

He sighed. 'I dunno.'

'You think she was telling the truth?'

'She was in tears over it ...'

'But was it just the booze talking?'

Chrissy shook his head. 'I dunno. But I ain't gonna say nothing about that until Christmas is over.'

Marie nodded.

'Problem we have now is to find some drink from somewhere ...'

'Oh, go and ask Rosie's mum if we can pass off one of her bottles as our own,' Marie said. 'Mr Shapiro'll bring that kosher stuff, we'll have enough. Mammy's always been worried about what people will think. They think what they think, is what I say, it's up to them.'

Chrissy smiled and wished he could be more like Marie.

'Rebekah! Time to go!'

'Coming, Papa!'

Becky picked up the bag of presents she'd made to go underneath the Lynches' tree and checked how she looked in her mirror. Tired and washed out if she was honest. Her cheekbones looked as if they were about to burst through her skin. She'd been glad to see that Solly Adler had made so much progress when she'd been to visit the family. She could've done without Sharon's occasional digs about Bernie, though. Not so long ago Sharon had run away from her 'intended', horrified by the way he looked after his accident. She had nothing to crow about – except, of course, for her upcoming wedding.

Becky put on her green felt hat and fixed it to her hair with a hatpin. It didn't go that well with her grey coat but it was the only hat she had that wasn't damaged in some way. It was unlikely, but if someone had got her a hat for Christmas that would be marvellous. Gloves too would be welcome. She slipped what had been a very good pair of leather ones onto her hands and grunted in annoyance when her fingers encountered holes. It was almost impossible for anyone to look good when there was precious little to eat and clothes were so badly made and drab.

But she was quite pleased with the presents she'd made. Everyone was to be given a little notebook made from the tissue paper her papa used to make suit patterns. This she'd cut into sheets and had then bound with silk, cut from an old dressing gown and glued onto pieces of cardboard. She'd given Solly one of these, much to Sharon's obvious disgust.

'Oh, a book,' she'd said dismissively when Becky had handed it over to him. Then she'd left to go back to the scullery and her preparations for Christmas.

Solly had smiled when he'd said, 'Thank you. I'll use it to write down me thoughts.'

And Becky knew that he would. Because in spite of everything he'd been through, the disillusionment he'd felt after the Spanish Civil War, the old Solly Adler was still in there somewhere. Which was why it was so strange he was marrying someone like Sharon Begleiter. Spiteful and vain, she didn't seem to have a useful thought in her head – although maybe, Becky thought, she was wrong about that. Maybe Sharon had hidden depths.

What she did feel she knew about Sharon and Solly however, was that they didn't love one another. She'd seen love: when her father spoke about her late mother; when Auntie Kitty had nursed Uncle Pat; and when Solly and Bernie had looked at each other all those years ago on Cable Street.

Chrissy dragged the table into the middle of the room and began to arrange an assortment of chairs around it.

Nell Larkin, already seated with her back to the range, said, 'I wonder if Mr Shapiro'll bring any of that wine?'

She'd given what had remained of the half bottle of gin she'd got from a Dutchman to Chrissy so they could all have a drop with their Christmas dinner. Nell knew that Kitty drank and she knew why and sympathised. To lose the reason for your existence was a bitter pill to swallow. For Kitty that had been Pat's death; for Nell it had all happened a long time ago when she'd left her family in Epping Forest.

People always thought that Romany girls, like her, were free with their sexual favours, but quite the reverse was true. Nell had disobeyed her family's code of behaviour by being free with her favours, and she'd been caught out. Her own people had then rejected her and it was made plain by them that she had better live elsewhere. Although until only a few years ago her mum and dad had still visited from time to time, that had all stopped. Then Rose had gone. Sometimes Nell felt as if the only constant in her life was the drink.

There was a knock at the street door.

'I'll get it,' Chrissy said as he raced past Marie and Aggie who were setting the table.

Outside stood Moritz and Becky Shapiro with what looked like armfuls of presents in their hands.

'Come in!' Chrissy said. 'Merry Christmas to you!'

'And to you too,' the old man said.

Becky looked around the faded, slightly smoky room and saw the one small decoration in the corner.

'Oh, a Christmas tree!'

'More like a twig, but yes, that's what it's meant to be,' Marie said. 'We've put our presents down there if you want to put yours down too.'

Becky piled her notebooks up underneath the tree's single glass bauble while her father placed two bottles of kosher wine on the table.

Nell looked up at him through a veil of her own black-grey hair and said, 'Oh, Mr Shapiro, you have done us proud!'

'I know you like my wine, Mrs Larkin,' he said. 'And because it's your Christmas ... '

She picked up one of the bottles and stared at it. He knew the label would make no sense to her as she had never learned to read. But he left her to it and sat down.

'Mammy's just getting herself ready,' Marie said as she placed a bowl of roast potatoes and parsnips on the table.

Becky, looking up from her place beside the 'tree', said, 'I thought that Dermot was at home.'

'He is,' Marie said. 'But he went out with some of his army mates last night.'

'Oh, I see.' Becky smiled.

'He should be back soon.'

But if he wasn't no one would blame him, except maybe his mother. They all knew that he was going abroad in the New Year. No one knew where or for how long, and that included Dermot himself.

The bedroom door opened then and Kitty Lynch came into the parlour looking an absolute picture in a blue velvet dress. Only Marie and Aggie knew it had been Mrs Rabinowicz the matchmaker's old day dress that their mammy had taken in to less than half its original size. But with her hair piled up on top of her head, and the cream silk shoes she had been married in on her feet, Kitty looked stunning.

Aggie breathed, 'Oh, Mammy!'

'Well, it *is* Christmas,' she said. 'And even without your father, there's no need for the rest of us to drop our standards.'

It was less than ten hours ago that Chrissy had held her head so she didn't choke on her own vomit. Now Kitty Lynch looked as fresh as a daisy. She seemed happy. Did she even remember what she'd said to him in the yard? If true, it was a terrible thing and Chrissy knew he couldn't leave it alone until he knew the truth. But now was not the time.

Everything in this room reminded Herbert of why he had left West Norwood to go to Soho over thirty years ago. It was one of the reasons why he'd become Tilly.

146

While his mother muttered and tutted in the scullery, he sat in a bald velvet chair beside the wireless, looking at a menagerie of dead things under glass domes. Sparrows and polecats, a raven and a group of dead kittens having a picnic – all dusty, miserable and old. Like his mum. The taxidermy aside, it was the bleeding antimacassars on all the chairs and the endless doilies and tablecloths that really got him down. Middle-class aspirations worn threadbare. And for what?

Herbert had never known his father. In fact, he had some real reservations about whether the man had ever really existed as a permanent fixture in their lives. All Herbert had known was this flat, his mum and some bloke he'd called 'Uncle Ben' until he'd finally died back in 1934. Referred to as the lodger, Uncle Ben had never slept with Herbert's mum, so far as he knew, but he had seen them have 'cuddles', which had really confused him as a child. Why had his mum cuddled a man who wasn't even related to her?

Cissy – Mum – came out of the scullery wiping her twisted, arthritic fingers against her apron. 'About ten minutes,' she said as she sat down in what had always been her chair.

'Okey-dokey.'

She smiled. With her thin grey hair pinned up in a bun and her face deeply lined with what she had always told Herbert were 'my worries about you', she looked a lot older than seventy. And it had got worse since she'd had to have all her teeth out in the summer.

'So, Herbert,' she said, 'I remember last time you came home, you told me about a young lady . . . '

He had. Over the years he'd often made up stories about imaginary girlfriends to keep his mum happy – and off his scent.

'Rose, was it?'

But this time the 'mystery girl' had a name. That hadn't been a good idea. It should have been, but as things had turned out, it had been a mistake.

'Yeah,' he said.

'So . . . ' She leaned forward in her chair, her twisted fingers curling in on themselves like snakes, waiting to latch on to any details.

Herbert sighed. Life with Rose and the nipper would have been hard but it would have given him the legitimacy his mum had always craved. After all, none of her other old lady friends still had an unmarried fifty-year-old son.

'It's not worked out,' he said.

'Oh. I'm sorry, love. Why not?'

He'd been afraid she'd ask him that.

Herbert shrugged. In his wide pinstripe suit he looked dapper but also, he always felt, a little bit shady too – especially when he shrugged. 'She was in the family way,' he said.

Cissy put a hand up to her mouth. 'Oh,' she said. 'And she wanted you to . . . '

'I couldn't take on a nipper too,' Herbert said. It broke his heart to say it and he felt tears gather in the corners of his eyes.

''Course not,' his mother said. Then she shook her head. 'Girls these days . . . '

Herbert didn't say anything. Not for the first time, he wondered whether Uncle Ben had taken him on in a way. But he said nothing. That was all in the past. Rose was still very current and what she'd done still really hurt. And not just because being with her would legitimise him as a 'normal' man, but because he was very fond of her. He'd saved her in a way and now she was moving on. But then, wasn't that what kids always did?

Cissy got up from her chair and said, 'I'd better go and finish off the spuds.'

148

'All right, Mum.'

As she passed him, she put a hand on his shoulder and said, 'Probably for the best, son. Given how things are with you.'

Herbert thought about asking her what she meant by that, but then decided against it. Although his mother had never spoken about it, and in spite of the fact she did occasionally ask him about girls, she knew.

Rose was excited and apprehensive. Walking hand in hand with Dermot down Bishopsgate, she was on the one hand the cat that had got the cream; on the other, well, she just didn't know ...

They'd left Tilly's in the early hours of Christmas morning. And although they'd all had a laugh with Til's 'girls', Dermot had been quiet and thoughtful afterwards. He was walking her home and they'd got as far as Piccadilly Circus when suddenly he'd turned to her and asked her to marry him. Rose hadn't known what to say.

'It'll mean the nipper'll have a name,' he'd said. 'And I've always cared for you, Rosie.'

She had thought at that moment he might have kissed her, but he hadn't. He'd just held her and said, 'Tell me you will.'

But still Rose had held back. How could she tell Dermot that the last thing she wanted was to be married in the fullest sense of the word? After what Kenneth had done to her, she had even less interest in the physical side of love. She opened her mouth, watching as her breath clouded in the chilly Christmas air, but no words came out.

'I won't ask anything of you,' Dermot had said then.

Did he know? She couldn't remember saying anything about not wanting to 'do things' with men? Or was he just assuming?

Eventually she'd said, 'We've always been mates . . .'

'Which won't change,' he'd said. 'I'll send you money. I'll keep ya. While the war's on you can go and live with your mum or my mum or . . .'

Would either Nell or Auntie Kitty even have her back after what she'd done? She'd asked him and he'd said, 'Of course they will! Reckon they'll fight over having you after they know we're having a baby!'

'But *we're* not,' she'd said.

He'd put his arms around her then and whispered, 'You leave that to me. We'll make that right and I'll be the baby's dad, I promise you. What do you say?'

What else could she have said? Living with Tilly would have been fun but also very hard work. Rose would have no income herself. All cooped up in that one little room with a baby and no other woman to help her, she could all too easily see herself going barmy. At the same time, she didn't want to upset Tilly . . .

And so she'd said 'yes' to Dermot and then they'd both run back to Tilly's little flat to tell her, with tears of joy in their eyes. Rose had always liked Dermot; in truth, she'd been a little bit in love with him all along.

When she took the wrapping paper off, there was a box Bernie knew was small enough to contain a ring. She hoped it didn't.

Heinrich smiled. 'Open it,' he said.

When she'd walked into the lounge after getting home from work on Christmas Eve, she'd been greeted by the sight of the biggest Christmas tree she'd ever seen apart from in a public place, complete with baubles and tinsel and a pile of presents at its base. There had also been, as now, champagne on ice.

Heinrich had said he wanted to give her the best Christmas ever. And now this ...

'What is it?'

His wife wouldn't give him a divorce and so not a ring, surely. No. But if it was ...

'Open it!'

The little box was covered in black velvet. She lifted the lid and saw what looked like two teardrops of ice inside. Earrings. Thank God. She looked up and smiled at him. 'Thank you.' She kissed him.

'Not new, I'm afraid,' he said. 'They belonged to my mother.'

'Oh ...'

His mother had died a long time before they had met. Why didn't these ... she peered at them hard ... diamonds belong to his wife?

'Each drop is a one-carat diamond,' he said. 'My father bought them in Vienna for their first wedding anniversary.'

'They're so beautiful, but ...'

'But nothing,' he said. 'Rest assured my daughter has everything else. I kept these and Mama's wedding ring which, one day ...'

She put her fingers to his lips. They'd always promised each other they would never talk of marriage unless that became possible and it hadn't.

He kissed her again then said, 'Fitzhugh wants me to go to Palestine.'

'Palestine?'

'Wants me to cover the activities of the Palestine Regiment. They're a mixture of British, Jewish and Arab soldiers. Unlike many of the Arabs, the men of the Palestine Brigade are committed to the Allied cause. But there's another reason I want to go that's got nothing to do with that.'

'What is it?'

He put a glass of champagne into her hands. 'Come and sit down.'

There was a roaring log fire in the grate. Its flames were reflected in the tinsel and the baubles on the tree. Momentarily Bernie felt guilty. What kind of Christmas was her mum having down in Spitalfields? she wondered. Not like this one, she was sure. Bernie sat down.

'You're not the only one snookered by our censorship laws,' Heinrich said.

He was referring to the way all her more visceral photographs of London, especially, the East End, were very pointedly not used by their *Evening News* employers.

'I know you want to say more,' Bernie began.

'About what London has been through? Of course I do,' he said. 'But, Bernie, there's another big story that's taking place at the moment. It's one I feel even more strongly about. And it's something I'm fairly sure you've never even heard of.'

'You've not told me?'

He took her hand. 'More misery is not what you need,' he said.

'I can take it, you know.'

'I know.' Then he shook his head. 'Bernie, you know that the British have a Mandate to run Palestine.'

"Course. Everyone knows that. Hitler's trying to take it from us. As you say, some of the Arabs are working with him.'

'Some, yes,' Heinrich said. 'Although we mustn't get carried away thinking all Arabs are bad. This brigade contains many Arabs. But we also must not get carried away with the idea that we, the British, are necessarily the good guys, as the Yanks say, in all this.'

Bernie lit a cigarette then asked, 'What do you mean?'

Outside the flat's big picture windows, if you didn't look too far into the distance, Pimlico seemed to go about its Christmas Day as it always had done – people walking to church, neighbours greeting neighbours, old people taking the Christmas morning air. Only if you looked towards Victoria and the ruins that ringed the railway station did the reality of what was happening strike home.

'Bernie,' Heinrich said, 'you know when we were in Berlin, we saw how the Nazis treated Jewish people . . . '

'How can I ever forget?' she said. 'Those stars they made them sew onto their clothes to show they were Jews . . . I hate to think what's happening now.'

'They're being killed,' Heinrich said. 'They're being systematically taken from their homes and killed.'

Bernie already knew that. Quite a few people did. Jews were being taken away and shot, not just in Germany but in all the places the Nazis had conquered – Poland, the Netherlands, France. It wasn't spoken about, just like the real scale of the suffering of the East Enders wasn't spoken about – in case such news damaged morale.

'But in spite of this, some of them are trying to get away,' Heinrich continued. 'Crossing the Mediterranean in small boats, trying to get to Palestine, the home we all left two thousand years ago.'

'I know some Jews want to live there,' Bernie said.

'But these refugees, these . . . Bernie, the Jews of Europe are not just running from the Nazis because they are threatening to shoot them – they're running away from forced labour camps, from their women being raped, from places you can't even begin to imagine.'

She put a hand on his knee. 'What places?'

'Death camps,' he said. 'I don't even know what I mean

when I say that but there are rumours, terrible stories, about whole towns where Jews are worked until they drop, starved to living skeletons, and then put to death. It's these places that people are trying to escape from and, when the British troops send them back across the Mediterranean, it is to these places that they are returned.'

'British troops are sending them back?'

'Yes,' he said.

'How do you know about this?'

'I know the right people,' he said. 'Even now, they tell me, a trickle of Jews manages to make it out of Germany. I need to see if it's true because if it is ... '

'Then we, the British, have some tough questions to answer,' she said. 'God Almighty, how can anyone send people to their deaths like that? How?'

He shrugged. 'I go on the tenth of January,' he said. 'I know it sounds very soon, but Fitzhugh only told me yesterday. Of course, I put the idea in his head some time ago.' He took hold of her hands again. 'I know the bombing has stopped, Bernie, but I still don't think we're safe here, not really.'

'There's a war on,' she said. 'Who *is* safe?'

He stood up and leaned against the mantelpiece, firelight reflected in his dark brown eyes. He said, 'I gave you my mother's diamonds because I love you but for another reason too. If the Nazis get here, I want you to get out.'

'I'm not Jewish, Heine.'

'They don't just kill Jews, Bernie,' he said. 'A girl with a lively mind and a camera is not someone of whom the Nazi regime will approve. You remember how the SS tried to break your camera when we were in Berlin? The only reason you got to keep it and your pictures was because you came from Britain, which wasn't in conflict with the Nazis back then.

'If they get here, sell my mother's diamonds and get out,' Heinrich said. 'Go to Canada. These are very fine stones, cut by an artist, they're worth a fortune. And if you can't get a fortune for them, then get as much as you need to run from Europe. I know you love your family and friends back in the East End, and believe me, if I could provide them with a ticket out too, I would. Just promise me you'll go in spite of that?'

Suddenly the diamonds seemed to have lost their lustre. She said, 'But Mammy and Dermot ...'

'Promise me!' Heinrich insisted. 'Please?'

Deep into their Christmas dinner, no one heard the street door open. Dermot heard his mother saying, 'So, Mr Shapiro, what do you call this wine?'

Becky's dad, who had his back to the door, said, 'I don't know, Mrs Lynch, just it's kosher is all I know.'

It was Aggie who spotted him first.

'Dermot!' she said. 'Where you been?'

His mother looked up. 'We kept you some dinner but it'll be half cold by now,' she said. 'Come and sit down.'

'I've brought someone with me,' Dermot said.

His mother cast her eyes to the ceiling. 'Well, if you're prepared to share with him then ...'

'Her.'

'What?'

'Share with her,' Dermot said.

The room became very quiet as a small figure entered. Nell Larkin saw it first. Her eyes widened and she said, 'Christ! Rosie?'

All around the table people murmured her name. Only Becky moved, or rather ran, towards her.

'Oh, Rosie!' she said, her eyes full of tears. 'We've missed you so much! Where have you been?'

She hugged her old friend. Becky's father meanwhile gave Nell yet more wine and said, 'For the shock, Mrs Larkin. For the shock.'

Rose, now in tears herself, clung on to her friend as if her life depended on it. 'Becky,' she whispered. 'Oh, Becky.'

'So where the effin' hell has she been?' Her face white with shock, Kitty Lynch finished what remained of Nell Larkin's gin in one gulp. 'Eh?'

Dermot smiled. 'Don't worry about where she's been, Mammy,' he said. 'It's where she's going that's important now. Me and Rosie are going to be married.'

Chapter 11

Boxing Day

'I can't hang on any longer, I'm sorry,' Heinrich said as he kissed the back of Bernie's neck. 'Adrienne and the children are expecting me.'

She tried to be 'grown up' about it when he had to go and see his wife and kids, but Bernie found his visits to them difficult, especially at Christmas. Whenever he went to see them she was left entirely on her own. People in posh flats like Heinrich's didn't mix with their neighbours like they did in the East End. They kept themselves to themselves – especially when it came to consorting with Jewish journalists and 'common' girls like Bernie.

Once he'd gone, she made herself a gin and tonic and lit a cigarette. Heinrich had a large library so she'd sit by the fire and read a book. Although many of them were in German, she eventually found a novel called *East Lynne* by Ellen Wood. It was an old, rather battered book and so she expected the story to be old-fashioned. But it was also irritating. Set in Victorian times, it appeared to be the story of some aristocratic lady who ran off with a bloke who wasn't her husband. Terrible things then happened to her and, if Bernie guessed right, she would probably end up dying in 'disgrace'. She wasn't in the mood to sympathise and so she set the book aside.

There was a bit of washing up to do in the kitchen and so she did that and then looked at her diamond earrings again for a while. But they depressed her. What if she really did have to sell them in order to leave the country? Could she do that with Mammy and her siblings and Becky still in England? She'd promised Heinrich that she would, but could she? And what about Rose? Bernie didn't even know where she was. How could she leave England without taking Rose along too?

Suddenly Bernie felt desolate. Much as she loved Heinrich and much as she appreciated how good he'd been to her, in that moment it wasn't enough. Maybe it was because Boxing Day was also the Feast of St Stephen, the day when all her Irish relatives used to descend upon their old flat and her dad would get the lot of them drunk. Oh, how she missed him! Her dad had always believed in her. Even when she was a small child talking about Egypt, for God's sake, he'd tell her that one day of course she'd go there, and she'd believed him. Part of her still did. If and when this war was over maybe she would go and see the Pyramids.

Bernie began to cry then. Thank God she'd managed to see her daddy before he died. It was her only consolation but was one that had been denied to her mother. Kitty hadn't got to Ilfracombe in time and Bernie knew how hard that had to be for her. But did that excuse the way she'd just ignored her own daughter at Pat Lynch's funeral? In part, but only in part.

With a fierceness Bernie hadn't experienced before, suddenly she wanted to go home. To hell with what anyone thought, she had to do it even if she must walk, or crawl, over broken glass . . .

Becky turned over and opened her eyes. For a moment she wondered who on earth had apparently crept into her bed when she wasn't looking and then she remembered that Rose had come back into her life again.

'Rosie . . . '

She opened her big green eyes and smiled. 'Morning, Becky,' she said. 'That was a good sleep, I have to say.'

She sat up and the two friends hugged.

'I still can't really quite believe you're here,' Becky said.

Christmas dinner at the Lynches' flat had turned into a full-scale booze-up once Dermot and Rose had arrived. As well as Moritz Shapiro's kosher wine, their stocks of drink had been boosted by some bottles of brown ale Dermot had brought with him and even a bottle of champagne that appeared from somewhere. The party hadn't broken up until the early hours of the morning when Becky had taken Rose back to her house and put her to bed. Nell Larkin, the grandma-to-be, had passed out in the Lynches' back yard.

Becky rubbed her head. Although she'd not got drunk she'd had enough to have developed a slight hangover. 'I'll get us some breakfast,' she said. She got out of bed while Rose flopped back down again.

'I'm not that hungry,' she said.

Becky looked at the girl's unfettered stomach and said, 'You feel full a lot?'

'Yeah.'

159

'Often happens at the end of a pregnancy,' she said. 'Baby can squash the stomach up.'

'Can it?'

Becky sat down on the bed again. 'Rosie, have you been seeing a doctor or a nurse since you've been pregnant?'

'No,' she said. 'I never knew about it for a long time.' Then she looked up. 'Dermot ain't really the father.'

Becky had never thought he was. His story about seeing Rose back in the spring just didn't make sense. Back then the Blitz had been on and Dermot had either been at work or in her father's Anderson shelter.

'So who is?' Becky asked.

Rose shook her head. 'Some bloke who worked at the Windmill,' she said. 'I was drunk.'

'He took advantage of you.'

'Yes.'

'So you've no idea when the baby's due?'

'Not exactly. It happened in May ... the ... you know ... '

There wasn't an ounce of fat on her stomach and so Rose's bump was all baby. 'So you've got to be about eight months,' Becky said.

'I s'pose.'

Becky took her hand. 'Then why is Dermot marrying you?' she said. 'If the baby isn't his?'

'He likes me and I've always liked him.'

'You have to do more than like someone to want to marry them, Rosie.'

She turned away. 'I do.'

'What? You love him?'

'I always have.'

Becky had suspected Rose held a torch for Dermot when they were kids. She remembered they once went to the cinema together in Limehouse. Rose had been full of it for days afterwards. But did Dermot love her? He was a nice boy, always had been, but he'd never, as far as Becky could recall, walked out with anyone. Girls had never seemed to be important in his life. And then there was Chrissy ...

Everyone knew what Chrissy Dolan was. Nobody said it except his drunken father and his awful brothers. But also no one would employ him, usually saying it was because of his weak heart. But it wasn't. It was because he liked men in ways that he shouldn't. And Becky wondered whether Dermot was like that too. But what would be the point of saying that to Rosie if she didn't already know?

Becky smiled. 'I hope you'll be really happy together,' she said. 'Do you know when you'll get married?'

'Dermot says we'll have to apply for a special licence,' Rose said. 'He's going to do that tomorrow. He's off again on the fifth. Out East somewhere.'

And that was another thing – what if Dermot died? Becky shook her head. So many worries and what was the point of any of them? Her papa had worried all his life and all he'd ever got for it was indigestion.

Becky put on her dressing gown and said, 'I'm going to go and see what I can find to eat. And make us all a cuppa.'

Jesus, but her mother was a loud woman! In spite of the mourning black she still wore twenty years after Kitty's father's death, Theresa Burke knew how to drink. Luckily there was plenty of it, courtesy of Kitty's brother Derek who had, as he put it, 'contacts' in the pub trade. Unfortunately, probably because his wife and kids were down in Sussex, he had come with precious little food.

'So what you going to feed us on this fine St Stephen's, Kitty?' the old woman said.

Maeve, Kitty's younger sister, a girl who had been born, as Theresa always said, 'simple', looked up expectantly.

'Bubble and squeak,' Kitty said. Which was true. Beyond fried potatoes and a bit of cabbage there wasn't much in the house.

'Jesus, God!'

Kitty's sister Concepta, tutted. 'Ma, be grateful.' she said.

'There is a war on, you know, Ma!' Kitty added.

She saw Dermot search around in his duffel bag, but she didn't take any notice until he pulled out a tin of Spam.

'There's this,' he said. And then he pulled out another tin. 'In fact, I've got two.'

'Ah, what a fine boy he is, the bridegroom!' Theresa said as she took her grandson's face between her hands and kissed him.

'I remember that girl Rose when she come to our street party for the Coronation,' Derek said. 'Pretty little thing.'

'When's she getting here?' Theresa asked.

'Soon.'

Dermot remembered the Coronation for a different reason. That had been the night of the robbery organised by Artie Cross, his old foreman, and Joey. The one that had gone wrong and resulted in the death of Fred Lamb.

Kitty took the tins of Spam from Dermot and gave them to Marie, who was once again doing all the cooking.

Theresa filled up her own glass with sherry and then passed the bottle to Maeve. 'Take a drop, not too much,' she said. Then she turned back to Dermot. 'So when's this wedding to be?' she asked.

'I don't know yet,' he said. 'I'll have to apply for a special licence tomorrow. It'll just be at a register office . . . '

'Not in church?'

'No. Er, Rose ain't Catholic, Gran.'

Theresa's face turned sour. 'Mmm. I wondered. Not Catholic and knocked up ...'

'Mam!' Kitty warned.

'Well, you can't be happy about it, Katherine!' she said. 'Girl's up the stick ...'

'Dermot had a bit to do with it too!' Concepta said.

'Yes, well ...'

Derek Burke, ever the family peacemaker, said, 'Ah, but it's St Stephen's and so we have to put the old year behind us and look forward. Here, maybe this year'll be the one the war ends!'

Dermot raised his glass of beer. 'I'll drink to that, Uncle Derek!'

'Good man.'

They toasted each other.

Aggie put more coal on the range and asked everyone if they wanted tea. Although they were drinking alcohol, they all said yes except for Maeve. She was drinking directly from the sherry bottle. Aggie, who was the only one to have noticed, said, 'Mammy ... Auntie Maeve!'

'Oh, Christ!' Kitty snatched the bottle out of her sister's hand and put it on the table. 'Don't do that, Maeve!'

But the woman just looked down at the floor.

'I can't deal with her when she's pie-eyed,' Theresa said.

'Then you shouldn't've passed her the bottle!' Kitty said. 'Jesus, Mother, you do some mad things sometimes!'

'No one made her drink it!'

'No, but she's ...'

'The poor cow's a simpleton, what can be done?' Theresa said. 'God gave her to me the way she is and so who am I to complain?'

'But you do.'

'Ach!'

Dermot looked at his uncle, who just shrugged. When his dad's brothers used to come round on St Stephen's it had always been a mad, but happy affair. But since Pat's death, the family left in London had all but disappeared. Now they were stuck with the Burkes – his grandmother, soft Maeve, Aunt Concepta, hopeless Uncle Derek and, later, his Aunt Assumpta, who was pregnant again.

'"I'm one of the ruins that Cromwell knocked about a bit . . ."'

They all turned and looked at Maeve.

'God help us, that's just what we need,' Theresa said. 'Maeve singing old music-hall songs!'

Then they all laughed.

'Oi! That you?'

Bernie had seen Rose's mother way before Nell had spotted her, but she'd said nothing.

'Yes, Nelly,' she said. 'It's me. Who'd you think I am?'

Nell Larkin hadn't changed. The sides of her feet still hung out of holes in her shoes, her hair was still like a black and grey cloud of tangles and she was still as thin as a fasting monk.

'Bernadette,' Nell said.

'Yes, Bernadette, that's me.'

Nelly smiled. Bernie couldn't smell booze on her but that didn't mean she wasn't drunk. Generally she only did smile when she was drunk.

'Where you going?' Nelly asked her.

'Mammy's.'

Bernie expected the woman to say something about her not being welcome there; instead she said, 'You'll never guess who's back home?'

'Who?'

Nelly smiled. 'My Rose,' she said.

Bernie was genuinely shocked. Rose had run away after stealing money from Mrs Rabinowicz. Bernie had thought her friend lost to her forever and felt ashamed now to have given up on her so easily.

'Turned up Christmas night, she did,' Nell continued. 'Up the stick she is. By your brother.'

This conversation, in the middle of filthy, mud-soaked Fournier Street, was rapidly resembling a dream rather than reality.

'My brother . . .'

'Your Dermot,' Nell said. 'But he's doing the decent thing by her. Just think – my Rosie, someone's wife . . .'

Bernie, who was wearing her only pair of high-heeled shoes, found herself swaying a little.

'Nell,' she said, 'are you sure about this? I mean . . .'

'Ask her yourself,' Nell said. 'She's still over at the Shapiros'.'

Bernie looked up at the tall, dark house where Becky and her father lived. Then she saw a curtain move in one of the upstairs windows where she identified a familiar face.

The three girls fell into each other's arms. For all of them there was so much to hear and to tell and yet at this moment all any of them wanted was to huddle close together. They all cried. When Moritz Shapiro walked into the kitchen to see what all the noise was about, he had to go away and leave them to it. This was, after so long apart, a moment just for the three of them. It was only when they were all thoroughly exhausted by their reunion that the girls sat down and really looked at each other.

Wiping her eyes with her handkerchief, Bernie said, 'Bloody hell, you're big, Rosie!'

'I'm pregnant.'

'Yes, I know! Your mum told me. Dermot . . . '

His name hung in the air between them. Out of everyone in the world, apart from Becky, Rose should have been able to tell Bernie the truth, but she couldn't.

'We met up again back in the spring,' she said. 'Which was when this . . . ' she looked down at her belly ' . . .happened.'

'God Almighty. And he said nothing to you?' she asked Becky.

'No.'

'Nor me.'

'When Der went in the army I thought it was all over,' Rose said. 'Then Christmas Eve, he come and found me.'

'Where? Where've you been?'

Rose told them all about the Windmill and what she'd done there. Not easily shocked, Bernie nevertheless found herself gasping.

'You lived with poofs?' she said. 'What, like . . . '

'Tilly's a drag queen but she does sometimes go with men for money,' Rose said.

'Rosie!'

'Well, it's true,' she said. 'The way them people behave up West is very different from how it is here. People used to call my mum a prozzie but she only ever done it because she had to. There's people up there do all sorts just for fun.'

Bernie knew what she meant. Although outwardly 'respectable', a lot of the middle-class people who were now her neighbours behaved in questionable ways from time to time. More than a few servant girls had been dismissed because they'd 'got themselves into trouble' – their disappearance bringing great relief to their masters. As Bernie's father and in fact all of the Commie boys had always said, the use of working women for sex was a class issue.

166

'So Dermot's over at Mammy's, is he?' Bernie asked.

'Yeah,' Rose said. 'I slept over here last night as there was no room left there and me mum's place is like it always was.'

A tip, as Bernie's mother had always called it.

'We're going over to Auntie Kitty's for St Stephen's later,' Rose said.

Bernie took a deep breath, then she said, 'Well then, I'd better come with you, hadn't I?'

The other girls fell silent until Bernie added, 'If our Dermot's getting married what can she say, eh?'

Becky knew that Kitty could say a lot but she kept that thought to herself and changed the subject. 'Hey,' she said, 'if you're getting married, Rosie, you'd better have a wedding dress!'

'What, in my condition?'

'Yes,' Becky said. And then a thought occurred to her. 'And I think I know where we can get you one.'

Chapter 12

Out in the yard he could think. Indoors they were all drunk or getting that way and Chrissy wanted to be on his own for a while. He'd not spoken to Dermot about marrying Rose and really he didn't want to. But he didn't feel right about it. Much as he loved them both, he couldn't imagine why it was happening. Although he'd never spoken of it, Dermot had surely always known that Chrissy suspected him. They'd seen each other look at other men over the years. But then maybe if Rosie knew too, that was all right? And if Dermot really was the father of her baby, what else could he do? Men like them often had families, though it usually meant someone ended up getting hurt.

'Penny for 'em?'

He hadn't heard Auntie Kitty come into the yard. She sat down beside him. 'You not come to use the khazi?' he asked.

'No, come to get a bit of air,' she said. 'Me ma, Concepta, Derek and Dermot are smoking up a storm in there, you can cut a knife through the smoke.'

He smiled as he watched her light a roll-up. It seemed as if an age had passed since he'd held her head while she was sick in the yard, and she'd told him her secret. Chrissy had wanted to get her on her own ever since. He thought about it for a moment and then decided there was no time like the present.

'Auntie Kitty,' he said. 'You know when you was sick the other night . . .'

'Oh, don't remind me!' she said. 'Ashamed of meself, I am. I know I need to cut down on the drinking . . .'

'You told me something then,' Chrissy said.

She frowned. 'Did I? Thought I was just being sick.'

'You did,' he said.

'Oh, maybe I did then,' she said. 'Probably rubbish.'

'Was it?'

'I dunno, was it? What was it about?'

She hadn't remembered. Either that, or she wanted him to ask her about it.

'You told me about a letter,' Chrissy said.

'What letter?'

He took a deep breath. If what she'd told him wasn't true, but just the drink talking, she'd lose her rag with him. But if it was true, then she needed to know she had to tell Bernie what she'd done. Chrissy had heard that Solly Adler was going to marry Sharon Begleiter and rumour had it that he didn't love her. And if Bernie still loved him then maybe there was still time . . .

'You told me you destroyed a letter Solly Adler sent to Bernie from Spain,' he said.

There was a very long silence. So long that eventually Chrissy had to take all his courage in his hands and look up at her. What he saw shocked him. Suddenly, in spite of her hair being newly washed and that lovely dress she'd got from the matchmaker, his Auntie Kitty looked old.

'Auntie . . . '

'Did I tell you that?' she said. Her voice was low, not much more than a whisper.

'I'm not making it up,' Chrissy said.

'No, no . . . ' She touched his arm. 'No, you're a good lad . . . '

She became quiet for a moment and then she said, 'You have to understand she was very young, my Bernie.'

'You shouldn't have done it,' Chrissy said.

'He, the Adler boy, had gone to war.'

'They were in love.'

Kitty turned hard eyes on him. 'She was a kid,' she said. 'I'm her mother. I had to protect her.'

Chrissy swallowed hard. 'When Solly come back from Spain, Bernie didn't want to see him.'

'He never wanted to see her!' she said. 'Never wanted to see no one, 'cause of his injuries.'

'She said she never got the letter he promised to send her and so she thought he'd gone off her.'

'She never said nothing about it to me,' Kitty said.

'Auntie Kitty, when you told me, you cried.'

'It was the drink . . . '

'No, you cried because you felt guilty.'

'No, I never!' She went to hit him and then stopped herself. Chrissy flinched.

'Sorry. Sorry,' she said, 'I . . . '

'You have to tell her, Auntie Kitty,' Chrissy said. 'Solly Adler's engaged to Sharon Begleiter and everyone knows he don't love her!'

'So? Bernie's with her bloke up West, living in sin! She's made her bed.'

170

'One that you helped her to make,' he said.

She looked away.

'You know I love you, Auntie Kitty,' Chrissy said, 'you've been nothing but good to me but Bernie's my mate and she's always been good to me too. You must tell her the truth.'

'And what good would that do?'

'I don't know,' Chrissy said.

'What good does the truth ever do? How would it be if the world knew all about the unnatural things you do?'

He might have expected this, but Chrissy gasped at her cruelty.

'Your love for men.'

'Then I'll go, Auntie Kitty, if you ...'

But she flung her arms around him, her eyes leaking tears. 'Oh, no, no, no! That's not what I want! You lovely boy, that's not what I want at all. I'm just ...' She pulled away and looked at him. 'I'm just an angry bitter old woman, like me ma.'

'No!'

'I am! I am! But when I done it, when I burned the letter, I was truly afraid for Bernadette, you have to understand that!'

'I do! But that doesn't mean you shouldn't tell her now.'

'What? Go up West and ...'

'Whatever it takes!' Chrissy said. 'I know you know it's the only right thing to do, Auntie Kitty.'

The wardrobe door made a terrible creaking sound when it opened.

'The whole thing could be gone into holes because of moths by now,' Moritz Shapiro said to his daughter.

But Becky knew that wasn't possible because her father replaced the mothballs in this particular wardrobe all the time. He'd made her mother's wedding dress himself. He always said it was his best work.

He pulled a long parcel covered in tissue paper out of the cupboard. Becky had only ever seen her mother's wedding dress once. As she recalled it was a long, slim silk dress decorated with Brussels lace.

'I always hoped you might wear your mother's dress one day,' he said.

She put a hand on his shoulder. 'Papa, Rosie needs it,' she said. 'You know what kind of life she's had and it's not going to get any easier. I want her to have a day to remember.'

'In a register office?'

'If they love each other, what does it matter?'

He unwrapped the parcel and laid the dress on the spare bed. Still snowy white, it had a high waist and, now Becky looked more closely, she saw that it was decorated with tiny seed pearls.

'Your mother was so small.'

'So is Rosie.'

'Yes, but she's . . . '

'It will fit her,' Becky said. 'Oh, Papa!'

'You know that girl cost me fifty pounds I could ill afford,' Moritz said. 'Mr Lynch, may God rest his soul, couldn't pay and if I hadn't remunerated the *shadchan*, my name would have been mud.'

'You did a good thing.'

'The girl stole money,' he said. 'For a good reason admittedly . . . '

'Which is why you covered her debt.'

'But it was still theft.'

'I know.'

They both stood looking at the dress. Becky knew that

Rose had done a terrible thing when she'd stolen from Mrs Rabinowicz. But she'd done it to protect her mother. If Nell's rent hadn't been paid there and then, she would have been flung out on the street and would by now probably be dead. And Rose herself had paid a price too. Exiled in the West End, it seemed she'd had some fun there, but also that she had been lonely. And she'd been part of an industry where girls easily lost their reputation and where she herself had been taken advantage of. It was lucky for her that Dermot had come along when he did. If he hadn't then who knew where Rose might have ended up?

Kitty said nothing. Everyone else welcomed Bernadette, the two youngest girls kissing and cuddling her. Even her grandmother Burke managed to say, 'Happy St Stephen's, Bernadette.' But Kitty kept her counsel. In her high-heeled shoes and smart black coat, Bernie looked every inch the professional woman she'd wanted to be. But she was also a married man's mistress and that was something that made Kitty's blood boil. How could a daughter of hers have become such a thing? But then, she knew the answer to that question.

'Anyone fancy a pint down the Ten Bells?'

Derek had finished all the beer and didn't have a taste for either gin or wine.

'I'll come, Uncle Derek,' Dermot said.

Nell Larkin nodded and Kitty's mother had already got her coat on. Once everyone had decided what they were doing, it seemed that only Kitty and Bernie were not going to the pub. Chrissy looked at the two women anxiously as he left. And then they were gone and, for a long while, there was nothing but silence.

'Would you like a cuppa ...'

'No, no, I'm fine,' Bernie said.

'Ah.'

The clock on the mantelpiece above the range ticked more loudly, or so it seemed, than it usually did. A scratching sound from behind the walls reminded the women that the building was plagued by mice.

'You . . .'

'I'm not going to give up either my job or Heinrich, Mammy,' Bernie said. She looked into her mother's eyes with a level of defiance that shocked Kitty. 'Daddy accepted it, and so can you.'

'Your father was dying. He didn't know what he was saying.'

Bernie didn't respond. Kitty had expected to be reminded that she hadn't been there when Pat had spoken for the last time. But then she felt bad for having that thought. It was unworthy of her and unworthy of Bernadette. The girl was a lot of things, but she wasn't cruel.

'He's a married man,' Kitty said.

'An unhappy one.'

'I don't care. Those whom God has put together . . .'

'Mammy, Heinrich and his wife were living apart before I came into his life,' Bernie said. 'I didn't steal him.'

'He seduced you . . .'

'No, he didn't! We both wanted each other!'

Ach!' Kitty turned her face away in disgust.

'And don't "ach" me,' Bernie said. 'You can be as disapproving as you like, Mammy, but you can see that my sisters and my brother love me. I'm sick to death of being stopped from seeing them by you.'

'You see Dermot.'

'Yes, I do, and I will go to see him and Rose get married if I can.'

'Oh, will you?'

'Yes!'

'And take your Jew ... '

'Ah, and that's where we get to the heart of it, don't we, Mammy?' Bernie said. 'You don't want me to be with Heinrich because he's a Jew. Just like you didn't like me having an innocent kiss with a man who was going off to fight in the Spanish Civil War. He was a Jew too, a comrade of my father's, your husband ... '

'Solly Adler was ... '

'He was someone I cared about and I know you were happy when he went off me ... '

'He didn't.' It just came out of Kitty without her even thinking.

Bernie rolled her eyes. 'Oh, so now you've convinced yourself that I gave him up? Nice try, Mammy. *He* gave me up. He didn't want me when he came back from Spain. You might have noticed he never wrote ... '

'He did.'

Chrissy had been right. Kitty had to tell her daughter the truth. This bitterness between them wasn't just Bernadette's fault.

'He wrote you a letter, from Spain.'

The look of confusion on the girl's face broke her mother's heart.

'No ... No!'

'You never saw it because I never let you,' Kitty said.

It took a moment to sink in and even then Bernie said nothing. She just went white.

'He wrote to you, telling you how much he thought of you ... '

'Where is it?'

'What?'

175

'The letter!' Bernie yelled. 'You stopped me having it! YOU read it! Where is it?'

Kitty looked down at the floor. Now it had come to it, she was afraid. Why had she told Chrissy about the letter when she was drunk? Because deep down she felt guilty . . .

'Where, Mammy?'

She'd denied her own daughter a chance of love. How could she? But Kitty knew why. 'He was . . . he is a Jew, Bernadette. We don't . . . we can't . . . '

'Oh, we can be together, Mammy,' Bernie said. 'Me and Heinrich . . . '

'Don't!'

'Yes, we sleep together, we have sex!'

Kitty put her hands over her ears. 'Bernadette!'

'It's true! Wake up, Mammy! The world is at war and nobody cares who is sleeping with whom except for bloody Hitler! And when the Yanks get here . . . '

'I burned it!' Kitty said. 'I read it, I saw that he had feelings for you, and I burned it!'

She hardly dared look at her daughter but, when she did, Kitty could see that Bernadette was shaking.

'I did it for the best,' Kitty said.

Her daughter turned to one side and then she ran out of the back door and into the yard. Kitty, head in her hands now, heard her being sick. When she finally came back in again and sat down at the kitchen table, Bernie's face was grey.

'Bernadette . . . '

'You burned a letter from a man who had feelings for me because you thought it was the right thing to do?'

Bernie's voice was low and and Kitty could feel the menace that lay beneath it.

'You were a child.'

'I was in love for the first time,' she said. 'When Solly didn't write to me, it broke my heart. Even when I think about it now, it brings me pain.'

Kitty began to cry then, and when her daughter said, 'You're a bigot,' she cried even harder.

'Did Daddy know?'

Kitty shook her head. Of course he hadn't known. Pat had never had time for religion or any other differences that pulled people apart.

'Of course he didn't,' Bernie said. 'Because if he'd've known, he would have told me and I would have run to Solly when he got home and told him that I loved him. And maybe we wouldn't still be together now, but it would at least have been our choice.'

And she was right. In trying to protect her daughter from the 'unknown', Kitty had taken away her control over her own life. And, God Almighty, it had taken drink and the just, simple good grace of a poor queer boy to make her feel the guilt and see what she had done wrong.

'Bernadette ...'

'So you're pleading now, are you, Mammy?'

'No. No, I ...'

'Because now I'm even more determined to keep on coming to my own home and seeing my own family,' she said. 'Not to see you, because I don't know whether I can ever forgive you ...'

Kitty felt Bernie's words strike to her heart and her crying became painful and bitter.

'But to see them and be a part of this family. And don't you ever try to stop me, Mammy. Because if you do, I will tell Dermot, Paddy, Marie and Aggie what you did and they will hate you as much I do.' Shakily, Bernie got to her feet. 'Now, I can't be here for a while and so I'm going out.'

177

'Will you tell anyone else about this?' Kitty sobbed.

'No, it's no one else's business. But I need to get away from you.'

And then she turned on her heel and left. Kitty looked around for something to drink to calm her nerves but when she found some wine she just threw the bottle to the ground. It had been the hard stuff that had got her into this mess. She was never, ever going to drink that filth again!

Rose looked like a princess from a story book. Becky had called her in when she saw her going back to the Lynches' flat from the pub. Dermot had stayed at the Ten Bells with his uncle, his aunt and his grandma.

Staring at herself in the mirror, Rose said, 'I don't even look as if I'm carrying.'

That wasn't strictly true, but Becky just smiled.

'Papa made it for Mama with great love,' she said.

'It's beautiful.'

And then suddenly she saw Becky's father reflected in the mirror. 'Oh!'

He walked into the room and said, 'You look lovely.'

'Oh, er . . . '

'You have black hair like my Chani, may God rest her soul.'

'It's very kind of you.'

'It is a *mitzvah*,' he said. 'A blessing. But, to be fair, Rebekah had to make me see that.'

Rose blushed. She knew he was referring to the money she'd stolen from Mrs Rabinowicz and that Mr Shapiro had paid back.

'I will repay you,' she began.

'No, no, that's not important,' he said. 'What's money in a world on fire? It's nothing. No, you wear my Chani's dress well, Rose, and then give it back so that Rebekah can wear it again some day.'

'Papa . . .'

'You think you'll be a nurse all your life, Rebekah?' He shook his head. 'You are a beautiful girl with a good heart. You will marry when the time comes, God willing.'

'I will take great care of it, Mr Shapiro,' Rose said. 'I promise I will.'

'Then take the dress with my blessing,' he said, and left the two girls together.

Rose said, 'Your dad's such a nice man. You know he let me mum shelter in your Anderson even when she was pissed? She told me.'

Becky began to help her out of the dress.

'He likes your mum,' she said. 'I don't know why it should be, but they get on. Will you live with her when you're married, Rosie?'

'She wants me to, so I expect I will,' she said. 'Ain't got nowhere else to go.'

'What about where you used to live in the West End?'

She shrugged. 'That all finished when Dermot found me.'

'Won't you miss your old friends from the theatre?'

'Yeah,' she said. 'They were nice, especially Tilly. She offered to look after me. But it's better this way. The baby'll have a proper father. I never had one and that ain't good. People look down on you. Not you and Bernie . . .'

'I know.'

'And Mum says she won't drink round the baby and we'll have Dermot's pay . . .'

Becky held the dress while Rose stepped out of it.

'And once the nipper's born, I can do war work,' Rose said. 'Do my bit.'

179

'Some would say you did that at the Windmill,' Becky said. 'Keeping up morale and all that.'

Rose put a hand to her mouth and then said, 'Kept something up!'

Then the two of them laughed together, Becky with a very red face.

There was nothing to see. Like all good citizens, the Adlers had their blackout curtains drawn and so all Bernie could make out was more darkness. She couldn't even hear their voices. It being winter the windows were closed. But she knew they were there. More specifically, she knew that Solly was at home.

As she stood in a dark shop doorway opposite the Adlers' flat, smoking, she wondered what Solly was doing, and thinking, now. She wondered whether his mum was with him, or Sharon was, or both of them. She'd never liked Sharon Begleiter ever since they'd worked together at Sharon's uncle's sweatshop. A spiteful gossip was what she had been; she'd even got Bernie the sack. In retrospect that hadn't been a bad thing but . . .

What she had to remember was that, in a way, Sharon was a victim of Kitty's meddling too. If Bernie had got back with Solly after the Spanish Civil War then maybe Sharon would never have had the chance to go out with him. But then maybe Bernie and Solly wouldn't have lasted as a couple anyway. But what really made her sad was how rejected he must have felt when he got home and she ignored him. He'd done as he said he would and sent her a letter from Spain. How was she to know she never got it? And now that she knew the truth, didn't Solly deserve to know it too?

Bernie wasn't sure what to do. She didn't even know why

she was spending so much time thinking about it. She was with Heinrich now and she loved him. Or did she? Why, whenever she saw Solly or heard things about him, did she feel such pain? God, he was marrying someone else! She had no right to interfere with that. And yet . . .

And yet when he'd been taken to hospital the night Wolfie Silverman died, Bernie had felt as if the world had ended for her.

Chapter 13

2 January 1942

Only Becky, Bernie, Nell and Dermot's uncle Derek went to the register office for the wedding ceremony. But Rose wore Chani Shapiro's dress just as she would have done if she'd married in church. It had come with a gauze veil that tumbled over her head and shoulders, held in place by a crown of wax flowers that Becky had hastily constructed from a domed floral display in her father's parlour.

Because Rose was under twenty-one, Nell had been required to give permission for her daughter to marry. Ashamed because she could neither read nor write, she'd signed the document with her mark, a simple scrawl that signified her consent.

At the end of the short, civil ceremony, Dermot had lifted the veil from his wife's face and kissed her so tenderly, Rose had felt her heart swell. Her new husband was never going to hurt her like all the other men in her life had. Back at Piccadilly

Circus where he'd asked her to marry him, he'd promised her he'd never make her do anything she didn't want. She believed him. He was so handsome and gentle, it broke her heart to think that her new husband would have to go and fight. But there was no way round it; all able-bodied men had a patriotic duty to do just that and Rose knew that her Dermot was not the sort of man to shirk his responsibilities.

When they got back to Fournier Street, the couple were met by their families and friends outside the Shapiros' house. Because the wedding had been arranged so hastily there'd been no time to book a church or public hall and so Becky had, yet again, persuaded her father to be the generous man he really was, but never admitted to being.

While Kitty Lynch made tea in the Shapiros' kitchen, all the guests who could brought food. The pooling of ration coupons even meant that a small wedding cake had been produced. Although largely made from carrots and parsnips and completely devoid of icing, it was saved by a pretty cardboard cover Marie had painted for it, featuring carefully rendered pink rosebuds and faux-icing swirls. Sardine-paste sandwiches and potato cakes called *latkes* made by the Shapiros' washing woman, Mrs Michael, made up most of the wedding breakfast as well as leftovers from Christmas such as eggless Christmas cake. Uncle Derek had once again come up trumps with the booze while Moritz Shapiro contributed two more bottles of his precious kosher wine. Once the pubs opened for the evening it was understood that most of the guests would decamp to the Ten Bells. But for the time being, just having what was the first party of her life in a parlour that was clean and, though old-fashioned, comfortable, made Rose's heart sing. Marriage and babies were the only things she'd ever wanted and now she was having both. Somehow the people who loved her had pulled this wedding together and there would even be photographs of her great day thanks to Bernie.

Had she been less concerned with herself, Rose would have been able to see how tired and drawn Bernie looked in spite of the brave face she was wearing for the wedding. Weighed down with fears for Heinrich's safety in Palestine as well as plagued by the spectre of the crime her own mother had committed against her, Bernie was struggling. But one person noticed and that person was little Chrissy Dolan.

Beyond Moritz Shapiro's workroom, at the back of the house, was a small yard. These days it was mostly taken up by the Anderson shelter, but there was still a small wooden bench outside the workroom door. Chrissy found Bernie sitting on it, smoking.

'Good do,' he said as he sat down next to her and took the cigarette that she offered.

'Rosie looked beautiful,' she said. 'I hope my photographs have done her justice.'

'I'm sure they will.'

She smiled. 'So what you up to then, Chrissy?' she asked.

'I get by,' he said.

'You'll miss our Dermot.'

'I'm glad he's happy,' Chrissy said.

Bernie put her arm around his shoulders and whispered, 'You'll find someone one day, Chrissy. I know you will.'

But before he could even think of an answer, a great cheer rose up from inside the house and they both looked up.

Bernie smiled, a little weakly, but then she said, 'Ah, that's my wedding present just arrived.'

Rose and Dermot stood in front of the parlour fireplace looking very stiff.

'No, no, no, no, no! You're film stars, not Queen Victoria and Prince Albert!'

Boris Bennett, legendary wedding photographer to the East End's fashionable Jewish elite, wasn't used to working in people's homes. Usually couples came to his studio on the Whitechapel Road, but this job was by way of being a favour. Bernadette Lynch, the *Evening News* photographer, was a friend of Walter Katz, an old German photographer that Boris had met when he'd first come to England twenty years before. As a professional courtesy to her, the famous wedding photographer had agreed to commemorate her brother Dermot's marriage to Rose.

After carefully adjusting the beret he always wore on his head when he worked, Boris shooed all of the guests out of Mr Shapiro's parlour and then said to the couple, 'Now ... they've gone so you can relax.'

The bridal pair, who were handsome and very young, giggled.

When the door opened Boris threw up his hands. 'What do you have to do ... '

'Boris, it's all right!'

Bernie Lynch was a lovely girl, tall and blonde, and would make someone a lovely wife herself one day. But like old Walter, she was a bit of a Commie. Word was that the paper knocked back a load of her pictures for being too grim.

'Oh, Bernie, this is a lovely surprise!' Rose said. She flung her arms around her husband. 'Me and Dermot, we don't know what to say!'

'Don't say anything,' Boris ordered. 'Just keep smiling and hold that pose!'

He looked into his camera and snapped. 'Handsome!' he said. 'Look like Errol Flynn and Vivien Leigh, you two do!'

'Get out of it!' Dermot laughed.

'You do! Swear to God,' Boris said.

Bernie walked over to Rose and hugged her.

'Boris can take portraits better than anyone,' Bernie said. 'And I wanted you to have the best, both of you.'

'And now you're my sister!' Rose squealed. 'Oh, Bernie, I always wanted a sister! I always wanted you and Becky to be my sisters!'

'And we always will be,' Bernie said. 'And that would hold true even if you weren't married to my useless brother.'

Dermot laughed and lit up a cigarette. 'Oi,' he said to his sister, 'watch it with the useless!'

Boris Bennett packed up his camera and said, 'Oh, well, I'll leave you all to your wedding now.' He squeezed Bernie's hand. 'I'll be in touch when it's ready, Bernadette.'

'Thank you, Boris.'

He left and, as the guests came streaming back in for some more leftover Christmas cake and fish-paste sandwiches, Bernie was content to fade into the background. She was glad her brother had married Rose but couldn't help feeling some uneasiness about it too. Maybe it was because she knew that Rose would be living back with her mum. Nell had started drinking as soon as she got into the Shapiros' house and, although she'd told Rose she wouldn't drink around the baby, Bernie wondered.

She walked to the parlour window and looked out into the street. It was only mid-afternoon, but already the sun was setting. Soon it would be night and Rose and Dermot would spend it in Nell's mean little hovel. But Rosie wanted it that way and so ...

Something in the street caught Bernie's eye. For a moment she thought it was just one of the old lampposts made strange in the dimness of the twilight. But then she looked again and saw that it was a person. A man, thinner than she remembered him, but . . . Bernie held her breath as she watched him smile at her.

Jumping back from the window, she put a hand up to her mouth and then ran out into the street. Could it be? God, if it was . . .

But Fournier Street was empty and quiet, save for the sound of the wedding guests, and there was no sign any longer of her brother Joey. Had she just imagined what she'd seen? Bernie hoped not.

A wedding was a wonderful thing. Two people in love promising to care for each other forever. Solly had been on his way to the market when he'd seen Dermot Lynch and Rose Larkin arrive at the Shapiros' house, the bride all dressed in white. They'd looked so happy. He couldn't even imagine what it was like to be as happy as they seemed. And Dermot's sister Bernadette had been with them. Tall, blonde and slim as a whip, she was even more beautiful now than the girl he remembered from before the war.

She hadn't seen him, or he hoped she hadn't. Now they'd all gone inside and yet he couldn't seem to move away. The sound of singing and glasses clinking drifted across Fournier Street to where he stood, alone, trying to hide from thoughts of his own imminent marriage. Sharon had it all arranged. He hadn't wanted to get married in synagogue but she was giving him no choice in the matter. Bloody woman wasn't even religious! It was all being done to impress her uncle.

'Got a light, mate?'

The bloke who'd spoken had appeared at Solly's side without making a noise. He was tall and muscular, his face heavily scarred, and Solly felt he should know him from somewhere, but he didn't.

'Here you go.'

He lit the roll-up in the corner of the man's mouth.

'Ta, mate.'

He sloped off rather than walked away and Solly thought no more about it until a couple of seconds later Bernie Lynch burst out of the Shapiros' house, looking wildly from left to right. Not wanting her to see him, Solly put his head down. When he looked up again, she'd gone.

He knew Bernie was living up West now with her posh bloke and so the last thing she'd need was him popping up again. Why she'd never so much as acknowledged his letter from Spain was still a mystery to Solly. Had she even got it? He'd poured his heart and soul out in that letter, written in various filthy foxholes around Madrid. Maybe it had been too much for her?

Whatever the reason, he and Bernie were not meant to be. And in the state he was in now, how could he even think about attracting a girl like that? No, he'd marry Sharon, they'd maybe have a few kiddies and, because Sharon came from money, he'd not have to worry too much. Her uncle would see her right, which meant that Solly could help his mum and even Ben, if he ever came home again. If he wasn't already dead. No one had heard from him for such a long time it was almost as if he no longer existed.

Solly was about to walk on towards the market when there was a scream from inside the Shapiros' house that froze his blood.

'Mum! Mum, I'm ... It's ... '

Nell Larkin had never sobered up so quickly in her life. She pulled the soaking satin and lace skirt up and away from her daughter's legs and said, 'It's all right, Rosie.'

'Mum!'

Nell looked over at Kitty Lynch who nodded and then shouted, 'Come on, away with you all! Out of here! Let the girl have some air!'

And while they looked at each other askance, the wedding guests quickly relocated themselves. It was all too easy to see what had happened.

Dermot said, 'Have her waters . . . '

'Yes, they've gone,' Nell said. 'And you can get out an' all.'

'Yeah, but . . . ' He held his wife's hand and, when she looked up at him, said, 'It'll be all right, Rosie.'

Nell got between them and shushed the young man away. 'Get out, you're not needed.'

In the end only Rose, Nell, Kitty, Bernie and Becky remained.

'Come on, let's get this dress off her,' Kitty said as she began to unbutton Rose's wedding dress.

'Mr Shapiro'll go mad!' Rose began to cry.

'No, he won't,' Becky said as she put her arms around her friend's shoulders and led her to one of the armchairs. 'Come and sit down. Your waters have broken, it's all right.'

'But the baby ain't . . . '

'Rosie, you don't even really know your dates, do you?' Becky said. She looked up and saw Bernie, standing over by the fireplace with a face as white as snow. 'Bern . . . '

A bit unsteadily, she walked over and took one of Rose's hands. 'If your little one wants to come out now, he won't be denied, kiddo,' she said.

'Yeah, but it's early . . . '

'Not THAT early,' Bernie said. Then she looked at Becky. 'Should we get her into a bed?'

189

Rose screamed. Her mother held her shoulders until the contraction passed.

'Yes,' Becky said. 'Upstairs to my bedroom.'

'Your bedroom?'

The two girls got Rose to her feet.

'It's the only one that's got a bed made up, apart from Papa's. I'll need her to lie down flat so I can examine her.'

'You're not a midwife!' Kitty said.

'No, but I've delivered babies.'

'When?'

'When the bombing was on,' Becky said. 'Now come on, we must get Rosie upstairs!'

It was a different bicycle, Dolly Adler was sure. Hyman Salzedo was riding something that looked like a delivery boy's bike, but without the basket at the front, going full tilt down the middle of Brick Lane, bloody mugging like a *meshuggeneh*. Dolly's grandfather always said that every village had its idiot back home in Poland and what was Brick Lane if not a village in all but name?

Mrs Rabinowicz, the *shadchan*, down on her luck since war broke out and not in her customary furs, shook her head. 'That boy should be in the madhouse,' she said. 'He's likely to run someone over!'

Actually it wasn't likely. Although Hyman rode as fast as he could, getting up any sort of speed on Brick Lane was difficult. Even with a war on there were people everywhere – barkers and bookies' runners, rabbis and good wives, and children, children, children. Many had come back to the city after being evacuated to the country in 1939, some with their parents' knowledge and others without. The ones who'd come without were known as the 'Dead End Kids' but, in spite of the rather rude name, they were neither criminally minded nor idle. Dead End Kids helped the fire brigade pull people out of collapsed buildings, they watched for fires and they helped bombed-out families move house.

'Oh, Hyman's all right,' Dolly said. 'Just a bit soft in the head. He means no harm.'

Mrs Rabinowicz sniffed. 'You hear the gypsy who robbed me is marrying the Lynch boy today?'

Dolly knew who she meant: Rose Larkin who had been a best friend of that lovely Bernie Lynch. But she said nothing.

'Where's the justice, eh?' Mrs Rabinowicz continued. 'And at the Shapiros' house too! Moritz Shapiro, such a gentleman, such a *frummer* – he must have lost his mind!'

Dolly hadn't wanted Solly to get too close to Bernie Lynch because, although she wasn't religious, the considered the *goyim* to be different. Marrying out was always complicated. But then again, was she happy about Solly marrying Sharon? No. She didn't trust the younger woman. Always a gossip, since the girl could first talk, Sharon was someone who'd liked to exercise power over people. She'd have the whip hand in her relationship with Solly, that was for sure. With her rich uncle and her widowed mother all dressed up like a dog's dinner, she had far more materially to bring to their marriage than he did. All Solly had was what remained of his good looks and the ruins of his politics.

Hetta, one of the street beigel sellers, just managed to get her basket of sweet rolls out of the way before it was knocked into by Hyman Salzedo.

'Ach! You little . . . '

She batted him away. But Hyman, still singing, fixed his eyes on Hetta and on the *shadchan* and Dolly Adler too, and said, '*Ipish*!'

'A bad smell? Where?' the *shadchan* said. Then she turned to Dolly. 'See? Mad.'

But by now Dolly's attention was fixed on Hyman. There was something especially intense about him today.

'Hyman?' she said.

He stopped his bicycle in front of her and his expression became grim. 'The *dybbuk*,' he said. 'The *dybbuk* – now!'

Dolly shuddered. A *dybbuk* was the spirit of a dead person who inhabited one of the living. Had he seen one? Did he expect one? What did it mean?

But then he rode off, singing again, and although Dolly felt dizzy for a moment, she soon recovered.

'That boy needs a rubber room,' Mrs Rabinowicz said. '*Dybbuk* indeed! Only rabbis can talk about such things. Who does he think he is?'

And then Hetta the beigel seller, recovered from her encounter with Hyman, said, 'Oh, you know the Larkin girl's gone into labour? At her own wedding. Fancy!'

Becky could see that Rose was extremely dilated. The baby could come very soon. But the more she panicked, the less likely it was that the birth would be easy. Becky smoothed her friend's brow. 'Breathe, Rosie, breathe deeply.'

'I'm trying!'

Her face was red and shiny with sweat but then her contractions were coming every two minutes by now. Her body was under maximum stress.

Nell Larkin had boiled up a pan of hot water, which she put in a corner of the room by the washstand. Kitty Lynch, now out of her posh wedding frock and wearing a long apron over a dress she'd made for herself out of khaki material, said, 'Rebekah, do you want me to ...'

'No, I'm fine,' Becky said.

Auntie Kitty might have had babies but she'd never delivered one so far as Becky knew. Her own tally was six, all delivered in the basement of the London Hospital, all under the most stressful conditions imaginable.

'Do you think we should call Dr Klein?' Bernie asked. She was sitting beside the bed, holding Rose's hand, but in such a way as not to be able to see what was happening underneath the sheet Becky had draped over Rose's stomach.

Nell Larkin snorted. 'She's having a bloody baby, she don't have a broke leg!'

'No, but ...'

'Can't afford no doctor!' Nelly continued. 'I never had one with her!'

'I can pay for it!' Bernie said.

Becky looked up at her. Poor Bernie. So brave in the face of the Nazis when she'd gone to Germany, so stalwart in her support of her lover Heinrich, it was odd to see her so squeamish about childbirth. 'It's OK, Bernie,' she said. 'Rosie's doing really well, aren't you?'

But Rosie's face reddened even more deeply and she screamed as another contraction hit her.

'Breathe! Breathe!' Becky said.

'I am! I am!'

But then as quickly as it had arrived, the contraction subsided.

'It's so strange', Rose panted. 'So strange ...'

Nell dragged a chair over and sat beside her daughter.

'I've some laudanum,' she said.

Becky said, 'Things are fine now, Mrs Larkin. But keep it for later if you like.'

Childbirth had been equated with the war by some

politicians. It was something to be got through in order to fulfil one's patriotic duty. But this analogy didn't always work. Pre-eclampsia and pregnancy diabetes, as well as some women's small pelvis size, made childbirth hazardous for some. Not that Becky thought Rose would be one of those. Not at that point anyway.

Chapter 14

The *goyim* were not that different from the Jews. When Rose had gone into labour, only the women closest to her had stayed. All the other women and the men had gone elsewhere, but they had separated along gender lines, as was right.

Moritz Shapiro hadn't planned on this wedding reception taking over his house for so long, but then no one had imagined that the bride would go into labour. The new husband, his hands fidgeting nervously around his glass of brown ale, sat in the yard smoking along with his uncle and his friend. The other men, mostly elderly, from Dermot's father's family had all gone down the Ten Bells, while the women sat in the parlour and talked.

No one had come from Mrs Larkin's family. But then that wasn't surprising. Gypsies who roamed around the highways and byways of Essex, especially Epping Forest, they weren't easy folk to pin down. And, he understood, there had been some sort of trouble, long ago . . .

Nell Larkin was not the type of woman Moritz usually

related to easily. For many years, and indeed up to the present time, she'd supported herself by selling her body. She was addicted to drink, probably as a result of her 'work', and had a mouth that could cuss like a sailor's. But for all that, when treated with respect, which he tried always to do, she could be good company. He recalled their conversations in the Anderson shelter with some nostalgia. But it wouldn't be easy for her once the baby had been born. He knew the idea was to get Rose on war work, and of course Dermot's military pay would help. But the Larkins' small flat was dark and squalid, and although he knew that Kitty Lynch would help as much as she could, she too worked and she too had her troubles.

He looked down at his Chani's wet and bloodstained dress and sighed. On the one hand it was just a dress while on the other it was all he'd had left of the woman who had been the love of his life. Of course, he wouldn't blame either Rebekah or Rose for the damage, but it was difficult not to be sad. Chani had been murdered by an intruder when Rebekah had been a young child and he still didn't know who that person might have been. It hurt and it always would.

Day became night and, although Becky had checked that the baby wasn't lying in a transverse position, he or she was still not keen to come out. From what she could feel, the baby was big and, as she listened to its heart, she was glad to hear that it was strong. However, with contractions only two minutes apart for four hours, Rose was beginning to tire.

Nell, her bottle of laudanum in her coat pocket, dribbled some water into her daughter's mouth and said, 'You holding up, girl?'

'I'm trying, Mum,' Rose said, and managed a smile.

It was hard for Becky, given her previous experiences of midwifery, to feel as uncertain of her own abilities as she did now. Maybe it was time to call Dr Klein? But then as Mrs Larkin had made very clear, there was no way she could pay for his services.

Rose suffered yet another contraction and then slumped into a distressed, partial sleep. Becky looked at Bernie whose eyes were huge with fear. The baby was stuck and Becky knew she didn't have either the strength or the expertise to move it.

She said, 'Auntie Kitty, can you go down the Ten Bells and get Dr Klein?'

Dr Alphonse Klein, when not tending to his patients, was usually to be found in the Ten Bells. Another doctor who liked a drink, by the name of O'Dwyer, was generally with him.

Alarmed, Nell said, 'No! No doctors! I ain't got . . . '

'Mrs Larkin, I can't do this!' Becky said. 'Rose's baby is stuck and I don't know why. I need help!'

Nell just threw her arms up.

Then Bernie said, 'Nelly, it'll be taken care of, all right? Mammy . . . '

But her mother already had her coat on.

He watched his mother run down to the pub. She'd looked upset, as if she was about to cry. Had the wedding between that gypsy and his brother already gone wrong? Joey Lynch didn't give a damn either way if he were honest. The only reason he'd come back to Spitalfields, or so he told himself, was to fence a few bits and pieces he'd got up West. He still knew a few faces here who wouldn't dob him in to either the coppers or his family. He still had respect in some quarters. And he was interested, in a way.

Word had reached him six months ago that his old man had

died and that Paddy was in the Forces. But this was the first time he'd seen Dermot in uniform. He looked like a ponce. Anyone in uniform was a ponce according to Joey. There was money to be made in the wartime streets of London and so why would anyone pass that up to die for their country?

Looters, if caught, were hanged. But Joey had given that up back when the raids stopped. Unless there was danger of bombs falling, people tended to take their valuables with them. Anyway now he had a new 'business' as well as plans for another, he hoped. Once the Yanks arrived there'd be some trades to be done that could work to his advantage. After all, Artie Cross, if he was still alive, owed him a favour, and if Artie was still living he was working at the West India Dock.

Where there were rich pickings for those in the know ...

Only Becky had been allowed to stay. The rest of the women had been told to go and, further, not to hover around the bedroom door.

'If I need any help, then Nurse Shapiro will provide it,' Dr Klein said as he shooed the women out of Becky's bedroom like a herd of sheep. 'Go and have a drink, ladies.'

Well, of course he'd say that because of course the man had been three sheets to the wind when Kitty went and got him from the Ten Bells.

And so Bernie, Kitty and Nell sat in Moritz Shapiro's kitchen and waited. For their own reasons, neither Kitty nor Bernie had much to say to each other. But they tried to make conversation, for Nell's sake.

Kitty began, 'What is your ... What's your reporter friend doing?'

Bernie looked up from the glass of brown ale she'd poured herself. 'Me?'

'Yes, your friend . . . '

'He's off to Palestine in a few days' time,' she said.

'Oh, so what . . . your flat . . . '

God, this was stilted! Bernie wanted to scream but instead she said, 'I'm staying in the flat. I'm working here.'

'Bet it's nice, the flat,' Nell said. 'If he's a reporter, your bloke.'

'He's not her bloke,' Kitty said. 'He . . . '

'He's my bloke,' Bernie cut in. 'And, yes, it's nice of him to let me keep the flat on, Nelly.'

'Got a good 'un there, girl!'

Kitty looked away.

'I've only ever had bad 'uns meself,' Nell continued. 'Never had a bloke let me live in his flat. I've always had to let 'em live in mine. But then I've only ever been with useless articles.'

'Heinrich is very far from being useless.'

Kitty looked up at the sound of his name. She hated that her daughter's man was a German. She felt compelled to tell Nell, 'He's a Jew. So not a Nazi.'

'Oh. Okey-dokey.'

Nell didn't care. Why would she? Men were men to her, all hell-bent on one thing most of the time and generally not much use. They all heard Rose scream and looked up.

'Them contractions was getting stronger when we left,' Nell said.

'Yes.'

And yet Bernie had seen the forceps in the doctor's bag and knew he would probably have to use them. Becky had whispered as much. They'd looked enormous, too big to go inside Rose's little body.

'I never had a minute's bother having any of my kiddies,' Kitty said. 'I always had Mrs Pepper come to help me, God rest her soul. Do you remember her, Nelly?'

'No,' she said. 'Why would I?'

'From Kent they were,' Kitty said. 'Romany people. Sarah Pepper was there for birth and death, it was what she done. Laid out Pat's granny and his poor sister who died as a kiddie. She knew things.'

'What?'

'I don't know! Things you people know ...'

'I don't know much.'

'You tell fortunes,' Kitty persisted.

Nell looked at her blankly.

Bernie put a hand out to her mother. 'Mammy, that's ...'

'She would've stayed with the dead, your Mrs Pepper,' Nelly said. 'You don't leave 'em, until they're in the ground. You have to watch ...'

'Can we talk about something else, please!' Bernie said. With Rose screaming upstairs in Becky's bedroom, talking about death made her feel anxious.

Her mother looked at her sourly.

Cousin Helen had fat fingers and so she was clumsy. As she pinned the bustle onto the back of the gown, she accidentally grazed Sharon's skin.

'Oi! Fatso! Watch what you're doing!'

Helen Sassoon cringed. She hadn't wanted to work on her cousin Sharon's wedding dress. Her dad had always preferred Sharon to her even though she was his only daughter. 'Fat' had been the word that had haunted Helen's life. She'd never been allowed to dance because she was too fat, she'd been excused PT at school for the same reason and, until the war had started, she'd always been on a diet. Nobody expected her to marry.

Sharon, looking at herself in a full-length mirror, said, 'You know Polly Rinder who works for Mr Nadel the furrier? She says I look like Claudette Colbert. I've always felt a bit French.'

'Claudette Colbert's American,' Helen said.

Her mother, Sharon's Auntie Evelyn, smacked her round the shoulders. 'She might be, but her parents was French,' she said. 'Soppy date! What you gonna do with her, eh?'

Sharon said nothing, but she smiled. Her Auntie Evelyn and Uncle Zvi had always praised her at Helen's expense and Sharon liked it. Of course, where Helen's brother Leslie was concerned, no one else got a look in, but then he was the boy. Fat, like his sister, Leslie was also 'handsome' in his mother's eyes and 'a genius' in his father's. Sharon had always thought Cousin Leslie was a lazy sod, but she'd never told his parents that.

'You chosen your veil yet, Sharon?' Cousin Helen asked as she began to tack the bustle onto the back of the dress.

'It's gotta be long,' Sharon said. 'I don't want one of them little things only goes halfway down your back.'

'Uncle Zvi'll do that for you,' Auntie Evelyn said.

'I want lace.'

'You'll get lace.' She smiled. 'Your Solly fixed up with his whistle yet?'

'I hope so,' Sharon said. 'I've left it to him and his mum.'

'Dolly Adler? Ach.' Evelyn shook her head. 'You best check, *bubbeleh*. That woman's always in the middle of troubles. Her Ben ain't been heard of for months. Please God, he ain't dead, but ... Then her Solly ... Her life is one disaster after another. Was from when she was a little 'un.'

Nobody, apart from Dolly, knew who her boys' father was. Only she looked away when one of the most respected men in the community caught her eye. Myths about Dolly Adler abounded – about how she'd once worked as a magician's assistant, how she'd been a show-girl and a prostitute. Some of the myths were true. To women like Evelyn Sassoon who envied smart, pretty Dolly and her handsome sons, it was all true.

'You'll have lovely *kinder* with him,' Evelyn continued. 'I know the poor boy's not what he was, but nothing got damaged down below, please God.'

Sharon didn't say anything. Just a week ago they'd 'tried' for the first time but nothing had happened. His mother had been out and he'd taken her into that tiny little boxroom of his. But there'd been no passion. It had been more like going through the motions. And, although Sharon wanted to do 'it', she wasn't that keen on seeing all his scars. If only a person could have a baby without a man. Or with a whole man who looked like Solly used to. At her age she couldn't afford to be picky but Sharon hoped with all her heart that she'd find a way to live with Solly that didn't mean she was on edge all the time.

If he gave her a baby straight away that would sort it out. If he didn't she'd be unhappy with him and she knew it. But at least she would be married and respectable and that was worth something.

'Soon you'll be a wife and a mother, please God,' Auntie Evelyn said. 'You know there was a Sephardic woman used to live in Hanbury Street who always used to say that heaven is at the feet of mothers. I asked her once where she heard that and she said it come from the Muslims she used to live with back in Persia. So it ain't just us as thinks that mothers are sacred.'

Helen looked up at her mother and smiled.

Evelyn said, 'Not that all of us can be mothers. But those as can, well, we're queens, ain't we? Queens!'

Sharon looked at herself in the mirror and thought that she was very much a queen.

Rosie cried as if her heart was breaking.

Dr Klein, who had seen most things in his thirty years as a family doctor, wasn't shocked but he was surprised. Tough little nuts like the gypsy girl generally kept their tears to themselves.

As he washed his hands in the bowl Becky had brought for him he said, 'You have a perfect little boy, Mrs Lynch, you should be delighted.'

'I am,' Rose stammered through tears. 'And I'm, I'm grateful and ... He's all I ever wanted ... All ...'

Her mother, who smelled strongly of beer, cuddled Rose to her and said, 'He's a smasher.'

'Can ... Can Dermot come and see him now?'

'Of course.' The doctor put those evil-looking forceps back in his bag and rolled down his sleeves.

'You know it's early hours of the morning, Rosie?' Nell said. 'Last I saw of Dermot he were drinking in the parlour with Chrissy and Mr Shapiro. Having a good drink they was.'

Becky, who had been downstairs about an hour before to get more towels, had seen them. Drunk as sacks, all three.

Dr Klein said, 'Well, if wetting the baby's head is in order then I'd better join the gentlemen.'

Becky helped him on with his jacket. 'Of course, doctor,' she said. 'And very welcome you are. I know Papa has some nice wine I'm sure he'd be glad to open, given the occasion.'

'Excellent!'

He left and Becky sat down on the bed next to Nell. She took one of Rose's hands.

'I know he's an old drunk, but Dr Klein's a good man,' she said.

'Dunno how I'll pay him,' Nell said.

'He won't take payment,' Becky said. 'His wedding gift to the happy couple.'

Rose, who had stopped crying, began again. 'Oh, that's so kind!'

'Ssshh, you'll wake the little 'un.'

And he was little. Six pounds and with hair as black and curly as a bull-calf's mane, Rose's baby squirmed and chirruped in her arms, occasionally opening his eyes and pulling what looked like smiles. He already looked a little like his mum and also, in his colouring, something like Dermot too, which was fortunate.

'What you gonna call him?' Nell asked.

'I thought I might call him after your dad, Becky,' Rose said.

'Moritz? It's a bit, well ... ' Becky felt awkward.

'He was born in your dad's house.'

'I know, but ... Rosie, we don't generally name babies after people who are still alive,' Becky said. 'It's not our way. But ... Moritz in English is Maurice and so why don't you call him that?'

Rose smiled.

'Nice name that,' Nell said. 'Classy. Maurice Lynch.'

They heard footsteps on the stairs and Becky got up.

'I expect that's Dermot wanting to see his baby,' she said and went to the door. 'Can I let him in?'

'Yes, and his mum,' Rose said.

She opened the door. Dermot Lynch, clearly unsteady on his feet, stood outside holding his cap in his hands. Behind him, Kitty peered over his shoulder.

'You can come in but do be quiet,' Becky said. 'Baby's sleeping.'

They walked in and Dermot stumbled over to the bed. He looked at the baby in his wife's arms and smiled.

'Oh, he's beautiful, Rosie,' he said. 'You clever, clever girl.'
He kissed her on the forehead.

'Gonna call him Maurice,' she said. 'After Becky's dad.'

Dermot smiled. 'That's handsome,' he said. 'A handsome name for a handsome boy.'

And then he began to cry. Becky, the only other person in the room who knew the truth about the baby's father, put a hand on his shoulder and said, 'You'll make a wonderful father, Dermot.'

Downstairs in the parlour, gruff male voices toasted the arrival of the baby. Another little soul born into the chaos and the courage of wartime Spitalfields.

Chapter 15

3 March 1943

He'd been called Hank. Hank the Yank. It had made her laugh partly because it rhymed and also because surely it was a made-up name. How could anyone be called something so silly?

But he'd been tall and muscular and he'd bought drinks for both her and Helen even though her cousin was more of a hindrance than a help. It had been Helen's idea to go 'up West', but Sharon had been all for it. Now that Solly was volunteering as an ARP warden every night, what else did she have to do?

The Paramount Ballroom on Tottenham Court Road was a magnet for American and Canadian servicemen. They came with their girlfriends or, if they didn't have one, soon found plenty of women willing to be their dates. Jitterbugging to the Ivor Kirchen Band, the whole place was awash with excitement and desire and even someone like Helen was asked to dance.

The spark between Sharon and Hank had been instantaneous. She was blonde and willing, and he, all muscles and cropped hair, had a hard-on like a rock for her. They'd done 'it' twice in a cubicle in the Ladies', and he'd been so desperate for her, he'd not had time to use precautions. If she hadn't been three months gone already, Sharon would have been worried. But she was already carrying what was probably her husband's kid and so, before she got too big, she was determined to have a bit of fun.

Helen had to know what she'd done, but she didn't say anything. She'd spent all night at the Paramount the same as Sharon and so she'd have some explaining to do to her mother when she got home, which was probably what was on her mind. Helen hadn't wanted to stay and it was only the promise Sharon had made to buy her breakfast at the Corner House on Coventry Street that kept her at the dance hall.

'We can have bacon,' Sharon said as the two of them entered the elegant entrance to Lyons Corner House just off Piccadilly. All Art Deco glamour, it made Sharon feel as if she was in a Hollywood film. 'I won't tell if you won't.'

Then Helen said, 'Don't your mother-in-law work here?'

Sharon stopped in her tracks. How could she have been so bloody stupid? Of course Dolly Adler worked as a 'nippy' at the Coventry Street Corner House! She turned on her heel and walked back out onto the street. All that sweet talk of Hank's had turned her mind. 'Honey' this and 'Sweetie Doll' that. God, it was so sexy!

'So what are we going to do now?' she heard Helen say.

The greedy pig wanted her breakfast and Sharon had promised.

'Come on,' she said as she took the girl's plump arm in hers. 'There's got to be a caff round here somewhere.'

But unbeknown to both girls, they had been seen. Dolly Adler, in a break from waitressing duties, saw her daughter-in-law and her cousin come and then go, and wondered why. She also wondered why Sharon hadn't been home the previous night.

Heinrich Simpson looked out of the café window and up into the skies above Fleet Street. Bernie, at his side, carried on drinking her tea.

Two nights before, the RAF and their allies had mounted a series of enormous bombing raids on Berlin, Heinrich's home city. And although none of his family still lived in Berlin, Bernie knew that the bombing of his old home had to affect him. There was also now the risk of retaliation by the Luftwaffe on London. Everyone knew it and there was a tension in the air that made people permanently nervous.

Heinrich hadn't been the same since he'd come back from Palestine the previous August. What he'd experienced in the Mandate had affected him deeply. While Jews died at the hands of the Nazis on mainland Europe, British troops sent those trying to escape to their ancestral lands back to their deaths. Done in the name of not wishing to provoke Palestine's Arab citizens into the arms of Hitler, Heinrich had also witnessed some real hatred for the refugees shown by British servicemen. He was beginning to feel as if, were the war ever to end, he too would prefer to go 'home' to Palestine.

He lit a cigarette. 'I'm probably in the office all day today,' he said. 'Unless something comes up.'

He had been working on a series of articles about his visit to Palestine ever since he got back. The *Evening News* would never publish them but he had talked about 'another' paper that was interested. From letters he'd received Bernie knew this was the *Jewish Chronicle*. She also knew he was providing context for stories about the raids on Germany, making sure the British public knew that our boys were striking at the very heart of the Nazi war machine. Giving people some hope. Because everything was about that now. London lay largely in ruins from the Blitz, and with food and clothing rationing in full swing, civilians lived lives of pinched, drab acceptance. Except for places where they didn't.

Now that America had joined the war on the Allied side, the streets of London and many other British cities were full of American and Canadian soldiers. Glamorous and well fed, it was these men, above all, who gave British women a reason to try and dress up when they could. Often carrying nylons and other rare items, the Americans were the undisputed kings of every dance hall and night club in London's West End. And although she would really rather have spoken to their 'women' than to the soldiers themselves, Bernie was currently working on uplifting photographic stories about the Yanks who were 'over here' and American life in general. If these men were going to play a part in the war, people needed to understand them.

'I've got Mrs Albertine coming into the office at ten,' Bernie said.

Heinrich finished his tea. 'What is it this time?'

Mrs Albertine was a New York socialite, resident in London since just before the war. She fancied herself an expert on her fellow countrymen. In reality she was far too distant from most of them, insulated by her wealth, even to guess at the way they lived or what motivated them to join the Allied fight. But her little contributions could be amusing and she liked Bernie, whose work she greatly admired.

'The life of an average American farm boy,' Bernie said. 'Apparently she was born on a farm.'

'A money farm,' Heinrich said bitterly. 'You know that when the Yanks have "won" this war, they'll run the world?'

'Maybe if they do win the war, they'll deserve to,' Bernie said.

He shrugged. Sometimes these days it was almost as if he didn't care. Not just about the world but about their relationship. Rose and baby Maurice had gone down to Dermot's Auntie Mary's place in Devon to get away from London and, when Bernie had visited them, Heinrich had barely said a word about her absence. Usually when she went away, he was all over her when she got back. But not this time.

Becky waved and the man in the tin hat, standing across the street from her, smiled back at her.

'Hello, Mr Adler,' she said to him. 'How are you?'

Solly walked across Black Lion Yard and stood in front of her.

'Not bad,' he said. 'Keeping the lights of the manor out, you know.'

'You do a good job,' she said. 'Not that walking about in the blackout is much fun.'

'You just off shift?' he asked.

'Yes,' she said. 'Back at six o'clock this evening. Just hope I can sleep.'

'Night work's hard,' he said.

She smiled at him. 'How's Mrs Adler?'

'Mum? Oh, she's fine,' he said. 'Since she got that letter from Ben back in January, she's been much more her old self. He should be coming home soon.'

'Ben was in Palestine, wasn't he?'

'Yeah. Dunno much more yet. Don't really know what happened to him out there. Just that he's been wounded and got treated in a hospital in Jerusalem. It was a long time before we found out.'

The family hadn't heard anything from Solly's brother Ben

for almost a year before they received his letter, out of the blue. Becky, although she would never admit it to the Adlers, had thought that he was dead.

She changed the subject. 'And your wife?' she asked him.

She'd heard a rumour that Sharon was pregnant although that had come from Mrs Rabinowicz, who had added that she thought it was unwise.

'They hardly speak these days, the two of them!' she'd said. 'If that girl is pregnant then it's to try and hold the marriage together.'

'She's OK,' Solly said. 'Still working for her uncle, you know.'

They'd married at the Great Synagogue in a lavish ceremony paid for, it was said, by Zvi Sassoon. Everyone in the least connected to the couple had attended and the bride had worn a gown that had made her look like a film star. Such a grand occasion had given everyone a bit of a lift at the time, a chance to dress up and have some good nosh and a drink. But Solly had been forced into the background at his own wedding. A scarred, slightly awkward man who walked with a stiff gait and had sad eyes.

He nodded towards a shop window, heavily strapped with blast tape. 'Didn't your mate used to work there?'

'Bernie? Yes,' said Becky. She looked more closely at the building. 'Looks closed to me.'

'Old Devenish and his family went down Surrey way,' Solly said. 'Got family down there. Don't s'pose he'll be back.'

Just before the war the photographer had been implicated in a scandal involving pornographic photographs. It was said he'd produced them in partnership with the jeweller who lived across the Court, Menachim Suss. But nothing was ever proved. Long ago Becky had been engaged to Menachim's son, but when it had come to the point of arranging an actual marriage she hadn't been able to go through with it. She hadn't loved him. At the time, she'd been besotted with Solly.

As they stood on the pavement, a thin fog up from the river drifted around their legs, Chaim Suss came out of his shop and, for a moment, looked at them. Then he walked away. Becky noticed that somehow, and in spite of rationing, Chaim had become fat.

'So how are you feeling, Mr Adler?' Becky asked. He had been one of her patients after all.

'Ribs still ache a bit, especially when it's cold,' he said. 'And of course me face'll never be the same again.'

Although his burns had healed, the one on his face still looked angry and his eye was permanently displaced. But the wound was clean and dry and Becky, at least, felt that it made no difference to Solly's looks. She still found him attractive.

'It's healed well,' she said.

'Down to you.'

She looked away for a moment. 'In part.'

"Course, the worst thing about that whole business was that we lost Wolfie,' Solly said referring to his best friend Wolfie Silverman. 'We both fell off the church roof but he was the one who broke his neck.'

Becky put her hand on his arm. 'We were all sorry ...'

'Good comrade,' Solly said. 'Good mate.'

He looked as if he might be about to cry and so she said, 'Do you still meet up with the comrades, Mr Adler?'

Solly, Wolfie and Bernie's dad Pat Lynch had been staunch members of the Communist Party of Great Britain for years. They'd all taken part in the Battle of Cable Street back in 1936 when local people had run the fascist Blackshirts under their leader, Oswald Mosley, out of the East End. It was at the Battle of Cable Street that Becky had fallen in love with Solly and where Solly had fallen for Bernie.

Solly seemed to pull himself together again. 'Oh, yes,' he said. 'When this war's done, this country'll need Socialism more than ever. Then the fight'll be for proper wages and a decent standard of living for all. And I tell you something, Nurse Shapiro, we won't be palmed off with half measures again, like we were after the Great War. Britain will really be a land fit for heroes or we'll want to know the reason why!'

She smiled. 'I'm so happy to see you've still got your passion for the Cause, Mr Adler.'

For a moment he looked a little flustered, then embarrassed. He said, 'Well, I'd best be getting on then, I suppose.'

'Me too,' she said. 'I must at least try to sleep.'

Their hands touched just briefly and he said, 'Nice to see you again, Nurse Shapiro. Please give my best wishes to your friends when you see them.'

He meant Bernie, of course.

'I will,' she said, and they parted.

Her mother's Romany family had come from the country, travelling around Essex and Epping Forest, but Rose hadn't been to those places. This was the first time she'd ever lived anywhere that could have been called the country. It was horrible.

Dermot's Auntie Mary was nice, but she was originally from London. The rest of the people in Ilfracombe looked at Rose funny and spoke with a weird accent she found hard to understand. And so when she was out with baby Maurice in his pushchair on that drab Wednesday afternoon, she was happy to see a small band of what looked, and more specifically sounded, like show people walking down Ilfracombe High Street.

She said to the toddler, 'Looks like the theatre has come to town, Morry.'

Little Maurice giggled. He was now just over one year old and interested in everything.

'Look! Look at that lady in the pink dress! Looks like a fairy queen, don't she?'

In reality there were only three 'performers', with two of them dressed in brightly coloured clothes. The third person, a man, wore a very natty suit and a trilby hat at a jaunty angle.

Rose squealed when she recognised him. 'Tilly!'

Herbert Lewis flung his arms in the air and said to the two 'ladies' beside him, 'I told you we'd find her. Rosie! How lovely it is to *vada* your *dolly eek*!'

Oh, the lovely sound of Polari, the language all the gay boys used to communicate privately. Only those in the know spoke it.

'Tilly! Tilly! Tilly!'

Rose began to run, Maurice giggling in his pushchair. As she got closer she saw who Tilly had with her – Dolores, Duchess of Greek Street, and, in flamingo pink, Doris. It was doubtful whether Ilfracombe had ever witnessed such a sight before. If she'd been in the mood to notice, Rose would have seen that everyone was staring at their group.

She flung her arms around Tilly's neck and said, 'What are you doing here?'

'We evacuated ourselves for a week. Thought we'd come down and see you.'

Rose had got Dermot to write to Tilly and tell her where she was going last time he came home on leave. Her mum hadn't been able to cope with baby Maurice. His crying kept Nell awake and then she'd got angry and started going out all night boozing again. Auntie Mary's place had been the only real solution. It was safe, the air was clean and, although it was boring for Rose, Maurice loved playing on the beach and going for donkey rides.

As befitted her assumed status, the Duchess kissed Rose primly on both cheeks while Doris winked at some farmer's boy who'd never seen anything like 'her' in his life.

'So where are you staying?'

'Streatham Sal's,' Tilly said.

'Streatham Sal?'

'She done fan dancing back in the twenties,' Tilly said. 'Then she married a farmer for some reason and come down here to be with him. Lives out in the middle of nothing with donkeys.'

'Oh,' Rose said. 'That sounds like Mrs Pickard. Her husband died recently.'

'That's right,' Tilly said. 'Streatham Sal she was, back in the day. Had men falling over themselves to spend time with her, she did.'

This was hard for Rose to imagine. Mrs Pickard, in spite of having her own farm, always looked like a tramp. Usually seen wearing tattered men's clothing and a battered bowler hat, she was about as glamorous as mud nowadays.

'You're here for a week?'

'Yes!' Tilly said. 'Thought we'd come and see you and treat little Maurice because that's what aunties do, ain't it? Oh, and I've got you a few things from up the Smoke.'

'Nylons,' Doris said.

'Really?'

Rose hadn't had stockings for so long she couldn't remember what they felt like. Bernie, using her old sewing skills from when she'd worked in Mr Sassoon's sweatshop, had sent her down a pair of trousers but Rose had not worn them yet because people here stared. Only the Land Girls wore trousers, not married women with children.

'We'll be going back to Sal's this afternoon so why don't you come with us?' Tilly said. 'Bring the little 'un so he can have a ride on the donkeys?'

'Oh, he'd love that!'

'I'm sure Sal won't mind if you stay over,' Tilly said.

'I'll have to ask Auntie Mary.'

Tilly smiled. 'All right then, girl,' she said. 'You go and ask her and we'll meet you here at three.'

Rose kissed them all and skipped away with little Maurice singing in his pushchair.

'Where'd you go last night?'

'Me and Helen went down the Duke of York,' Sharon said.

Dolly crossed her arms over her chest. Just in from work, she'd found Sharon alone in the flat and had taken this opportunity for a 'chat'. As soon as Solly was in, she knew she'd have to shut her face. For his sake.

'Duke of York on Turk Street?' Dolly asked.

At the Bethnal Green end of Brick Lane, the Duke of York was a pub she didn't know well, but she knew a few blokes who did.

'Yeah.'

Dolly lit a cigarette and said, 'Liar.'

'I beg your pardon, Dolly?'

All fake indignation, Sharon pushed past her mother-in-law and left the scullery. Dolly followed her.

'I saw you this morning,' she said. 'Outside my Corner House. If you was in the Duke of York last night, what was you doing round Piccadilly this morning?'

Sharon sat down and pretended to read a magazine. 'Must've been someone looked like me.'

'Not many look like you, Sharon. Not many that cheap, thank Gawd.'

216

Sharon looked outraged but was smart enough to stay quiet.

'It was you and your Helen,' Dolly said. 'She, poor kid, looked as if she'd just lost a shilling and found fourpence. What did you do? Take her to some dance hall where you could pick up Yanks?'

'I was at the Duke of York,' Sharon said. 'Ask her if you don't believe me.'

'And what's the point of that?' Dolly asked. 'She'll just say whatever you want her to say. No, I think I'll go down the Duke of York tonight and ask around.'

Sharon shrugged. 'We were there.'

'Yes, but for how long?'

Sharon looked away. 'I'll tell Solly how spiteful you are,' she said.

'Oh? Then I'll tell him you're taking the piss out of him!' Dolly said. Her face flushed with anger, she continued, 'I don't know what you're up to, Sharon, but I don't like it. Going out to pubs when you're expecting ...'

'Girls do it all the time now.'

'A certain type of girl, yes. And pubs around here I can just about tolerate, but dance halls up West ...'

'I ain't been to no dance hall!'

'Then why do you smell as if you've been selling yourself in an alleyway?' Dolly retaliated. She sat down in the chair opposite her daughter-in-law. 'I know you only married Solly because you was frightened of being left on the shelf. I saw how you looked at him after he had his accident.'

'Your precious son ain't so innocent!' Sharon said. 'He could hardly bear to touch me until last Christmas! And then only when he was drunk ... imagine how that made me feel. Still mooning over that Irish bitch ...'

'Solly married you!'

'Yes, but if he's not being a real husband then what's that worth?'

'You're pregnant, aren't you?'

The room went silent and cold. Solly had taken to having short, unsatisfactory sex with his wife sometimes and so was, probably, the father of Sharon's child. But she couldn't be sure. Not really.

'If I stay round this flat all the time, I'll go mad.'

'No one's stopping you from going out,' Dolly said.

'Not to work, no . . .'

'Go out with your husband!'

'He don't want to go out and you know it! And also, when's he gonna go out, eh? He's got his tin hat on doing his ARP . . .'

'He's doing his bit!'

Sharon went quiet. There was nothing that could be said against people 'doing their bit' and she knew it.

Dolly got to her feet and said, 'Can't sit here all day . . .'

Sharon smirked. She had a day off work and, as Dolly knew only too well, she wasn't planning on doing anything. She never did.

Unable to stand it anymore, Dolly stood over her and said, 'I don't give a shit what you do, truth be told. You can fucking die of the clap for all I care. But you harm or humiliate my son or that child you're carrying and I will put you in a coffin. You hear me?'

White now, and truly afraid, Sharon nodded her head. Then when Dolly had gone she closed her eyes and thought about something far more pleasant. What Hank the Yank had done with her last night . . .

Chapter 16

Even though she couldn't see inside because of the blackout, Kitty knew that Nell Larkin was in the Ten Bells because she could hear her voice. Nobody swore like Nell when she really got going. Sounded like she was steaming.

Kitty walked on by. Even when she'd been drinking after Pat died, she'd tried never to be seen drunk in public. Boozing at home wasn't good either but it was better than making a fool of yourself. But then Nell was different from her in all sorts of ways.

Kitty had thought her neighbour might settle down when Rose and the baby went to live with her. But poor little Morry had just made things worse. Not an easy baby to pacify, his crying, and the round-the-clock nature of looking after a young child, had agitated Nell and sent her back to her old life of drink and abusive men. And although Kitty could have taken Rose and Morry in, with Aggie, Marie and Chrissy all at home too it would have been difficult for everyone. When Pat's sister Mary had offered to take them in down in Devon it had seemed like a perfect solution. And, as far as Kitty knew, Rose and the baby were fine. But now they'd gone it did mean Nell was free to go off the rails.

Drawing level with the Shapiros' house, she saw Becky leave for work in her nurse's uniform. Although she was talking to Bernie again, Kitty still didn't approve of her lifestyle and resented the fact that both Becky and Rose appeared to see nothing wrong with it. Kitty's world was falling apart and there was nothing she could do to change that. If this war ever ended, then a world that was completely different would be the result and how would she cope then? What would it be like and would there even be a place for her in it?

'Ma?'

She turned around. The voice was familiar but the look of the man was not. He was dressed in a flash striped suit, a fedora tilted over one eye.

'Joey?'

He'd drifted out of the twilight and was now standing in front of her at the top of the area stairs.

'What are you doing here?' Kitty asked.

'Come to visit,' he said.

He looked relaxed, a fag hanging out of one corner of his smiling mouth. But Kitty wasn't fooled. She knew that if Joey wasn't in the Forces he was up to no good. All the young men had gone, except for the sick and the lame. He was neither.

'I don't want your sisters to see you,' she said. 'What do you want anyway?'

'Me? Nothing,' he said. 'It's what I can do for you, Mammy.'

'Do for me?' She shook her head. 'Your poor father sent you away even though it broke his heart. I'll not go against his wishes even if he has passed over.'

'You know where I live, Mammy? Up West. I got a flat of me own and everything. I'm a businessman.'

'You're a killer.'

He said nothing.

'You admitted it yourself,' she said. 'You killed Mr Lamb.'

'I . . . Well . . . '

'Don't try and deny it!' she said. 'Your father told me everything. I don't want you near our girls. I want you to go away now and never come back here again.'

He shrugged. 'Your loss.'

'I don't think so.'

'I'm only here because I want to help you,' Joey said. 'Can't bear that me poor old mum's still living like this.'

'Like what?'

'In this shit hole.'

Kitty wanted to hit him. Where had he got the idea they were any worse off than anyone else?

She said, 'We're at war, much you seem to care about your country, but we are. Everyone's struggling and everyone's poor, but we're . . . '

'All in it together?' He laughed. 'No, we're not, and you're a fool if you think we are. Some people are making money out of this war. Some are getting rich.'

'You, I suppose.' She held up a gloved hand. 'I don't want to know.'

'When this war ends, I'll have money and a business that's legit. And you, Mammy, will be treated like the bloody Queen.'

Fed up with his fantastic ramblings, Kitty pushed her son aside and began to walk down the steps to her flat.

'I don't want your dirty money made from other people's misery,' she said. 'Get away from here and don't come back – ever.'

'Your loss.'

And then he was gone. God Almighty, he'd looked for all the world like one of those foreign gangsters who ran brothels and drinking dens up West. Kitty wanted to cry to relieve the tension in her chest but found she couldn't. She was too angry for that. She opened the street door and then slammed it behind her as she went inside.

There was tension in the air. The bombing of Berlin two nights before had been heavy. People were talking about the possibility that maybe the most recent raids had broken the Germans' resolve. But Becky wasn't convinced. The Nazis had bombed the guts out of London back in 1940/1 but no one's resolve had been weakened then. In fact, it had strengthened. Why would the Germans be any different?

Folk of a more pessimistic nature, like her father, reckoned that reprisals would come soon. Someone as arrogant and nationalistic as Hitler couldn't possibly tolerate his capital city being bombed and not try to take revenge. The big question was, when would that happen?

Nurse Caitlin Moore, a very young girl from Deptford, came and sat down next to Becky. They didn't know each other well but they both smiled a greeting. A nice cup of tea before going onto the wards was something a lot of the nurses liked to fit in if they could. They drank in silence for a few moments and then Becky said, 'Did you manage to get some sleep today, Nurse Moore?'

'A bit.' She smiled. 'Me dad's a docker and so he ain't used to being quiet. He was banging pots around in the kitchen.'

'I bet your mum doesn't like that!' Becky said.

The other girl's face fell. 'Mum died,' she said. 'Back in 1940.'

Becky felt terrible. She put a hand on the girl's shoulder and said, 'I'm sorry.'

She shrugged.

'Mine too actually,' Becky said. 'But a long time ago, before the war.'

She hardly ever thought about her mother, murdered by a burglar when Becky was a child. The culprit was still out there somewhere. What was the point of dwelling on such things? Nurse Moore's loss was much more recent.

'Did your mum die in a raid?' Becky asked.

She nodded. 'And me little brother. He was only eight.'

'That's terrible.'

Nurse Moore didn't say anything for a while and then, looking around to make sure no one was listening, she continued, 'I come home and found them. What was left of 'em. It's why I'm a nurse, so that maybe I can help one day . . . '

'We help every day,' Becky said. 'I've seen you on the wards, Nurse Moore, and believe me, you are helping every moment you spend in this hospital.'

The other girl smiled. Then she offered Becky a cigarette, which she refused.

'Just me and me dad now,' she said.

'Same as me,' Becky said.

'Nurse Shapiro, you're educated,' Caitlin said.

'Well, not really . . . '

'Do you think that the Jerries are going to bomb us again? Because of Berlin?'

Becky thought for a moment. Deliberately being negative about things was frowned upon, seen as unpatriotic. But lying was never justified.

She said, 'I imagine they'll do something.'

'Do you think it'll happen tonight?'

'I don't know.'

'Because me dad's at home tonight and he won't go down the shelter. He says he feels as if he'll be buried alive down there. When I'm with him, he'll go, but if I'm not, he won't.'

A lot of people felt like that. Becky's own papa wasn't keen on the Anderson, especially if he was on his own.

Her tea finished, she stood up. 'We just have to hope for the best,' she said. 'Believe me, I am praying for a quiet night.'

Solly hadn't meant to open up a can of worms, but the can in question came and presented itself to him. As soon as Dolly went out, Sharon said to him, 'I want you to stop your bloody mother treating me like dirt.'

At first he said nothing. He knew that Dolly didn't like his wife and he knew why, but this was not a conversation he wanted to have.

But Sharon persisted. 'Well?' she said. 'You gonna answer me or what?

He'd still thought he could ignore her. But then she said something that meant he had to respond.

'What kind of man lets his missus be insulted by his mother?'

That hurt. Solly, who'd been in the middle of getting ready to go out on his ARP duties, stopped and said, 'What did she say that upset you so much?'

'Well, you know me and Helen went to the Duke of York up Turk Street last night?'

'I know you said you was going, yeah. And?'

'Well, we did go and then we stayed over with Helen's friend Judith. You know, she lives on the Boundary, on her own on account of her . . .'

'I've heard of Judith, yes,' he said. 'Reichman.'

'Spinster, yeah, very respectable,' Sharon said. 'Helen and me met her in the pub and then went back to her place because it's nearby, and also, Solly, because when you're on duty, I don't like being here on my own with your mother.'

'Don't you?'

'No.'

He nodded. He really didn't want to have this conversation now or at any other time. But she'd raised the subject and for how much longer was he going to ignore what Dolly kept on telling him?

'And if I go and ask your cousin or Judith Reichman, they'll say you all stayed at her place?'

'Yes,' said Sharon defiantly. 'Why wouldn't they?'

'And the people in the pub? Will they say they saw you there last night?'

There was a momentary pause, which told Solly all he needed to know. If he'd cared he would have been hurt, but that was something he hadn't done for Sharon in a very long time, if ever.

''Course,' said his wife.

'Until closing time?'

She shrugged. 'Most of them was drunk by then.'

She was probably right about that. But Solly also knew she was working things to her own advantage. And so he dropped his bombshell.

'Mum says she saw you and Helen up West this morning.'

There was a pause. He didn't look at her but he heard the air she sharply expelled from her lungs.

'Well?'

Sharon looked at him, her eyes burning. 'Your mum tells lies about me.'

'Does she?'

Sharon stood up and put her hands on her hips. 'Always meddling, the old *yente*! Always in our business! Can't never be alone with me own husband because of his bloody mother! How do you think that feels?'

'Mum only wants what's best . . . '

'For you, yeah!'

'For both of us and the little 'un.' He walked over to his wife and made her sit down. 'You mustn't get yourself worked up . . . '

Sharon began to cry. 'Then why'd she say them things about me?' she asked. 'It ain't true I went up West! It ain't!'

He sat down beside her. Dolly Adler, like all the mothers Solly knew, was never really going to take to any woman one of her sons married. In her eyes no one would ever be good enough for them. So Sharon had a point there. And it was true that whenever Solly was on his own with his mother, Dolly poured out a constant stream of criticism about Sharon. On the other hand, Sharon did like to dress flash and go out whenever she could. And because he couldn't dance any longer and wasn't keen on boozing in pubs these days, he was partly to blame for that because he never wanted to go with her. Sometimes he wasn't even sure he felt anything for Sharon at all. But he did for the baby. Even though it had yet to be born, he loved it.

He took his wife's hand. 'Look,' he said, 'let's not talk about it anymore, shall we?'

'I never wanted to! You brought it up!'

He hadn't but he didn't want to make things worse by saying so and he had to go out.

'I'll have a word with Mum,' he said as he put on his tin hat and lit up a fag. 'You're right, it ain't fair.'

'Good.'

He went to kiss her but Sharon turned her face away. She often did that, and, as he often did, he let it go.

'I'll see you later,' he said.

The people of Spitalfields were good at keeping the blackout. They'd had plenty of practice. Solly made his way down Brick Lane carefully in case he fell over some unexpected object or even person on the pavement. He was due up Bethnal Green that night and would have to walk past the Duke of York on Turk Street to get to Cambridge Heath Road and his post for the night. And although he felt for Sharon, he also knew that he'd pop into the pub and try and find out what time she and her cousin had left last night.

'Woolton Pie!'

It hit the surface of the big oak table like a hot and heavy lump of concrete.

Tilly said, 'Gawd blimey, Sal, what's that made of? Shell-casings?'

Streatham Sal, one-time fan dancer now known as Mrs Pickard, was not a natural in the kitchen. She was far happier out in the fields with her animals. 'Take it or leave it,' she said.

'Is there anything to go with it?' Dolores asked.

'Like what?'

'I dunno. Spuds?'

'Spuds are in it, you daft mare!' Sal said. 'It's bleedin' Woolton Pie, nothing but spuds, turnips and carrots.'

'Gravy?'

'In the sodding pie!'

In order to help people cope with meat shortages, the Ministry of Food under Lord Woolton had come up with the recipe, which was made from potato pastry filled with mixed vegetables and vegetable gravy. Since it was often bland and tasteless, many people hated it. But not Rose, who thanked this strange woman in the bowler hat very much for her dinner and got stuck in.

While Sal went out to feed her donkeys, Tilly sorted through the inside of the pie with her fork.

'I thought Sal'd at least kill a rabbit for us,' she said. 'They're all over the place out there.'

'I don't think Sal's one of them as likes killing things,' Doris said. 'Remember that boa she had when she was in her snake-dancing phase? Robert, she called it. I ask you! Used to take it to the vet when it was off its mice.'

Little Maurice was in bed upstairs in the room where Rose would spend the night, which left her free to have a meal with her mates and maybe even a few glasses of something. She was, after all, quite safe around Tilly and the other 'girls'. When they'd finished eating the Woolton Pie as well as some very strange bottled fruit Sal had provided, they all sat around the fire in the big farmhouse living room and swapped news. Not that Rose had too much to tell.

'I don't know how you manage to live out here,' Tilly said.

'Dermot's Auntie Mary's a nice lady,' Rose replied.

Tilly just grunted. Both Doris and Dolores watched her closely. As soon as Dermot's name was mentioned, Tilly always pulled a sour face. All the 'girls' believed that Dermot was a 'gay boy', but only Tilly thought that Rose should be told. The others knew why. Tilly herself had wanted to make a little family with Rose and Maurice, a prospect Dermot had taken away. But that was no reason to make the girl unhappy and, after all, Dermot and his family were providing well for Rose and her nipper.

'Well, I couldn't live out here,' Tilly said.

Sal, who most people thought had dropped asleep after her dinner, said, '*You* can't live anywhere that isn't populated by pimps and mucky photographers.'

Tilly pretended to be shocked. 'Oh! You!'

They all laughed. But they all knew that it was true. Eventually Doris said, 'Anyway Rosie and Morry can't come back at the moment even if they wanted to.'

'Why not?' Tilly asked.

'Because of that big raid on Berlin,' Doris said. 'Honestly, Till, do you ever pay attention to anything important? The Jerries'll get back at us for it – they'll have to. And if that's the case, London's nowhere for a mother and child to be.'

'Won't happen,' Tilly said. 'Rose can come back any time she likes. It'll all be fine, you mark my words.'

Sal shook her head. 'Oh, don't be so bloody ridiculous, Tilly,' she said. 'Even if there's just a chance of more raids, it's not worth taking. It may be dull down here to your way of thinking, but at least it's safe.' Then she added, 'And there are donkeys. The world's a better place for them, as I know.'

Nobody dared disagree with her there.

The inside of the Duke of York on Turk Street boasted its own self-contained smog. A floor-to-ceiling wall of cigarette and pipe smoke hit Solly full in the face as soon as he pushed in through the blackout curtains protecting the door to the public bar. This wasn't a pub he knew well or that really knew him. But he was acquainted with a few of the regulars including Judith Reichman, Sharon's cousin Helen's friend. And although Sharon had described Judith to him as a 'spinster', she actually came across as more of a gangster's moll from an American film noir.

Solly watched as an old stevedore called Jim O'Callaghan lit the cigarette between Judith's ruby-red lips and then bought her a drink. Like her parents before her, Judith was a home-working, respectable seamstress. Unlike either of them, she was also an alcoholic.

Once the old stevedore had been engaged in conversation by his mates, Solly went over to Judith and asked if he might sit down. She looked at him with some suspicion in her eyes but she agreed and so he sat. Thin and angular, Judith Reichman could certainly put away pints of brown ale and she finished the drink the old bloke had bought her in very short order. Solly offered to buy her another.

'Why?' she asked. 'You trying to get me tiddly, are you? I'll tell your Sharon on you, Solly Adler!'

But she was smiling as she said it and he laughed too. When he came back from the bar with her pint she thanked him 'very kindly', and it was then he asked her where she'd been the night before and who she'd been with.

'With your missus,' she said. 'You knew she was out, didn't ya?'

'Yeah.'

'Mind you, Helen's actually my friend. She'd have stayed on for the lock-in if Sharon hadn't took her home,' Judith said.

Solly didn't want to give Judith the idea he hadn't known where his wife had been that night and so he said, 'Right.'

But his heart was racing as he took in what Judith had just told him. Sharon had said that she and Helen had stayed with Judith. Unless they'd gone back to her flat later?

But then she smashed that notion with, 'I said they could've stayed round mine after – all girls together and quite respect-able – but they never.'

Chapter 17

Legend had it that El Vino on Fleet Street was housed in the former premises of a Victorian Hall of Mirrors. In spite of extensive damage to the area, many of these mirrors remained intact.

Bernie Lynch sat at the back of the building, nursing a glass of port bought for her by a barrister from the nearby Inns of Court whom she'd got to know. Giles Beaumont was a typical middle-aged bachelor whose fondness for a drink was attested to by his large stomach and ruddy complexion. He had a quick mind, however, as well as a passionate belief in social justice. He'd picked Bernie's brains about the East End on more than one occasion and she had unofficially consulted him on a couple of legal issues she'd come up against. She'd been glad when she'd met Giles on the street outside Carmelite House and he'd suggested a drink. Going home to Pimlico had become a dismal affair ever since Heinrich had returned from the Middle East. Though she could understand and sympathise with his depression over the plight of Jews trying to flee to Palestine, it was a problem that neither of them would ever be able to solve. Dwelling on it seemed pointless.

Giles cut through her thoughts with a single word. 'Jowls,' he said.

She looked at him and blinked. 'Beg pardon?'

He put a hand up to his chin. 'I have jowls,' he said. 'You know, the pockets of loose skin men get below their cheeks when they grow old. I'm looking at them now in this mirror.'

'You're not old!'

'I beg to differ.' Turning to a man on the adjacent table, who sat slumped over a small glass of sherry, Giles said, 'My learned friend, if I may have your ear for a moment?'

'Of course,' the other man replied. 'Yes?'

'If I may venture to ask: would you say that I am old? In your opinion, having known me for a great number of years . . . '

'Oh, undoubtedly,' the man said. 'In fact, I'd go so far as to say that you're closer to the grave than almost anyone else in this bar.'

And then he turned back to his drink and said no more. Bernie laughed. Contrary to popular opinion, many of the barristers and judges she had come to know, mainly through Giles, were witty and entertaining.

'So don't look at yourself in the mirror,' she said to Giles.

'Bit difficult in this place, old thing,' he said.

'We could swap seats?'

'We could, but then that would prove beyond reasonable doubt that I am vain.'

She laughed. It was so nice to have a drink with a friend even if the ever-present threat of enemy reprisals hung over everyone's head.

Giles offered Bernie a cigarette, which she took, and they both lit up.

'Does Herman the German still have family back in the Fatherland?' Giles asked in his usual irreverent way. He'd called Heinrich 'Herman the German' for years, to his face as well as to mutual friends. It was meant affectionately. Giles knew full well that Heinrich was also Jewish.

'No,' Bernie said. 'At least, he doesn't think so. His close family are over here and the others, well, he's not sure where they are ... '

Giles looked at her and bowed his head a little. 'I see.'

Rumours about where Germany's Jews might have disappeared to had been circulating for a couple of years although people rarely spoke about this. Only Heinrich and a few other Jewish people in the media attempted to get the story out. But with limited success so far.

Bernie was about to change the subject when the air-raid sirens began to wail. She sprang to her feet.

'Oh, Christ.'

Lots of drinkers joined her, but not Giles. As people began to pile out into the street to go to the nearest air-raid shelter, Bernie said, 'Come on, Giles! The Jerries are here!'

He looked up at her and smiled. 'You go, old thing,' he said. 'I've only just started this bloody drink.'

'So bring it ... '

A woman's high-heeled shoe caught Bernie's ankle as she pushed by, desperate to get out.

'Ow!'

'Sorry!'

'Giles?'

He looked as settled and immovable as the white cliffs of Dover. A confirmed bachelor, Giles had no one in his life beyond an ancient mother in Dorset. And Bernie knew that underneath the blasé exterior he was really quite sad. So she sat down again.

'Well, if you're staying then so will I,' she said.

'Oh, no! Dear Bernie . . . '

She lifted her glass to her mouth.

'I insist,' she said. 'Anyway, who wants to be in some horrible public shelter stinking of piss and fear, eh?'

He smiled. 'They make 'em tough down your way, don't they, Bernie Lynch?' he said.

She didn't answer because she didn't need to. Tough was something East Enders did with their eyes shut.

Becky ran. Holding onto the front of old Mrs Tomlin's bed, guiding the wheels, while Caitlin pushed from the back, they had to try and get to the hospital basement before the bombs started falling. It was a drill they'd got out of the way of doing since the nightly raids of 1940/1 had ceased. This wasn't lost on Mrs Tomlin.

'Thought we'd done with all this lark,' she said as they rounded a corner and belted down a corridor that was quickly filling up with other beds, nurses and patients.

'We bombed them a couple of nights ago,' Becky said.

'Should've finished the bastards then, shouldn't we?' the old woman replied. 'Bloody Germans! They was trouble back in the Great War and they're trouble now!'

Not wanting to get into a debate about how bad Germans were, Becky tried to see what was happening at the end of the corridor. There was some sort of bottle-neck involving a group of doctors who appeared to be arguing about something. Under her breath she muttered, 'Come on! Come on!'

Back on Fournier Street she hoped her papa had remembered to go and knock for Nell Larkin before he went down the Anderson. Some people said Rose's mother had taken to 'seeing' American servicemen, although Becky wasn't so sure about that. Nelly had aged considerably since the beginning

of the war and Becky doubted she'd be able to get herself to
the places the GIs liked to go. Becky couldn't really see Nelly
at a dance hall. Unlike Sharon Adler. Solly's wife was always
out and about while he was on ARP duty, or so the rumour
went. The worrying thing about it was that the rumour came,
it was said, from Sharon's own mother-in-law.

Becky looked up at the ceiling as if she expected to see
Luftwaffe planes flying overhead. Strangely there was no
noise yet so maybe the Jerries had been picked up by radar
farther out than usual. Becky looked at her watch. It was
already fifteen minutes since the sirens had sounded and they
still weren't anywhere near the basement.

Caitlin shouted down the corridor, 'What's going on?'

Some of the older nurses looked at her with disapproval.
Doctors were talking amongst themselves at the top of the
corridor and one never disturbed them, raid or no raid.

Minutes passed. Old Mrs Tomlin said, 'What's this bleedin'
carry on? I could be kipping now!'

She had a point.

Then all of a sudden Dr Pierce was at Becky's side. He said,
'Nurse Shapiro, I'd like you to take Mrs Tomlin back to the
ward now and then come with me.'

She looked at him and frowned. 'Doctor?'

Smoking one of his ragged roll-ups, he breathed into her
ear, 'There is no raid but we have another situation . . .'

'Another . . . ?'

He put his hand to her lips. 'Careless talk, Nurse Shapiro,'
he said. 'Do as I ask, please.'

She bowed her head. 'Doctor.'

When he'd gone, Caitlin said, 'What was that all about?'

'Got to take Mrs Tomlin back to the ward. False alarm
it seems.'

Mrs Tomlin rolled her eyes. 'False alarm? What is this country coming to? Couldn't hold a piss-up in a brewery, any of 'em!'

Just the noises, more animal than human, were hellish. The look of it was far, far worse. Even though the light was dim and rain continued to pour down in stair-rods from the darkening skies, Solly could see blood. It filled the small spaces left between the tangled limbs and crushed heads, the mangled hands and mouths twisted in agony or death. Only in Spain had he ever seen anything like this, but that had been in the heat of battle. Here there was no battle, no raid, no danger, not a Luftwaffe plane in the sky. Only a staircase descending down into the bowels of the earth, piled high with bodies either dead or dying.

Bethnal Green Tube Station had been dug out back in the 1930s. Tunnels had been built, entrances and even a booking hall. But then the war had come along and it had never been put into service, except as a place where local people might shelter. It had seen a lot of use before that awful evening of 3 March 1943. People had slept down there, cooked, laughed, cried and found safety. Now all they discovered was death.

Solly, like all the ARP wardens, police officers and medical staff who attended the scene, didn't know what had happened or how. All they knew at the time was that the air-raid warning had turned out to be a false alarm. Unfortunately this knowledge had come too late for the three hundred-odd local people who had poured down into the station, their feet slipping on the rain-slicked stairs.

Mainly women and children, those who had fallen first had been at the very bottom of the staircase, while those who came after had piled down on top, unable to see what had already happened by the light of the single twenty-five-watt light bulb suspended over the stairs.

Then the screaming began. Solly put his hand up to his head and said, 'We've gotta get them out of here!'

But an older, cooler-headed man took his arm.

'Not until the medics get here,' Wilf Irons, Senior ARP Warden, said. 'If you don't know what you're doing, you could make their injuries worse!'

'Yeah, but can't we at least get the ones off the top?'

Those who had come last, unable to see what was happening below, were attempting to get up, sometimes standing on the people beneath.

Irons didn't answer and so Solly launched himself down the stairs and grabbed a woman's flailing arm. Less than five minutes before he'd been miserably wondering how he would broach the subject of her previous night's activities with his wife. Now that seemed not only a million miles away but also so petty as to be unworthy of consideration.

'Well, I have to say, this is a very civilised raid.' Giles Beaumont raised his glass of port in a toast to the ceiling of El Vino's.

'Must have been a false alarm,' Bernie said.

He shrugged. They'd passed a pleasant half-hour, drinking and talking about all the things they'd like to do once the war ended. For Giles, this meant more time spent in El Vino's and less at his Chambers, while Bernie wanted to travel. It was something she had wanted to do as a child and its allure had never faded. When she'd been really young this passion had revolved around a desire to visit Egypt and the Pyramids. And she still wanted to go there, especially since her father, who had always encouraged her dreams, had died. But what would be left of Egypt after the war? she wondered. Would it even still be possible to go there should the country have fallen into Nazi hands? No one knew, but that didn't dull her desire. And neither did any thoughts she might have about leaving Heinrich behind or in Palestine. Maybe they could go to Palestine together as he had suggested once . . .

When the front door of the pub smashed open, Bernie didn't look up as she imagined it had to be people coming back from their air-raid shelters, gagging for alcohol. But it wasn't. When she didn't hear voices, Bernie glanced over to the front door where she saw a weedy teenage boy, standing clutching at his cap.

'Sidney?'

He was the office dogsbody, tea-boy, and sometimes unofficial messenger.

The boy wiped his nose with his shirtsleeve and said, 'Miss Lynch! Where's all the other . . . '

'Down the shelters,' she said. 'What is it, Sidney? You got something for us?'

He looked as if he had a story to tell. His face was white and he was out of breath. He must've just come from the *News*'s offices in Carmelite House.

He gulped. 'It's big . . . a disaster at Bethnal Green Station . . . '

'My dear boy, Bethnal Green doesn't have a station,' Giles said. 'Bernie dear, he's having you on.'

'No!'

She put her hand on the boy's shaking shoulder. 'No, Giles,' she said, 'there is a station, it's just never been used. What disaster is this, Sidney?'

'At the station,' he said. 'On the wire, it said people fell there. Loads of them are dead, Miss Lynch. Loads.'

Bernie didn't even say goodbye to Giles. She picked up her

cigarettes and her handbag, finished her drink and ran out of the door.

She hadn't even thought to bring a coat. Inside the ambulance, Becky shivered at the cold and wet outside as well as the nature of the task ahead of her. The shock of what she'd heard settled into her mind and her bones. There'd been no raid but people had been killed, somehow, at Bethnal Green. Not even the ambulance driver, Marie Lynch, Bernie's sister, knew any more.

'That new station at Bethnal Green is where I've been told to go,' she'd said to Becky as she'd got into the ambulance. 'God knows why.'

She'd put her foot down, though. Bells ringing, tyres screeching. But then Marie's was just one of a fleet of ambulances that left the London Hospital for Bethnal Green that grim, rainy night in March 1943. Later known as the Bethnal Green Tube Disaster, the medical staff were on their way to one of the biggest civilian catastrophes in British history. Not that anyone outside those intimately involved with it would know anything about it for many years to come.

When they arrived at the site of the mothballed station, hardly anyone official seemed to be about. Just one copper and an ARP warden. By the light of their torches, they were looking down into a hole in the ground.

Dr Pierce walked up to the policeman. He was about to speak when he too looked down into the ground and then fell silent.

Becky, still at Marie's side, grabbed her arm and they looked at each other as the faint whimpers, screams and groans of those underneath began to filter out to them. And then through the rain came the smell of blood.

*

'Well, give us a hand then!'

The woman staggering beside Solly, clinging to his shoulder, moved like a sleep-walker, slowly, eyes half-closed.

Other coppers had arrived since he'd gingerly stepped into the gloom of the stairwell and removed first two children and then this woman from the top of what had turned out to be a much larger incident than he'd imagined. Although he couldn't see anything much by the light of that one tiny bulb, what he could see convinced Solly that few people, if anyone, had made it to the station booking hall. Later he would learn that he was right. Nineteen steps led down to the first landing and no one, so far as they could tell, had made it beyond that point.

The woman by his side fainted and an elderly doctor stepped forward to catch her.

Solly, looking through the smoke from the doctor's fag, said, 'It's like a human pyramid down there. You'll have to lift them from the top and work your way down.'

'All right.'

The doctor laid the woman down on the pavement where she was quickly attended to by a nurse. In the meantime still more coppers had arrived and a system for removing people from the top layers began. It didn't take long to reach the dead. Although hardened, to some extent, by the Spanish Civil War and the Blitz, Solly Adler hadn't been prepared for the dead baby he removed from its dead mother's arms.

For a moment he just looked at it. The copper working beside him found a toddler alive and passed her up to her mother who was crying at the top of the stairs. Solly held the baby out, but no one took it from him. He climbed the stairs, tears in his eyes, and had almost reached the top when someone gently took the dead infant from his arms.

For a moment, he thought he was seeing things but then, of course, she would be here. Of course she would.

'Nurse Shapiro . . .'

'Mr Adler.' She held the infant, all covered in blood, to her breast and said, 'I'll look after this little one. You have no need to worry about her anymore.'

He nodded. Then Becky was gone. Solly made his way back down the stairs. They hadn't had to go far into this hellish pile of human flesh to discover the dead. He wondered as he lifted a dead boy of about ten in his arms what terrible sights they were going to uncover at the bottom of the pile.

'Mr Adler?'

It was Nurse Shapiro again. Now without the baby, she stood in front of him, her arms outstretched to receive the body of the boy.

'Come on,' she said, 'we need to make a human chain so we can get everyone out as quickly as possible.'

Solly knew this. Of course he knew it! And yet it was almost as if he was doing everything in slow motion. He felt cold and clumsy and, although it was raining, didn't seem to feel wet. Nurse Shapiro took the boy from him and then passed the small body to another nurse at her back. In less than a second she was looking at Solly again, waiting for whatever or who-ever he pulled out next.

Bernie had detoured into her office in Carmelite House to retrieve her camera and then she'd hailed a cab to Bethnal Green. Cabbies were usually good sources of information and so she asked him if he knew anything about the 'raid' that hadn't been a raid.

'Word is that some new anti-aircraft missiles we've got sound like bombs falling,' the cabbie said. 'But don't quote me on that, miss. Careless talk and all that.'

He'd picked her up outside Carmelite House and everyone in London knew what went on in there. Plus she had her camera with her.

'Know anything about this trouble down Bethnal Green?' she asked.

He paused for a moment and then said, 'Not really. But I know it's bad.'

'What is "it"? Do you ...'

'I was born in Bethnal Green,' the cabbie said. 'Barnet Grove.'

Bernie knew it. An area teeming with kids, just like Fournier Street. If nothing else, the East End was about kids. The birthing and the looking after them, the having far more of them than a family could afford to feed. Because what else could you do? Bernie now knew there was plenty you could do, but why do it when so many kids still died in infancy? What was the point in living if you left not a trace of yourself behind? If all your life meant was a job that made you die young after years of unrelenting poverty?

These days, when she went back to the East End, Bernie didn't feel the same nostalgia for it as she'd felt on first leaving the manor. Now it seemed to her that any cheery Cockney faces she did see on the streets belonged not to people bravely 'making the best of it', but to fools blinded by government propaganda and fobbed off by official lies. As she looked out of the cab window into the wet streets outside all she could see were dim figures dressed in grey, living ghosts attempting to make something called life of the shattered world they continued to inhabit.

When they reached the mothballed Tube station, these grey shadows were joined by coppers in sopping capes and the grey and red, once white, coats of the doctors and

242

nurses who, she could now see, were carrying bodies that did not move.

Caitlin was crying. She'd just put the body of a little girl down on the ground and covered it with a sheet. She had her hands over her face and was howling. It wouldn't do. Becky knew what the young nurse had been through when her own family had died, but they couldn't have this.

Ripping Caitlin's hands away from her face, she said, 'You've got to pull yourself together! We're here to help these people and we can't do that if we're falling apart!'

'But I can't . . .'

'Yes, you can! You can and you will!' Becky said. She held the girl's shoulders and looked into her eyes.

For a moment Caitlin looked as if she might burst into sobs again, but then she took a handkerchief out of her pocket and wiped her nose. She nodded.

'Good girl,' Becky said. Then she hugged her. 'I know it's hard, but we have to be here for them. Alive or dead. We're all they have.'

And then she saw, over Caitlin's shoulder, something that made her blood boil. In fact, it was something so awful Becky could barely believe her eyes. And no one else, it seemed, was doing anything about it.

Becky let go of her colleague and ran towards the figure leaning down into the stairwell – with a camera.

'Oi! You!' she yelled.

A tall man by the look of it. The figure turned to face her.

'Becky?'

She stared at her friend. 'Bernie?' Then she lost her temper. 'What the bloody hell are you up to? Do you know what's just happened here?'

Solly Adler, going back down the stairwell yet again, looked at the two women for a second, particularly at Bernie, and then turned away.

Bernie strode forward and took Becky's arm, dragging her aside.

'What's happened?' she said urgently.

'There's been an accident. Why am I answering your questions? What are you even doing here?'

'We heard something was going on,' Bernie said. 'Unless someone gets in and prints the story, with photographs to prove it, they'll cover it up!'

'Who will?'

'The government,' Bernie said. 'They censor everything!'

'Some things, yes,' Becky said. 'For the sake of morale and ...'

'That's a load of rubbish and you know it. They cover up things they could have done something about! They don't want us to know about their mistakes.'

Becky pulled away from her. 'I haven't got time for this.'

She began to walk away.

But Bernie followed her. 'All these rumours about Jews being rounded up and shot by the Nazis are true,' she said.

Becky turned on her. 'I know that!'

'But do you also know that our government prevents Jews who have managed to escape Europe from entering Palestine?'

Becky blinked. Behind her, Solly Adler, the police and her colleagues from the London Hospital were bringing out only corpses now. Bernie grabbed her arm. 'Remember Hallsville School?' she said. 'Remember how local people were sent there to wait for a bus that never came?'

Not all East Enders knew what had happened when Hallsville School in Canning Town had been bombed back in

September 1940. There had been no coverage of the incident in the press. Anecdotally seventy children had died when the school was bombed but the real figure was closer to seven hundred. Local families had been advised to go to the school to wait for a bus that would take them out of the city. But the bus never came. The Luftwaffe did.

Reference to Hallsville made Becky stop in her tracks.

Bernie put a hand on her arm. 'Look down that stairwell and tell me whether you think it should have been left like that?' she said. 'Dark and slippery. And what about this false alarm?'

'Nurse Shapiro!'

Dr Pierce was holding up someone who appeared to be alive.

'I have to go,' Becky said. 'I'll talk to you later.'

Chapter 18

The ARP Wardens, the police and the medics worked all night to rescue as many as they could from Bethnal Green Station's stairwell. But as light began to dawn, it became painfully obvious that at least half of those involved in the incident had died. Now that all the victims had been taken either to the London Hospital or laid out in St John's Church, most of the rescue workers had gone, to be replaced by a load of kids.

They started coming in large numbers at about seven. Looking for parents, grandparents, brothers and sisters, friends. Along with the kids came other hacks from Fleet Street, later to the scene than Bernie and with little clue as to what had actually happened. One of them, a slimy type she knew worked on the *Mail*, was offering kids money to tell what they knew. But they didn't want his money, they just wanted to know where their parents or big brother or best pal might be. And there was no one there to tell them.

'I thought you'd've gone home by now.'

Solly Adler appeared before her eyes as if by magic. His

familiar face, scarred and now covered in dirt and blood, gave Bernie a jolt.

'Can't you do anything for these kids?' she asked as she lit the last cigarette in her packet. It had been a long night.

'What?' he said.

'I don't know. Tell them the truth.'

'Which is what?'

'People died here,' she said. 'Someone fell and ...'

'It only takes one,' he said. 'I saw it in Spain. A stampede where no one can keep their footing.'

'But it shouldn't happen.'

'No,' he said. 'But it does. And we've been told to keep mum about it. So that's what we'll do.'

The old Solly Adler she remembered from the Battle of Cable Street wouldn't have kept mum about anything, especially if it concerned ordinary people.

She looked down into the stairwell again and said, 'How many do you think have died?'

'I don't know,' he said. 'I lost count.'

And then they stared at each other and, with his eyes still fixed on hers, he began to cry. She felt such a surge of tenderness for him, she took him in her arms and let him lay his head on her shoulder. She heard him say, 'Oh, Christ, Bernie girl, what is happening to us?'

Did he mean the two of them, the East End or the whole country? And did it even matter?

She stroked his grey streaked hair and said, 'It'll be all right. It will.'

Her daddy had said something similar whenever any of them got sick or were unhappy about something. It meant nothing and was usually a lie, but it was comforting. At least it always had been to her.

'But it won't, will it?' he said.

She felt him pull away from her. Now, in the brightening light of the morning, he looked older and thinner, worn beyond reason.

'Because look at this place,' he said. 'London's a wreck! We can hardly feed ourselves! We can't sleep or think or even love like sane people. My wife's expecting and what sort of world are we bringing that nipper into, eh? And I don't even know whether it's mine!'

He stopped talking, put a hand up to his mouth and just stood there. Oh, God, what did this mean? Had Sharon been playing around? Or was this simply paranoia born of what she knew were Solly's own regrets about his disabilities?

Bernie reached for him again and he fell into her arms.

Three children under five had died. One after the other, like dominoes falling. Three little bodies laid out on a trolley behind a curtain at the entrance to the ward. Becky knew she couldn't think about it. While the living still screamed and groaned from their injuries, she had to tend them; she couldn't let her mind wander from the task or she would be lost.

Caitlin had finally buckled under the strain in the early hours and one of the porters was being sick in the sluice. Dr Pierce, his mouth still clamped around the end of an unlit roll-up, was trying to administer morphine to a woman screaming swear words into the air because of the pain she was suffering. Becky looked down at her shoes, which were slipping on the lino floor, and saw that they were covered in blood. This was like being in hell. Worse, it was like being back in the eye of the storm of the Blitz. But this time the Germans were not to blame.

She'd just bent down to wipe her shoes with a tissue when Matron Dawkins came onto the ward and walked over to her. She was a big woman with arms like hams and a voice that had, it was said, been cultivated at a posh finishing school in Switzerland.

'Nurse Shapiro,' she said.

'Yes, Matron.'

'In the absence of Sister Domenico you are the most senior member of nursing staff on duty.'

'Yes, Matron.'

Sister Domenico had collapsed from exhaustion hours ago. A tough birdlike woman from Little Italy in Clerkenwell, Pia Domenico had taken more than her fair share of stick about her background – Italy being an ally of Germany – but it had been the Bethnal Green Tube incident that had finally broken her.

'I want you to tell your nurses that we are to keep what happened at Bethnal Green last night to ourselves. No details of this incident are to be spoken of outside this hospital and no one is to talk to the press under any circumstances. There are some grimy individuals hanging about outside, I gather. They are to be avoided. Do you understand?'

So Bernie had been right. They were hushing it up. 'But what about people who come to look for their relatives?' Becky asked.

'You will have no contact with them,' Matron said. 'They will be dealt with by the police.'

'Yes, but what if I'm going home and people see my uniform and ...'

'You are not to engage in conversation with them!' Matron's eyes blazed. She wasn't accustomed to being questioned. 'Say you know nothing, politely, and walk on.'

'Yes, but . . . '

'Are you defying me, Nurse Shapiro? Because if you are, then maybe it might be better for you to go home now until you return to your senses.'

Becky lowered her gaze. There was nothing else she felt she could do. Matron in imperious mood was a force to be reckoned with.

'No, I'm fine, Matron,' she said.

'Good.'

Matron pulled herself up to her full height and left.

Becky's first instinct was to run away and hide her fury in some distant corner of the building. But she had wounds to dress and stories to listen to – stories she could tell no one else. How did this help the war effort? But then she knew the answer to that question.

It seemed that no one in authority had told the people of London that the new anti-aircraft missiles now in use over the capital sounded almost exactly like enemy bombs dropping. What had happened the previous night had been a false alarm but countermeasures, in the shape of returning anti-aircraft fire, had been taken and it was this that had caused people at Bethnal Green Tube Station to panic.

But no one who didn't need to know that was going to. All she could hope, though it made her flesh cringe even to think about it, was that one of Bernie's photographs made it into the *Evening News* that night. Even though Becky knew that was impossible.

Bernie told Solly everything. She told him what her mother had done with the letter he had sent her from Spain, why she'd done it and how she'd kept it a secret for so long.

Even knowing that the building behind them was full of

dead bodies hadn't deterred them from seeking what little privacy they could find in the churchyard of St John's Bethnal Green. Sitting on what remained of an old bench beneath trees dripping with rain, Bernie said, 'I thought you'd gone off me when you went to Spain.'

He took her hand. 'And I thought you'd given me the heave-ho, too, because I didn't hear from you and you never come to see me when I got home.'

'You weren't easy to visit,' she said. 'Holed up in your mum's flat.'

'I thought I'd lost everything,' he said. 'Including you.'

She looked away. What was done was done. They both had other people in their lives now and time had moved on.

'I talk to Mammy, but I still find it hard to forgive her,' Bernie said. 'She had no right to meddle in my life even if I was only sixteen.'

'But you've done well for yourself,' Solly said. 'Your swanky job and ...'

'Mammy still sees me as a fallen woman,' Bernie said. 'Heinrich ... Mr Simpson ... is of course the villain of the piece in her eyes for having seduced me away from my family. But it wasn't like that.'

Solly offered her a cigarette, which she took and lit up. Then he said, 'Do you love him?'

'Heinrich?'

She had to think about it. Did she? He was a fascinating man to live with, educated beyond anyone she'd ever met before, and he was kind and, when he wasn't getting worked up about Palestine, caring. He'd do anything for her and they had experienced a lot together. They'd laughed a lot. But did this equate to love?

'I dunno,' she said eventually. 'I suppose I do.'

251

'Are you in love with him?'

And that was the difference. 'No,' she said, without hesitation this time. 'Are you in love with Sharon?'

He shook his head.

She sighed. 'So why ...'

'Why did I marry her? Because she wanted to marry me,' he said. 'Though I think it was more about me as I was before I went to Spain than it was about me now, with me wooden leg and me scars ...'

'Handsome Solly Adler the Communist Firebrand,' Bernie said, smiling.

He smiled. 'Yeah, that's it,' he said. 'That's what I was. But now ...' He shrugged.

'We can't change what happened in the past.' She smiled as she caught him looking at her shyly. 'But we can make the most of the present. You said something about Sharon going out with other blokes ...'

'I think she does, she's never in,' he said. 'And yesterday I caught her out in a lie about where she was the night before. Mum's certain she's up to all sorts. But then Mum never liked Sharon right from the start.'

'Why not?'

'Thought she was flash,' he said. 'Didn't like her family, thought she didn't love me ...'

'But she does?'

'Does she? I dunno,' he said. 'I know I don't love her ...'

He looked at her with those black, intense eyes and Bernie looked away. She didn't want him to declare his enduring love for her, that was the last thing she wanted! Or was it? Not exactly, but as an excuse it would have to do.

'But you need to think of the baby,' she said.

'And if it isn't mine?'

'You'll have to prove it.' She shook her head. 'But what for? Chances are it is your baby, and even if it isn't – what good does it do, making our kids even more unhappy than they are now? Look at these poor nippers round here . . . Some of them lost their parents, their brothers and sisters, their mates . . . and no one can know because it was them high up in government who made this mess. Not good for "morale" . . . '

'Yeah, but what's that . . . '

'It's got nothing to do with you and me, I know,' Bernie said. 'Because there is no you and me. There's you and Sharon and the baby and there's me and Heinrich.'

He put out his hand to cup her face. 'I want to kiss you, Bernie Lynch.'

'But you mustn't,' she said. 'You must go home to your wife and try and sort things out with her while I go back to my office.'

He lowered his hand and looked away.

Bernie knew what he was going to say, she remembered that sharp self-pity he'd shown when he came home broken from the Spanish War. It had almost made her push his existence from her mind. Almost.

'We were kids, Solly,' she said. 'Leastways, I was. Now we have to be grown-ups.'

'I still love you,' he said. 'Have done ever since I first saw you sitting on top of that barricade on Cable Street.'

In spite of herself, Bernie smiled at the memory. Sitting on that roadblock made of chamber pots and old mattresses, holding on for dear life to her first-ever camera. The best day of her life.

Bernie stood up. 'I have to go.'

'Bernie girl . . . '

She began to walk away. 'No,' she said. 'We're not having

some sort of strange chin-wag about our regrets. It don't do no good. I'll see you around.'

And then she left. Only when she reached Bishopsgate and got on the bus for Fleet Street did she allow herself a tear. Solly still loved her but now she had to go and persuade her boss to print one of the photographs she'd taken in Bethnal Green. She knew he wouldn't, but she had to try, for the sake of all the broken bodies she'd seen down that terrible stairwell. That was real to her; Solly was not. He was married and his wife was expecting even if the baby wasn't his. It didn't matter. Like Bernie, he'd made his bed a long time ago and, also like her, he now had to lie on it.

'Mr Shapiro!'

Moritz Shapiro looked over his shoulder.

'Mrs Lynch,' he said. 'Good day to you.'

'Good day.' Then she took his arm. 'Here, you heard anything about some accident up Bethnal Green?' she said. 'Nell Larkin was going on about it.'

'Mrs Larkin?'

'Heard something in the Ten Bells last night. Sitting on her area steps first thing, trying to get rid of her hangover, she told me about some accident up there.'

'I know nothing,' he said.

'Our Marie never said nothing when she come in from driving her ambulance last night. Your Becky home yet, is she?'

'No,' he said. 'She sometimes does a double shift these days.'

'Well, ask her,' Kitty said. 'Anyway, got to be off to work.'

She left to go and catch her bus.

Moritz walked up to Brick Lane where people seemed strangely quiet. Usually there was at least one fight going on, not to mention barkers yelling out the dubious virtues of their wares. But not today. When the war had started it had been like this. No one wanting or able to break the very delicate balance between calm and panic that gripped the streets back then. But as he looked more closely at the passersby, Moritz noticed that sometimes singly, sometimes in a group, certain people were crying. When he caught their eyes, these people turned away. Grief, if that was what this was, could he knew be a very private thing, confined to family and close friends. He had few family members and very few friends.

'Mr Shapiro.'

Again a woman's voice behind him! What was this?

'Can I have a word with you, please?' Marie Lynch said.

In her brown trousers and white shirt, her hair dyed blonde, Marie looked a lot like her sister Bernadette these days.

'Yes?'

'Have you got time for a cuppa, Mr Shapiro?'

Choosing to stand rather than sit wasn't a choice but a necessity. While the *News*'s editor Frank Fitzhugh looked at the first print she had hurriedly developed, Bernie needed to pace. Although why she was agitated she didn't know. There was no way on earth Fitzhugh was going to publish this or any of the other photographs she'd taken at Bethnal Green.

He looked up at her and said, 'Sit down, Bernie.'

She finally gave in. Fitzhugh passed her a cigarette, which she lit from the lighter on his desk.

He said, 'I caught a rumour as I came into the office this morning. But this is . . .'

'I was there all night,' Bernie said. 'It was carnage. The sirens went off and people fled down the stairs to the unused station. But it was raining and there was only one light bulb working down there. So you've got a lot of people on the stairs, then the new anti-aircraft missiles fire and they sound like bombs dropping. People panic and, just to make everything even worse, a bus pulls up outside the station and another load of people get out and join the others on the slippery stairs. Someone fell over down the bottom, or that's what the copper I spoke to thought. No one could see what they were getting into or how close the exit to the ticket hall actually was. People were crushed, suffocated ... ' She stopped for a moment to collect herself. 'It was like the worst of the Blitz, the very worst.'

Fitzhugh looked up, his face grey and tired. 'Have you shown this picture to anyone else? To Heinrich?'

'No,' she said. 'I came straight here from Bethnal Green.'

'You'd better go home and get some sleep,' he said.

She shook her head. 'I don't want to close my eyes, to be honest,' she said. 'Nervous about what I might see.'

'That you might see this?'

She couldn't look at the photograph again. A tangle of dead limbs and staring eyes.

'You know I can't publish it,' Fitzhugh said.

She nodded.

'God knows what an image like this would do.'

'They were killed by neglect,' Bernie said. 'Everyone knows that people shelter in the Tube stations. Bethnal Green wasn't safe. Somebody should be held to account. Just because these people are working-class ... '

'I know your views on class, Miss Lynch, I think we all do,' he said.

'With respect, my views are justified, sir,' Bernie said. 'If these people came from Chelsea or Kensington there'd be an outcry.'

He said nothing. But she knew he knew she was right.

'I'd never get it past the censors,' he said. 'You know that.'

'Yeah.'

He handed the print back to her.

'But I had to try,' she said. 'For my own self-respect. These are my people, Mr Fitzhugh. I know it doesn't always suit the *News* to remember where I come from, but I have a duty to the East End that goes beyond just poking my nose down there once in a while, when I need a good morale-boosting story.'

He just looked at her. It was time for her to go, she knew. But still Bernie persisted. 'I believe . . . '

'I'm trusting you either to destroy that image and any others like it or to put these pictures somewhere out of harm's way,' he said as he stared back at her. 'Failure to do that will result in dire consequences for you, Miss Lynch. You're a brilliant photographer, absolutely committed to your craft. Please do not spoil things for yourself by disobeying me.'

And there it was. For all the years of being 'Bernie', one of the 'boys' and in some senses an 'equal', she was being put down by a man who was not only her superior but a member of a higher social class too. Her daddy had been right all those years ago when he'd first joined the Communist Party. There was no way the workers could have anything but antagonistic relationships with the upper classes. And while she accepted that Fitzhugh's hands were tied on the issue of the photograph, she also knew she had been told in no uncertain terms to 'know her place' too.

The range wasn't putting out much heat and so the three of them sat as close as they could to it, nursing their cups of tea.

Moritz Shapiro shook his head. The story Marie Lynch had just told him was so bad as to be almost fantastical, but also, sadly, he could all too easily believe it. When Hallsville School got bombed back in 1940 at least seven hundred people died. But no one outside the East End had the slightest inkling of it.

'How many died?' he asked the girl.

'I don't know,' Marie said. 'I went off shift at midnight but Becky carried on. Best you ask her when she gets in.'

'She'll be in bits,' Chrissy Dolan said. 'I would be.'

'Ah, but Rebekah, with respect, is a nurse, Chrissy,' Moritz said. 'They have to get used to such sights.'

'Not like this,' Marie said. 'If you'd seen it, Mr Shapiro ...' She shook her head.

'Why didn't you tell your mother, Marie?' he asked.

'Because she'd shout up and down the street about it,' the girl said. 'And perhaps that's the right thing to do. But we was all told to shut up about it if we wanted to keep our jobs. Becky too, she might come home and not say anything to you.'

'So why did you?'

Marie wrung her hands. 'Because I can't bear it!' she said. Tears glittered in her eyes and Chrissy stroked her arm. 'And I wanted to warn you. Because if Becky don't say nothing to you, I think you need to know she will be suffering inside. And I know that you, Mr Shapiro, can keep quiet.'

'People were talking in low voices on Brick Lane today. Some of them crying openly. I knew something was wrong,' he said. 'But I thank you for the warning, Marie. Rebekah has many sorrows she must deal with; this further one I will prepare for. But, you know, your mother does suspect something.'

'About Bethnal Green? How?'

'Apparently Mrs Larkin heard something about the incident in the Ten Bells last night. She told your mother this morning when they met on the area steps.'

Chrissy shook his head. 'Nell gets worse and worse!'

'Because her daughter left her.'

'She was getting drunk around little Maurice,' Marie said. 'Rose couldn't have that!'

'I know, but . . . '

'Anyway Rosie's better off down in Devon,' Marie said.

Chrissy raised an eyebrow. 'You never liked it there.'

'I never had a nipper to look after,' Marie said. 'But it gives our Dermot some peace of mind, knowing they're both safe away from the East End.'

Chrissy got up and walked out the back door. Whether it was because he wanted to use the lavvy or for some other reason, he didn't say. But once he'd gone Marie said, 'He misses our Dermot something awful. Like a brother to him. But we ain't heard a word for months.'

'From Dermot?'

'No,' she said. 'Daren't say nothing about him in front of Mammy.'

'I'm sure Dermot will return,' Moritz said. But he didn't feel good when he said it. Dermot had always been a boy who could stand up for himself, but he also had a soft heart. If called upon to do so, could he kill people? Moritz was unsure.

'Nurse Shapiro!'

Solly couldn't run and she knew it and so Becky stopped in the middle of the pavement and waited for him.

'Mr Adler,' she said, when he drew level with her. Then, realising he probably, by the look of him, hadn't been to bed either, added, 'Are you all right?'

'Are you?'

Although they'd seen each other, they hadn't spoken privately at Bethnal Green the previous night. Becky had seen Solly speak to Bernie with whom, in spite of her protestations that she'd been taking photographs to inform the public, she still felt aggrieved. How could anyone, let alone her friend, do such a thing?

'I'm fine,' she said. 'And you?'

Solly shrugged. 'A bit tired.'

'It was a long night . . . '

'It was.'

Of course, he'd been told to keep his mouth shut just the same as she had.

'Are you going home?' asked Becky.

It seemed strange that he had been outside the hospital, far from Bethnal Green and his home on Commercial Street, at the same time as she had, but there it was.

'Eventually.'

Did Solly want to talk about last night? She could understand it if he did. She wanted to talk – desperately – but she knew she wouldn't. And neither should he.

'Well, I must go home myself now,' Becky said. 'It's been a long shift and I have to try and get some sleep and have something to eat if I can . . . '

'I don't wanna talk about . . . ' Solly looked down at the ground, his lips trembling. 'I can't, and I don't suppose you can either. I need to talk about Bernie . . . Miss Lynch . . . '

There had been a time, when she was younger, when what he'd just said would have filled Becky with dread. Back when she had been childishly in love with Solly herself. But not now. In fact men, apart from her father and her patients, played little part in Becky's life these days.

'What about Bernie?' she said.

They walked along together: Becky straight-backed and smart, Solly limping along at her side.

'I don't think she's happy,' he said.

'How do you know?'

260

'We talked this morning at ...'

So Bernie had stayed on after Becky had gone. What on earth had she been doing?

'She was watching kids come to see if they could find their parents ...'

'We can't talk about this,' Becky said.

'I know.' Solly bowed his head for a moment and then he said, 'She told me she don't love that bloke she's with.'

Becky stopped in her tracks. She couldn't imagine Bernie saying that, she just couldn't. Heinrich was a good man, bright and ambitious and just like Bernie in so many ways.

'You must have misheard,' she said.

'No. She said she weren't in love with him, that's what I meant, *in* love ...'

Ah, that made sense. To be *in* love was different and, when people had been together for some time, the romantic side of things could fade. Or so she'd heard. Not that it was anybody else's business.

Becky said, 'Mr Adler, you are a married man. I'd strongly suggest ...'

He took her arm roughly and pulled her into an alleyway. Becky, suddenly afraid, said, 'Get off me!'

He pushed her up against the side wall of the old Bell Foundry.

'I still love her, do you hear?' Solly's black eyes darted from Becky, back to the Whitechapel Road and down into the darkness of the alley. 'I love her!'

For a moment they looked into each other's eyes and then, suddenly, he kissed her on the lips, hard. And although it felt like the unwanted assault that it was, Becky did not pull away. The kiss was more than a kiss – it was a way for him to let out his aggression. How had he got to be this way?

As he drew back from her, Solly said, 'That cow I married, she don't want me . . . '

Lost for words, Becky wiped her mouth and then removed his hand from her arm.

'That's not Bernie's fault,' she said, once she'd caught her breath.

He didn't say anything. Had Bernie told him that her mother had destroyed the letter he'd sent to her from Spain? If she had, then why? She had another, better life away from the East End these days. And yet Becky also knew that Bernie still hankered after Solly.

Breathing heavily, leaning against the facing wall, he said, 'I'm sorry, I . . . '

'I should think so!'

'She, Bernie, seeing her again . . . it got me all . . . Nurse, forgive me, I know it's not your fault.'

Becky shook her head. If Solly Adler was no longer in love, if indeed he ever had been, with Sharon Begleiter, then that was his business and his alone. Word was that Sharon was pregnant. If that were the case it could explain why she didn't 'want' him. But Becky had no desire to pursue this any further. She pushed herself away from the wall and walked back onto the Whitechapel Road.

When she finally got home to Fournier Street, she was relieved to see that her father was out. Becky didn't want him to see her with eyes red from holding in tears and a face pale with exhaustion. Most importantly, she didn't want to have to answer any awkward questions. What had happened at Bethnal Green and then on the Whitechapel Road were things she wouldn't speak or even think about again.

Chapter 19

8 May 1945, VE Day

'Come on, gel! Gotta get up, get yer glad rags on. We're going to a party!'

Rose lifted her head high enough from the pillow to see her mother dancing around the room with little Morry holding onto her skirts.

'Get up, Mummy!' the three year old said. 'Party!'

Nell, a bottle of brown ale in one hand and a fag in the other, looked down at the toddler and sang, 'We won the war! We won the war! Ee-aye-addio, we won the war!'

Little Maurice clapped his hands with excitement.

Rose sat up. She and Maurice had come back to London from Devon in April 1943, just after Tilly and her pals had visited Ilfracombe. When they had left, Rose hadn't been able to stand the quiet of the countryside any longer. And with no news from Dermot she wanted to be home with her mum, however uncomfortable that might be. And it was. Two years on, Nell was still drinking and, although she saw her men elsewhere these days, her habits remained erratic and often dangerous.

They'd finally heard from Dermot at the end of 1943. Everyone was so relieved. Kitty got almost as drunk as Nell the day the letter arrived. But then in June 1944, as part of the biggest Allied fighting force ever assembled, he had taken part in the Normandy landings. The efforts of those men involved in the D Day operation had made VE Day possible. As far as Rose knew, Dermot was now somewhere with the British Army in Germany.

Rose rubbed her eyes. 'What party's this?' she said. She'd heard that there were going to be street parties all over the manor.

'Trafalgar Square!' Nell said.

It was then that Rose noticed the way her mum was dressed. High-heeled shoes, a skirt that showed her knees, lipstick – and she'd piled her hair up in dozens of thick Victory Rolls.

'What you want to go all the way up West for?' Rose asked.

She knew that Tilly and the old Windmill gang were going to be celebrating up West, they all lived there. But for her, with Morry in tow, it was just too far.

'There'll be dishy Americans!' Nell said. 'Don't you wanna see the dishy Americans, Rosie?'

'I'm married, Mum,' she said.

'I only mean to look!' Nell said. 'You daft cow! Now come on, get yer glad rags on!'

'I ain't going up West, not with Morry.'

Her mother frowned. 'What you saying, chavvie? Kitty Lynch'll have the little 'un. You and me can go and have some fun.'

But Rose doubted that. Although she knew her mother

loved her, she also knew that the first thing Nell would do was get drunk. Then she'd start throwing herself at men half her age – and some would take her up on the offer. Fun for her, for a bit, until someone choosier rejected her and she started crying. Rose knew she couldn't take it and, Victory in Europe Day or not, she also knew she wasn't going to put Morry through it either.

'Mum, I'm gonna stay round here,' she said.

'Oh.'

Nell looked crushed. It made her cheeks sink into the gaps in her jaw where, over the years, she'd lost teeth.

'It's a long way to go and he'll get tired,' Rose continued. 'But you go off and enjoy yourself. It'll be a good laugh, I reckon.'

'Would've liked to have you with me,' Nell said. 'And you know Kitty'd have . . . '

'I want to be with my son,' Rose said. 'We've won the war and, when Morry's bigger, I want to be able to tell him I was with him on the day we celebrated that.'

Nell nodded her head. Then she said, 'You rather I stay round here too, Rosie?'

Rose smiled. She knew her mum was gagging to get up West. 'No, that's all right. You go and enjoy yourself, Mum.'

The car still hadn't moved. Heinrich hadn't wanted her to come down and see him off and so Bernie had just stood at the kitchen window looking down at the roof of the old Vauxhall Cadet he'd had when they first met. He'd loaded his luggage into the boot over fifteen minutes ago. Was he changing his mind? Was the thought of leaving her, leaving England, finally too much for him?

They'd talked about it for days, his desire to go to Palestine.

He'd begged her to go with him. But she couldn't. Mammy and the kids needed her, or that was what Bernie told herself. In fact, Kitty was earning good money now at Tate's and Marie was enjoying her driving. But how long would any of that last when the men came back? And what about Solly Adler?

They'd only seen each other once since the day of the Bethnal Green disaster. They'd met, by chance, up at Paddington Station in late 1944. Solly had been seeing off Sharon and their little daughter Natalie who were going to stay with relatives in Bristol. Bernie had just waved goodbye to her Auntie Mary. Nothing really happened between them. Although when their fingers touched it had felt as if a bolt of lightning had entered Bernie's body, they hadn't been able to go through with it.

Without a word, she'd walked him to a cheap hotel she knew and they'd booked a room for an hour. But they'd only talked – and kissed. The first time that happened, Bernie had felt it would never end. She hadn't wanted it to. They'd both become aroused and had wanted to take the next step, but couldn't, fearing what that would make of them.

She'd said, 'I don't want to be the other woman. Not again.'

'Then I'll marry you,' he'd replied.

But she'd shaken her head.

'Why not?'

'Because you've got a baby now and because ...' She'd thrown her arms up in despair. 'Because there are still things I want to do. Now the war's over I can go places I couldn't before. I can take the pictures that I want to.'

He'd looked as if he'd just been punched, which in a way he had. She'd taken him in her arms and tried to comfort him then. But he had pushed her away.

That had hurt and she had cried. They'd agreed never to meet again.

But if things had been difficult between Heinrich and her before that time, they became even harder afterwards. She'd never told him what had happened with Solly, but she felt he somehow knew. She had no evidence for it, but what she had done still haunted her dreams. Just like Palestine haunted Heinrich's.

Bernie saw the car move off and began to wave, but then realised he couldn't see her. Was she supposed to cry now? She didn't feel like it. Why? Was it because Heinrich had refused to wait until they'd celebrated VE Day together? She'd wanted him to stay for that but he'd insisted that he needed to make a start for Dover. Then he'd given her the keys to the flat and told her that he'd paid the rent up to Christmas. With his wife and children in Canada, it was his last responsibility and he had honoured it like a gentleman.

Unable to watch anymore, Bernie turned away from the window and lit a cigarette. She had a job and, for the moment, somewhere to live, but what was to come next, she couldn't imagine. She knew she couldn't afford to pay the rent on the flat on her own when Heinrich's money ran out, but where else could she go? Her mother's old flat was already heaving with family as well as Dermot's old friend Chrissy and, when the boys came home, it would be even more crowded. Little Paddy had always been a messy sod and Dermot, Rose and Maurice would have to move in too. Dermot would never consent to live with Nell. Bernie would either have to find somewhere else or move someone into this flat to help pay the rent. But who?

There were going to be parties and celebrations all over London although, as far as she knew, no street parties in the flats. Not that a street party would cure what ailed Bernie. But at least it would make her feel more at home.

She remembered that party they'd all been to for the King's Coronation back in 1937. They'd all gone – Bernie, Becky and Rose. It had taken place on her uncle's street in Stratford. It had been on that day that Rose and Becky had discovered Solly had survived and come back from Spain. Bernie had found out the following day. Everyone had said that he had lost his fighting spirit – and his looks. But he hadn't, not in her eyes. He'd simply become a more muted, if angry, version of himself. And she had still loved him. But what was the use of thinking about that now? She put her coat on and picked up her camera. Exhibiting a confidence she didn't actually feel, she left the flat.

Kids were everywhere, waving Union flags, piling up bits of scrap and broken timber in the street. Dolly Adler called down to them, 'Oi! What you doing there?'

'Bonfire, missus,' one boy said. 'Victory bonfire!'

Dolly shook her head. 'There's gonna be a party down there later,' she said. 'You'd better not make a mess!'

'We won't!'

'Make sure you don't or I'll give you a clip round the ear meself!'

She pulled her head back in and watched as little Natalie toddled in from the kitchen.

'Hello, darling!' Dolly said. 'How are you today?'

The little girl, as dark-eyed as her father, her cheeks dimpled like her mother's, smiled.

'Nana,' she said.

'You coming to the party with Nana later?' Dolly said. 'Get a nice sandwich and some jelly?'

Whether the sandwiches the women of Commercial Street would bring would be 'nice' or not depended, Dolly imagined, on how you felt about Spam. Not that it mattered much either way. There'd be flags and funny hats and beer and a sing-song. A lot of people would probably dance too, Dolly included. She just wished that Ben was home to give her someone to dance with. Still in Palestine, he wouldn't be back for a long time. But at least she knew he was safe. Now that the Nazis had been defeated she could rest easy in her bed about Ben. Not so Solly.

In the last year he'd become, if anything, even more unhappy. Dolly would have liked to blame that piece of rubbish he'd married. But she was wise enough to realise that how he was wasn't all Sharon's fault. Since Natalie had been born, she'd calmed down a lot and now seemed to be content to stay at home with her little girl, most of the time. Dolly did know that Sharon wanted to go up West to join in all the big celebrations that were going to go on up there, but whether Solly would let her was another matter. The West End would be heaving with American and other servicemen and Dolly was still convinced that they weren't unknown to her daughter-in-law. But now that Sharon appeared to be behaving herself, she kept her mouth shut.

Solly walked in dressed in the only suit he possessed and kissed his mother on the cheek.

'Looking forward to the party?' he asked.

'I'm looking forward to seeing little 'un enjoying herself,' she said as she bent down to ruffle Natalie's dark curls. 'You look nice, Sol.'

'Thought I'd make a bit of an effort,' he said. 'Big day.'

'One you done your bit towards making possible,' she said.

'Well, I ... I ... ' He reddened.

'And don't say you never,' Dolly said. 'Because you did. ARP done miracles and we couldn't have managed without you.'

269

Solly sat down and lit a fag. Then he said, a little nervously, Dolly felt, 'Sharon's gonna go up West with Helen.'

Fat Helen, the cousin Sharon had knocked about with during those months when she was first pregnant. Dolly had never been able to work out which one of them had been the ringleader of those little adventures. Although Fat Helen was a mousy thing and so it was unlikely to have been her.

'She taking Natalie?' Dolly asked, knowing the answer.

'Nah,' he said. 'Be packed up Trafalgar Square and Piccadilly, I reckon. No place for a nipper. Anyway you want Nat to be here with us, don't you?'

'Yes,' Dolly said. 'I'd also like Sharon to be here, but then . . .'

'Don't go on about it, Mum,' he said. 'Not again. All that stuff between you and her's in the past. Let's leave it there.'

'Yeah, but . . .'

'I said, leave it.'

And so Dolly changed the subject. In fact, she stopped talking to Solly altogether and concentrated on Natalie until, about an hour later, she heard the front door open and then shut as Sharon left the flat without a word. Then she just looked at her son, whose face had gone quite grey.

It was the doctors who first started passing the bottles around. Brown ale, stout – even a couple of bottles of wine from who knew where. All the nurses took the booze gratefully, offering in return any fags they'd been able to purloin from American or Canadian servicemen. Standing on the steps of the London Hospital, they watched as kids ran by waving flags and women set up tables for a party outside the Tube station. Life went on, victory or no victory, but Becky had just come off shift and was going to go home and change to go up West with Caitlin once she'd shared a drink with her colleagues.

Old Dr Pierce, his mouth still clamped around a roll-up, raised his bottle of Guinness in salute and said, 'This is to our brave nurses without whom we wouldn't have made it through.'

All the nurses smiled, some of the younger ones giggled. All the doctors echoed his sentiments as well as people passing on the Whitechapel Road.

'God bless our nurses!'

'You're all a bunch of ruddy angels!'

Becky felt slightly embarrassed. Nursing was her life. It wasn't something she felt was difficult or unusual. She just did it. It was as natural to her as breathing.

Caitlin gripped her arm. 'It'll be so much fun when we go up Town,' she said. 'There's going to be soldiers, sailors and fly-boys! We can have our pick!'

It would be fun to let off steam after so many years plagued by fear and anxiety. But Becky was less convinced about how much she was looking forward to being leered at by a load of servicemen. What she'd seen, of the Americans particularly, didn't fill her with confidence. Polite almost to the point of parody, they were also, to Becky's way of thinking, pushy too and that she didn't like. And with so much booze flowing as well, there was a good chance she was going to get quite a lot of, in her case, unwanted attention. Men were such insecure and driven creatures!

It had been men who had started the war; in fact, started every war there had ever been. And the destruction they set in train was terrible. Not people like her father, of course, but men who either didn't possess or had abandoned the moral compass Moritz Shapiro had always lived by. She wanted none of them and thought that she never would. Even if she was going to have to put up with them for Caitlin's sake. The girl was so happy and so hopeful for the future, of course she wanted to have a good time today.

'We can't just put Spam in the sandwiches,' Chrissy Dolan said to Kitty Lynch. 'We've got jam, so why don't I make some with that too?'

'Oh, blimey, how many times, Chrissy?' Kitty said. 'That jam's been at the back of the cupboard since before the King's Coronation! It's probably older than you are!'

'Well, let's get the lid off and find out,' he said.

Kitty shook her head. 'If something green and 'orrible comes out, don't blame me,' she said.

After several attempts, Chrissy managed to get the lid off and found that the stuff in the jar wasn't jam at all, but honey. Golden and almost transparent, it smelled faintly of flowers.

'This is beautiful!' he said.

Aggie, who had been sitting down reading, came over and dipped a finger in the battered old jar.

'That's honey all right,' she said, 'and it's delicious.'

Kitty said, 'Ah, well, I was wrong. If it's honey you can use it. Pure as a virgin's knickers, honey.'

The Lynch kids and Chrissy laughed. Ever since Kitty had taken that job at Tate and Lyle's she'd become far more earthy and, at times, downright rude. She was also, when she wasn't thinking about Pat, more relaxed. Bernie was no longer decried as a bad example and, although she still liked a glass or two, Kitty no longer drank to excess and alone. It wasn't that she was getting over Pat's death, but she was getting used to it.

A knock at the front door probably meant that one of the other women in the street wanted to set up the party tables. Kitty took off her apron and went to answer the summons.

But what she saw wasn't a neighbour but her eldest son. She immediately went outside and shut the door behind her.

'What do you want, Joey?' she asked. 'I told you before not to come here!'

'War's over,' he said. 'New world now, Mammy. I think we need to put our differences behind us.'

He looked like a cheap lawyer in his sharp dark suit, a Homburg on his head, even a briefcase in his hand.

Kitty said, 'What are you supposed to be, done up like that?'

He was her son and she would always love him, but she couldn't like him, not after what he'd done.

'I work for a firm up West,' Joey said. 'In the lending game.'

Was he saying he was a pawnbroker? Or did he work for one? Then she realised what he was and said, 'You're a money-lender's muscle.'

If she wasn't much mistaken he had a set of knuckledusters and a flick knife in that briefcase. She knew the type.

'I'm a partner,' Joey said.

'In what?'

From inside the flat, she heard Aggie call out, 'Who is it, Mammy?'

'No one,' she called back. Then she whispered to her son, 'Go away. I won't tell you again!'

He smiled. 'And I won't stop trying, Mammy.'

She leaned towards him and smelled liquor on his breath. 'You murdered Fred Lamb,' she said. 'A good man's death is never forgiven!'

'Oh, but I didn't kill him,' Joey said.

'You did! You told your father . . .'

'No!' His face creased into a leer. 'Dad was so keen to blame Artie and I weren't having it!'

'So it was that bloody foreman from hell . . .'

'No, it weren't,' Joey said. 'And it weren't me neither!'

'So who was it then?'

'I ain't no grass!'

Kitty folded her arms across her chest. 'And you still ain't telling the truth neither,' she said. 'Whatever you are and whatever you done, you'll always be my son, but I want no more of you. You hear me?'

He said nothing.

'Today's supposed to be a happy day for everyone but I don't want you to be part of ours. You ain't got no place here.'

'Mammy ...'

For a moment she saw pleading in his eyes and then she saw calculation too. Joey had never done anything that didn't bring some advantage to himself.

Kitty pushed him up the area steps and into the street. 'Go,' she said. 'And just to keep you on the straight and narrow, next time you come here I'll call the coppers. Go up West and break people's fingers for a living. You are dead to me.'

And that, finally, seemed to hit home. His face turned pale and he began to walk away.

Over the other side of the street, Moritz Shapiro watched this exchange with a frown on his face. But he didn't say anything. Kitty knew he'd recognise Joey but she just nodded her head to the old man and then went back inside the flat.

Chapter 20

The words 'Displaced Persons' didn't even begin to sum up who people like Leon Blass really were. High up in the Harz Mountains, one of the most beautiful and spectacular parts of Germany, there were camps for 'such people', but no one would say who they really were.

Leon had ended up in Bergen-Belsen concentration camp. A mathematics teacher by profession, he told Dermot Lynch he had once been a very fat man.

'So fat I had three chins,' he said.

Dermot watched the laughter on his face reverberate down every one of Leon's pitifully exposed ribs. A 'living skeleton' was how Leon had described himself when Dermot had picked him up off the ground in front of the former Kommandant's office in that terrible, evil place. Leon had been one of the few they'd found who had been conscious. Hundreds, thousands, had died where they had dropped, innocent, brutalised victims of the Nazi war machine. For days, Dermot had wanted to kill every German he came across. He hadn't. Instead he'd simply beaten, smashed teeth and lying jaws and spat at their pitiful, terrified women in the street. There was nothing that was ever going to make this better, nothing.

But he hadn't come to hut five to sit with Leon and the only other person who could speak, a woman called Berta, to relive the horrors of Belsen. He'd come to tell them something good.

'The war is over,' he said.

This wasn't unexpected. With Hitler dead, by his own hand, since 30 April there had been little impetus for the Nazi regime to continue. But now, officially, the Germans had surrendered.

Leon nodded. 'That is good,' he said. 'You must be happy.'
'I am.'

Dermot sat down beside the old man and smiled. 'And you?'
'I will wait to see what happens next,' he said.

Some of the squaddies he'd served with would have wondered what Leon was talking about, but not Dermot. He'd seen the lines of people criss-crossing Germany and France. 'Displaced Persons' who didn't really belong anywhere anymore, looking for shelter. Further south, in southern France and Italy, thousands of Jews waited to get onto boats going to Palestine. Mainly they were prevented from doing so. But there was a rumour that the British Mandate in Palestine might be coming to an end and that a homeland for the Jews, in that ancient place, was being discussed at the highest level.

'You must get well first,' Dermot said.

Berta, a small bundle of rags on the bed opposite Leon's, reared up and said, 'He'll never be well, stupid boy!'

'The doctor . . .'

'Oh, in his body maybe,' she said. 'In his mind . . .' She shrugged. 'You will be lucky to be well up there, English soldier boy. After what you have seen.'

He knew what she meant and he agreed with it, but said nothing.

'We will always carry this horror,' Berta went on. 'But that is an honour too.'

Dermot frowned. 'How?'

How could witnessing the darkest, most depraved acts in human history be an honour?

'Because when we speak, when we horrify people, then maybe that will prevent them from doing something like this ever again,' Berta said. 'You have family back in England?'

'Yeah,' he said. 'Got a wife and a three-year-old boy, Maurice.' He smiled. Even though the boy wasn't his blood, he was Dermot's son and always would be. Rose had promised.

'You must want to be home now the war is over,' the old woman said.

'Yes. They're having a party in the middle of London today. Great big one,' he said.

'You wish you were there.'

'I do.'

Dermot shared his cigarettes with the two old people and then, after a pause to savour the flavour of the tobacco, Leon said, 'I had a son. He was a good boy. But when they came to take us all away, he resisted. They shot him in front of my eyes. He was twenty-three.'

Rose wished that Morry would let her put him down for a minute as her hip hurt. But he'd become clingy again in the past two weeks and would hardly let her have a moment to herself. And she was dying for something to eat.

The trestle tables set out down the middle of Fournier Street were heaving with all sorts of food and drink. Sandwiches, mainly Spam or dripping, faggots in gravy, mock egg salad

277

made with mash and carrots, and all sorts of cakes that may or may not be real. For the last few years elaborate cakes, for weddings and birthdays, had been made out of painted cardboard. But all of today's looked real and Rose felt her mouth begin to water.

Nell was long gone, up West, but almost immediately the Lynch girls, Marie and Aggie, had come to call and now the whole family was out on the street.

'Rosie, do you want me to hold him while you get some nosh?' Chrissy Dolan asked.

Rose smiled. He was a nice boy, very thoughtful. 'Morry's a bit clingy at the moment, ' she said. 'If I give him to anyone else he yells his head off.'

'Ah, give him over here to his grandma!' Kitty Lynch reached out and took Maurice from Rose's arms. The little boy immediately howled.

'Oh, God,' Rose said.

But Kitty held the boy tight and said, 'You go and get yourself some food, girl. He'll calm down, won't you?'

Maurice cried bitterly.

'Ah, that'll be enough of that nonsense now!' Kitty said. She jiggled the boy on her hip. 'Come on, let your poor mother have some fun!'

She walked him down towards the Ten Bells, jiggling and joggling as she went. Rose stuffed a dripping sandwich in her mouth. As usual there'd been nothing to eat back at her mum's flat.

People came with their contributions to the party – beer, more sandwiches, cake – even some home-made lemonade provided by the family of costers who lived down Elder Street. Mr Shapiro had been busy and came out of his house carrying a large tray of beigels filled with salt beef and mustard. Much better than dripping that was and so Rose quickly finished her sandwich and grabbed one.

'Take two,' Moritz Shapiro said. 'One for your little Maurice. He needs good meat.'

'And hopefully now we'll get it all the time!' some drunk bloke said as he passed by and swiftly swiped a beigel for himself.

'Oi!' Chrissy yelled. 'That ain't for you!'

The bloke ran away. Moritz Shapiro shrugged. 'Ah, let the man have a beigel, Chrissy,' he said. 'I don't know him from Adam, but who cares? Today in victory we share, and we come together, and we are all brothers and sisters under God.'

It was difficult to remember sometimes how stiff and forbidding Moritz Shapiro had been before the war. Older and wiser now, the fear and privations of the last five years had softened him, something he himself would freely admit.

A piano turned up, pushed by one of the pot men at the Ten Bells. Nobody knew where he'd got it, but once he sat down and started to play, nobody cared. Fournier Street was now filling up with adults and kids, and the sound of crying babies was enough to wake the dead.

Then Becky and her friend Caitlin came out of the Shapiros' house in clean, pressed nurse's uniforms and everybody cheered. Rose knew that they were going up West to join in the big celebrations and felt a little twinge of envy. But she also knew that she didn't want to be parted from Morry, and Trafalgar Square and Piccadilly Circus were no places for little children. Also Becky needed to have some fun. She'd worked hard all the way through the war and Rose hoped her friend would really let her hair down now. Even though she knew that she wouldn't. Because Becky was someone who didn't let go or even really show she had emotions, not now. Feeling sad for her, Rose ran up and hugged her.

'You have a right good jolly up!' she said. 'You dance and sing and have a good drink and ...'

Rose felt tears come into her eyes and said, 'Find yourself some lovely man to dance with!'

But all Becky did was kiss her on the cheek and smile. Did she even know how lonely she was? Or was her loneliness just in Rose's mind?

Three street congas, and an endless string of men offering her drinks, got Bernie from Pimlico to Trafalgar Square. It was chaos. Seen from the Mall it looked like a vast ants' nest. Thousands of people in uniform or tattered, grey Utility clothing swarmed around Nelson's Column, climbing up on the four bronze lions. When she got closer, Bernie could see others splashing about in the fountains.

Music came from all directions at once. Big bands, jazz, even Vera Lynn's pure tones rising above the chatter, the shouting and the whoops of joy. There would be bluebirds over the White Cliffs of Dover now that there were no more Spitfires and Messerschmitts continually flying across the Channel. To be safe from the threat of invasion was, Bernie realised, a strange and unsettling notion. Strange because that fear had been with them all for over five years, and unsettling because nobody knew what would come next. So much had been lost, not just loved ones, but also homes, businesses, the fabric of towns and cities damaged, if not beyond repair, then almost. In London, would the Underground ever work properly again? Would anyone be able to repair the ruptured sewers? Would her mammy and the kids ever have somewhere decent to live that had running water and electricity?

All these people were celebrating a brave new world with

their beer, their jitterbugging and, from what she'd seen en route from Pimlico, a lot of canoodling. Bernie wished them well and hoped that the brave new post-war world would make them all very happy. But she couldn't join in. It wasn't just because Heinrich had left her. She had been sad to see him go but she'd understood his decision. Sometimes ideas were bigger and more important than people and maybe that was what this Brave New World was actually going to be about. Having said that, Nazism had begun as an idea . . .

Bernie recognised the big-band trumpet sound of the Glenn Miller Band and felt her toes begin to tap. The tune of 'Pennsylvania 65000' was infectious! Then a GI, so tall and handsome she could hardly believe he existed, held out his hand to her and said, 'Wanna dance, baby?'

And suddenly she did. Whoever he was, he whisked her away into the thick of the crowd and, in the shadow of Lord Nelson atop his column, kissed her full on the lips.

Solly was usually a good dad. He looked after little Natalie more than her mother did, but on this occasion he wasn't going to and his mother was all for it. She had taken Natalie from him when they left the flat.

'Why don't you go down the Ten Bells and get yourself a drink?' she'd said.

'I've got Nat . . . '

'No, you ain't. Give her to me.'

She'd then pushed a pound note into his hand and sent him on his way. The poor sod was wound tight like a spring because of his so-called wife. Still off out when she could get away with it, sometimes offhand with him and the little 'un. Sharon had improved a bit but she still wasn't like a proper mother. Dolly had always known that marrying her was a bad idea. But Solly had been an adult so what could she have done?

In a secret place in her heart, Dolly still regretted that he hadn't walked out with Bernadette Lynch. God alone knew what went wrong there. But there was no denying that the girl had done well for herself, even if she was now 'living in sin'. Dolly hated that expression. Living in what 'sin' and by whose standards? All the men in her life had been 'in sin', even the father of her boys. A very honoured member of the Jewish community he was, the bastard. Not that she'd ever loved him. He'd raped her and she'd got pregnant with Solly, then he'd had another go when she was working as a magician's assistant on the music halls. The result of that had been Ben. Both lovely boys, but both born out of the fear a young girl had felt of a much older man who wanted to have sex with her without protection, tenderness or even any great desire. Dolly wondered whether Solly would end up like her – going out with people just for the sake of company.

Commercial Street was heaving with kids and, although she could just about smell some of the food laid out for the Victory Party, the main odour pervading the district was that of horse dung. Deliveries to the market stopped for no man or celebration and, although a number of the traders had motor vans these days, the majority of them still used horses and carts. Tatty old nags most of them, not like the two she saw tied to a bus stop across the road. Big and jet black and perfectly still they were, like statues.

Dolly pointed to them and said to Natalie, 'Look! Big gee-gees!'

The little girl's big, black eyes widened. 'Oooh!'

'Yeah. Wonder who they belong to, eh?'

Dolly put Natalie down on the ground and then walked her across the road towards the horses. A man, thin and shabbily dressed, a soft pudding-basin hat on his head, walked towards them.

'These your horses?' Dolly asked.

'They are.' He had a countrified accent, which was also slightly foreign-sounding.

'They're lovely.'

He nodded.

'What are their names?'

'Blackbird and Raven,' he said.

Natalie stroked the horses' flanks while the beasts stood completely still.

'I've not seen you round here before,' Dolly said. 'Where you come from?'

'The forest.'

He was a gypsy or a tinker. They rarely came into the city but maybe the prospect of a VE Day party had tempted them in. Dolly wondered whether their women would appear soon with baskets full of pegs and offers of fortune telling.

But then she felt a familiar touch on her shoulder that made all the hairs on the back of her neck stand up. She turned and looked into the thin, dark face of someone who had left the streets of London a slip of a boy, and come back a tanned, muscular man.

'Ben!' she said as she flung her arms around her son's neck. 'Oh, why didn't you tell us you was coming, you soppy date?'

He just stared into her eyes, smiled and then said, 'Surprise.'

The girls were exhausted. Hot and sweaty from all the dancing they'd done, with feet that ached so badly they could hardly walk, Becky and Caitlin had staggered into St James's Park and flopped down on the ground. Some people, mainly American servicemen and their girls, were still jiving amongst the trees and around the fires that had been lit all over the park. But many others were lying on the ground, like the girls, too exhausted to carry on. Waiting for a second wind.

Caitlin lit a cigarette and said, 'I think I'll need a few more beers before I carry on dancing.'

'That or take those shoes off,' Becky said. She was sitting up, looking at the tiny pair of scuffed high-heeled shoes by Caitlin's side.

'Yeah, should've worn work shoes,' the girl said. 'But they make your legs look so short and dumpy, don't they?'

Becky smiled. Nurses' brogues were not the most stylish footwear, but they did the job and, because she'd not worried about her own appearance for a long time, apart from being smart and clean, she didn't mind them. But even Becky hadn't worn brogues today. VE Day was a once-in-a-lifetime celebration and so she'd dusted off a pair of old court shoes that one of her aunts had given her years ago. She'd also dressed up. While most people were still wearing Utility shades of brown and grey, Becky's father had run her up a beautiful skirt made of red velvet.

It had attracted quite a lot of attention in Trafalgar Square, which was one of the reasons why she was so tired now. Men obviously liked to dance with a girl who looked colourful. Some men also liked to take girls into parks and almost have sex with them on the grass, if the couple who were rolling about together under a nearby tree were anything to go by.

Caitlin had seen them too and said, 'Blimey, that blonde'll have to drink a bottle of gin when he's finished with her!'

Becky shook her head. It was a joke but it had its serious side. This romance and booze was all very well, but as nurses both Becky and Caitlin wondered how many unwanted pregnancies might be brought about as a result. How many women would turn up at the London, bleeding and vomiting after trying to 'get rid'.

Caitlin closed her eyes and Becky looked over towards the lake. Much of the park was still taken up with vegetable allotments and so, although there were places to sit, it remained off-limits. So when she had a sudden urge to go paddling in the lake she knew that she had to resist. Walking on someone's prized potatoes and marrows wasn't something she wanted to do.

The noise made by the probably millions of people on the streets of central London didn't make for a restful feel but the music, even when it was loud and vibrant, made her smile. It was so good to be able to listen to music and not feel as if you were taking lightly what was happening in the world. And it had improved, or started to. What Bernie had told her about the Jews being turned away from British Mandated Palestine had made her feel uneasy. Heinrich had gone out there to do what he could to help. As her papa always said: *Jews helping Jews as always.* Bernie didn't think Heinrich was ever coming back and she must be sad about it. Becky had no idea what her friend was doing to celebrate VE Day.

Becky turned onto her side where she was treated to what Auntie Kitty would have called 'an eyeful'. The determined serviceman, American by the sound of him, had his hand up the girl's skirt and she was making moaning noises while he kissed her full on the lips. Becky tried to look away, but still found herself staring. And so, when the young man did come up for air, she was able to see the blonde's face. Whether Sharon Adler saw her or not was another matter, but Becky suddenly wanted to get up and go elsewhere very badly.

Shaking Caitlin awake, she said, 'Come on. Let's go home and have a dance and some drinks with our own kind.'

Caitlin sat up. 'What – back down East?'

'Yes.' Becky stood. 'Back home where we'll have a good old knees-up and, if we get too tired, we can go and sit in our house. I think I'm done with it up here.'

He said he knew her, but she didn't know him. In fact, the look of him, all sunburned, nut-brown skin, with clothes that hung on his thin frame like old rags, made Rose feel nervous.

'How'd you know my mum?' she asked him as he took a handful of dripping sandwiches from the table nearby and shoved them into his mouth. He didn't seem like her mum's usual type; he was neither loud nor drunk so far as Rose could tell.

The man chewed thoughtfully. He had two large, black horses with him whose coats were so glossy that they shone.

Mrs Adler had brought him over to see her. Her son, Ben, had just come back from the army and so she was very excited and a little bit drunk. She'd said, 'This bloke is looking for your mum. I think he's a travelling lad, you know . . . '

Rose knew that Mrs Adler had been trying to be kind when she hadn't used the word 'gypsy' but it didn't really matter. Rose knew what Nell was and what she'd passed on to her daughter. She watched Kitty show off Maurice to a group of women outside the Great Synagogue.

She said, 'Me mum ain't here. She's gone into town.'

The man looked at her blankly.

'You can wait if you want . . . '

Rose could only vaguely remember when her grandparents used to come into London on horses. They'd been ragged too and their horses had been old nags, not like these magnificent beasts. She stroked a horse's muzzle.

'They're beautiful,' she said.

'They're for your mother.'

'You what?'

'Horses – for your mother. I owe her.'

'What? You're gonna give these horses to me mum?' Rose shook her head. 'She ain't got nowhere to keep 'em. We've only got a flat and I've got a little 'un . . . '

'A little 'un? Where?'

'Over there.' She pointed to Kitty who was holding little Maurice by the hand.

The man stared. He carried on staring for far longer than Rose felt was usual and so she said, 'Mum ain't probably going to be home tonight, so she can't see you today, and you certainly can't leave these horses here.'

He tore his eyes away from the little boy and said, 'I ain't leaving them.'

'No? You said you'd give them to Mum . . . '

'Wanted her to see 'em,' he said.

'So you're not giving them to her?'

Rose was confused.

'You tell Nelly that I'm taking them up to Appleby, to the Fair,' he said. 'Two perfect stallions. When I get back, I'll give her the money I'm paid for these two fine boys, raised by me own hands.'

Rose shook her head. 'Why?'

'Why what?'

'Why are you going to give Mum the money you've earned?'

'Because I owe her.'

'Owe her for what? Who are you?'

Normally a stranger on Fournier Street would attract attention, but not on a day like this when the street was full to bursting.

The man took the bridles of both horses into one hand and began to turn them around.

Rose moved to follow him. 'Who . . . '

'Tell Nelly it's Nelson as called,' he said.

She repeated it. 'Nelson.'

'Yes,' he said. 'She knows me.'

'Yes, but I don't!' Rose said.

He began to walk his horses through the crowds and soon he and they had disappeared entirely. Only his voice could still be heard. It said, 'I'm your father.'

Or did it? Rose felt herself go cold. Had he really said that or had she just been imagining it?

The Ten Bells was so full of people, word was that the beer would run out soon. Those who hadn't managed to perch at the bar or get a seat inside sat or stood outside. Bernie caught Solly's eye immediately. He was sitting on the ground between his mum and some bloke in uniform who could be his brother Ben. She hadn't seen him for so long, she really didn't know.

She was glad she'd left the West End and come East. All the mad jollity around Piccadilly Circus and Trafalgar Square hadn't been what she'd needed. It had been a strain. Coming home had been a good idea and she'd already seen her ma, little Morry and one of her sisters who had all greeted her with hugs and kisses. She'd come to the pub to buy some bottles of brown ale. Now, clutching four to her chest, she said, 'Hello, Mrs Adler, Solly . . . '

They both smiled in that soppy way people did when they were as drunk as sacks.

'And Ben,' Solly slurred. 'You know, me brother?'

So it was Ben. Well, he'd grown. Ben Adler stood up politely.

'Bernadette Lynch?' He shook her hand. 'Blimey, you look smart. It's nice to see you.'

'You too,' she said.

'Bernadette is a photographer on the *Evening News*,' Solly said. 'Done well for herself.'

'Is that so?'

'Yeah,' she said. 'So you're back and ...'

'Not demobbed yet,' Ben said. 'Back to Germany in a week. But it's been so long, when I got the chance of leave, I jumped at it. Never even seen our little Natalie. I couldn't wait.'

The little girl was nowhere to be seen.

Dolly Adler, whose face was a little flushed now, said, 'She's off with her other grandma down Brick Lane. Got some party of their own down Sassoon's.'

'Oh.'

Years ago Bernie had worked at the Sassoon Garment Factory for Sharon's uncle Zvi. She'd hated every minute of it, largely because of the way Sharon and some of the other girls, who admired her, had made her feel excluded. But now that Sharon had Solly's child, of course her family had to have time with little Natalie. She'd looked to be a very sweet little girl the one time Bernie had seen her.

'Not that her mother's with her,' Dolly continued. 'Gone up West, doing Gawd knows what ...'

'Mum!'

Solly shot a look at his mother and Dolly shut up.

Ben said, 'Do you want to have a drink with us, Bernadette? Sorry, we can't offer you a chair or nothing ...'

'Oh, no,' she said. 'Thanks. I just come down the pub to get some more beer for Mammy. We've family come up from Wapping and me Uncle Derek's here from Stratford.'

'Well, you have a smashing time then,' Ben said, and then he sat down on the ground again.

Bernie left them and began walking down Fournier Street. Someone had put up tables in Christ Church graveyard and she even saw one old girl sitting on a headstone. This final victory had gone to everyone's heads. No longer having to be afraid all the time was like getting out of prison. And it had been marvellous when they'd heard that Hitler was dead. Not usually one to revel in the death of another, Bernie felt that in his case it was the only just outcome. Hitler the mass murderer was dead and now the Russians, God bless them, were going to make the Nazis pay. And she still had a job. And her mother was talking to her again.

Her life looked good on the surface. But below it was another matter because below there was the shadow of Solly Adler. Even though she was sad that Heinrich had gone, she also knew she wasn't as sad as she should be. And that was because of Solly, whom she could never have and should never go near again. Because he was married and a father and . . .

Becky's dad came up to her then and bowed slightly in that funny old-fashioned way of his.

'Ah, Bernie with supplies,' he said. 'I think your uncles could do with a drink. It's very good to see you.'

'And you.' She smiled at him.

Three of her uncles stumbled forward and took the brown ale bottles from her hands without a word. It was good to see that the war had not dampened their resolve to have a good time.

'Rebekah has gone to the West End with one of her nurses,' Moritz Shapiro said. 'Caitlin. I think they've both been working so hard at the hospital they feel they need a change of scene.'

'Of course,' said Bernie. 'Nurses like them have kept this country going, no one can begrudge them having some fun now.'

But then his expression changed. He appeared to be looking over her shoulder.

'Mr Shapiro . . .'

'But I was wrong,' he said. 'Maybe the West End was where she wanted to be, but Rebekah has returned to us now. Look!'

Bernie turned and saw the amazing red velvet skirt before she actually saw her friend. Then she ran towards her.

From above, with bonfires burning in the road, surrounded by people sitting around telling their war tales, Fournier Street looked like something out of a previous age. VE Day had been a long one and now that night had come, Becky, Bernie and Rose had all gone to sit up on the top floor of the Shapiros' house with the big weaver's window wide open. Rose, as she had sometimes done as a kid, dangled her legs out over the street. Becky and Bernie sat on the windowsill, the latter smoking a fag. The Shapiros' house was taller than most and, with the attic room in darkness, they could see all the lights and bonfires of a newly reborn London.

Of course night-time hid many bomb sites and ruins but it also revealed structures that were newly lit up, like the Tower of London, Christ Church and Liverpool Street Station.

Becky was the first to speak. Seeing Sharon Adler with that American in St James's Park had shaken her and she had wondered what, if anything, she was going to do about it. On the one hand, Solly was the woman's husband and so he had the right to know, but on the other, did Becky have the right to interfere in other people's lives? And if she did speak up, would what she said be looked on as malicious tittle-tattle?

'It'll be a very different world from now on,' she said. 'I don't think things'll go back to the way they were before the war.'

'Maybe not,' Bernie said. 'Although Mammy says she reckons a lot of the jobs at Tate's will be taken away from the women and given back to the men when they return. She shouldn't lose hers because she's always done women's work, but a lot of them'll have to go back to being at home.'

'Not sure I could do that,' Becky said.

'So don't get married.'

'No danger of that!' she laughed.

Rose said, in that disconnected way she sometimes did, 'I saw me dad today.'

Bernie and Becky both turned to look at her.

'You what?'

'Me dad,' she said. 'He come here with two black horses . . .'

'When?'

'This morning, before you come,' Rose said. 'He was a gypsy man and he said he wanted to see Nell.'

'Said that to you?'

'No, to Mrs Adler. So she brought him to me and he said he wanted to see Nell, because he owed her some money. So I said she was up West, which she still is, and then he said he was going to sell those horses to pay my mum.'

'What for?' Becky asked.

Rose shrugged. 'Then he left like he'd never been here.'

Bernie frowned. 'So how'd you get from some bloke turning up with two horses to him being your dad?'

'Because as he left, he told me,' Rose said. 'His name was Nelson, like the sailor.'

'And now he's gone?'

'Yeah.'

'To sell the horses?' Becky said.

'Up Appleby. That's the big horse fair where all the gypsies go every year,' Rose said. 'When he comes back, he'll have money which he'll give to my mum.' She shook her head. 'I'm a bit worried about that.'

'Well, father or no father, I'd look out for this bloke when he does come back from the horse fair and take that money off him,' Bernie said. 'If you are his daughter then he owes you more than he owes Nelly. Besides, we know what your mother'll spend any money she gets on.'

Rose nodded. 'If it's a lot of money maybe me and Dermot and Morry can get our own flat. I'd like that. Some place down Wapping where your granny lives, Bernie.'

'I'd be careful not to live too close to that old cow,' she said. 'She'll soon have you running errands for her. And don't tell her if you've got any money neither or she'll have it off you.'

'I hope it works out for you, Rosie,' Becky said. 'But, you know, if I came into any money, I think I'd like to move out of London to the countryside.'

Rose pulled a face.

'Yes, I know you didn't like Devon, Rosie, but there are other places,' Becky said.

'Like where?'

'I don't know. Essex?'

'Lot of gypsy people there,' Rose said.

'I still haven't travelled nearly as much as I want to,' Bernie said.

'Could you go and visit Heinrich?'

She knew she could, he'd said he'd love to see her in Palestine. But she knew that she wouldn't. There was a great big world out there, a bit battered and bruised right now, but Bernie knew she still wanted to see it. All of it.

The girls sat in silence for a moment until Rose said, 'I don't care too much about what I do so long as I'm with Dermot and Morry.'

'You're lucky you've got such a lovely husband and son,' Becky said.

But Rose noticed that Bernie didn't say anything. When she did speak it was to change the subject.

'So what we gonna do with our lives now no Nazis want to kill us then, girls?'

'What – apart from being with Dermot and Morry?' Rose asked.

'Yes. What do you want to do?'

She thought for a moment and then said, 'I think I'd like to meet that Nelson properly. I'd like to know me dad. You've both had dads and it looks like a good thing to have one if the bloke is nice.'

'It is,' Becky said. 'And I'd like to carry on living with my papa, I'd like to carry on nursing, but I'd also like to move somewhere green and clean where maybe I can try my hand at growing things. It's not a big ambition but ... Bernie? What about you?'

'Me?' She shrugged. 'Like I said, travel. I'd like to get better at my job. And ... and I'd like to be with someone. Not a man like Heinrich. He's wonderful but he has to do what he can for his people. I understand that. No, I'd like someone just for myself, who wants to do what I want to do, someone I can share everything with.'

'That's something we all want, I think,' Becky said. 'I'd like to meet a man, maybe ... But in the meantime, I've got a fine job, I've got Papa and ... ' she put her hands out to her two friends '... I've got you.'